CALYPSO

Ben Cero

iUniverse, Inc.
Bloomington

iUniverse books may be ordered through booksellers or by contacting:

iUniverse
1663 Liberty Drive
Bloomington, IN 47403
www.iuniverse.com
1-800-Authors (1-800-288-4677)

Because of the dynamic nature of the Internet, any web addresses or links contained in this book may have changed since publication and may no longer be valid. The views expressed in this work are solely those of the author and do not necessarily reflect the views of the publisher, and the publisher hereby disclaims any responsibility for them.

Any people depicted in stock imagery provided by Thinkstock are models, and such images are being used for illustrative purposes only.

Certain stock imagery © Thinkstock.

ISBN: 978-1-4502-9265-8 (sc)
ISBN: 978-1-4502-9266-5 (ebook)

Printed in the United States of America

iUniverse rev. date: 01/19/2011

One

"**Substantive** evidence justifies our indictment of the white American yachtsman for the brutal and senseless slaying of one of our black launch operators."

Ward Perez stopped in mid-stride, stunned by that resonant pronouncement in the precise diction of Brits, unlike the Calypso brogue generally heard on Saint Vincent and other Caribbean islands. He searched across the street fronted by two- and three-storied commercial buildings of Georgian architecture. Milling locals interspersed with tourists as well as vehicular traffic intermittently blocked his view of a television interview of an impressive black man—actually a tall mulatto with full mustache and graying sideburns.

Having sailed into port on his thirty-two-foot sloop, Ward headed to register at the Customs Port Office of Kingstown, the capital city of Saint Vincent and the Grenadines. He had only half a block to go, but became distracted by the hoopla of the television cameras focusing on two guys in suits and ties . . . in the midday sun.

Pulling down the visor of his blue cap with its New York Yankees logo to shade his eyes, he scanned the activity and recognized the white guy as an American commentator he'd seen on the tube, but couldn't recall his name. The impressive mulatto didn't ring any bells.

Curiosity impelled him to cross to the circus atmosphere, requiring he dodge traffic. Spotting two white guys near a panel truck displaying the World-Wide News legend, he sidled up to the one balancing a camcorder on his shoulder. "What's this about?"

"You don't know about the murder?" the cameraman asked in a voice obviously American.

"Just sailed into town. What happened?"

"Watch your ass," warned the shorter one, a blond with a clipboard filled with papers. "Two weeks ago they arrested an American yachtsman, claiming he murdered a black launch operator."

"Without enough evidence to convict him for littering," the cameraman added.

"The indictment had to be based on something," Ward said.

"All they have," the blond said, "is a body, but no weapon and not a single witness."

"Torchy, the guy got killed," the cameraman added, "could have been zapped by a dozen people who hated his guts." He eyed the newcomer obliquely, taking in his dark hair and burnished complexion.

"Hard to believe," Ward said. "I'm a retired New York City detective with twenty-eight years in the job. Man, we had to conform to specific rules of evidence to make a bust righteous."

The cameraman gaped at him. "Ex-cop, and you're a yachtsman?"

"A boatman. My rebuilt sailboat only qualifies me as a seafaring drifter. By no stretch of the imagination am I a yachtsman."

The cameraman took in his garish shirt splashed with pineapples and palm trees—contrasting with his worn and faded khaki cargo shorts and scuffed sneakers.

After gesturing to Ward's Yankee cap, the cameraman proffered a handshake. "Joe Kling. I'm from New York too. This here's Bill McVey, our editorial director, from some farm burg in Maryland."

"Ward Perez." He shook hands with both, while grinning at McVey's pretended objection to debasing of his hometown. But it didn't escape him the way the blond's blue eyes reexamined him upon mention of an Hispanic name.

Feigning unconcern, Ward asked: "Who's the impressive black guy? Well, almost black."

"Byrum Josephs," McVey said, "Prosecutor of Saint Vincent and the Grenadines."

"The hump that indicted the American yachtsman," Kling added.

"That's the reason for this interview," McVey said, "to let them know the eyes of the world is on them to prevent them from railroading the American."

"A few questions, Mister Prosecutor."

That strident pronouncement triggered Ward to swivel about to the reedy voice of the American interviewer. Half a head shorter than the prosecutor, the white guy swaggered with confidence that bordered on arrogance.

Adjusting his sunglasses, Ward studied the guy and remembered his name, having seen Jack Hower on the tube rendering caustic commentaries on high-profile stories. Referred to by his detractors as Texas Jack, he always impressed Ward as one hard-assed conservative who made lock-and-load Buchanan sound like a bleeding-heart liberal.

"We're trying to give you the benefit of the doubt, Mister Prosecutor," Texas Jack drawled. "But the paucity of evidence begs the question: Did Ogden Christopher murder that launch operator, or—considering Torchy's reputation and countless enemies—did someone else?"

"Our position is too obvious," Prosecutor Josephs replied in resonant voice, "to be obscured by a biased press determined to whitewash a murderer simply because he is a rich and white American."

"Is that it?" Hower asked. "Are you truly interested in prosecuting a specific murderer . . . or rich, white Americans?"

"Our sole interest is justice. But in keeping with British custom, I implore you to permit this matter to play out in court, rather than on television. Given proper—"

"Can you present conclusive evidence to justify your indictment, Mister Prosecutor?"

"Indubitably, but in court, not on television. We in these islands do not pre-try our cases in the media, as practiced in your country. We—"

"Please understand, Mister Prosecutor, that our only interest is reporting what occurs, without imposing prejudicial opinions."

"If, in truth, you refrain from infusing bias, then report how Ogden Christopher murdered a local launch-tender." The prosecutor pointed his index finger at Hower and cocked his thumb. "Report how a rich, white American shot down a black working man." The prosecutor uncocked his thumb and jerked his hand, simulating the discharge of a pistol. "Report a cold-blooded murder."

Hower sneered at the prosecutor's extended finger. "One last question, sir: How true is the rumor that Christopher has been offered absolution if he pays a fine of one million US dollars?"

"A blatant fabrication, typical of the American media. We do not ransom off our felons, nor accept bribes to exempt miscreants from standing at the bar of justice. Nor, may I add, do we—"

"We have it from reliable sources, Mister Prosecutor."

"Reveal your sources. Let those persons be questioned in the media-glare, as I am being, not hide behind the veil of inference. Let—"

"We never divulge our sources."

"Quite right, especially when they lack credibility. Admit it, Mister Hower, this imputation is a figment of fiction, another ploy of the American press, meant to prejudice—"

"Sorry, sir, we're out of time—can pursue the subject at a later broadcast. This is Jack Hower reporting live from the Caribbean island of Saint Vincent."

"I challenge you to publicly validate that specious and malicious denouncement." Frustration contorted the prosecutor's face upon seeing Hower's people turn away while detaching cameras and microphones.

"That's roughshod," Ward said. "First Hower disparages the prosecutor then curtly dismisses him. Where'd he scratch up those innuendos?"

"We've turned over rocks on the island," McVey said.

"Any of it substantiated?" Ward asked.

McVey scowled, but brightened a moment later. "You interested if Jack's amenable to hiring you as an investigator?"

"Hell yeah. I can use extra bread, living on a pension."

"Hey, Jack," McVey called to the interviewer. "Meet Ward Perez. He's an

ex-New York City detective, available to dig into the Christopher business."

"Perez? New York City?" Hower repeated as he approached. "You one of the Puerto Ricans got on the force back in the seventies and eighties to mollify the liberals clamoring for affirmative action?"

"That a problem for you?"

"Yes, considering that I championed those denied employment, despite being more qualified than most of the

BEN CERO

minority applicants. In my judgment, so-called affirmative action negates equal opportunity."

"Doesn't surprise me," Ward said as he spun away and stomped across the street and into the Customs Port Office. Of course that nasal-talking honky scorned hiring a New York Puerto Rican. He'd more than likely expound the lop-sided argument that affirmative action denied non-minorities opportunities they'd never been deprived of in the first place.

Yes, there'd been improvements in race relations during the intervening years, but enough ethnic repugnance lingered to stimulate resentment. He, like so many others, had been scarred by years of contending with bigotry.

Screw them all, especially that prick. He filled out the form, a procedure he'd become familiar with, having performed it in countless islands while traversing the Caribbean archipelago.

A uniformed clerk perused it and his passport, then chuckled. "Best you mind you manners while you here, mon. American yachtsmen be victimized these days."

"Yeah, just witnessed your prosecutor out there getting scathed by World-Wide News about some yachtsman alleged to have killed a local."

"Mon, that prosecutor send folks to prison to make a reputation for he'self, whether they deserves it or not. True, he a long-head, but have he'self a Gypsy-mouth."

Ward blinked, baffled by the calypso colloquialisms. He'd heard them uttered by West Indians he'd dealt with in New York as well as in the various islands he'd visited, but struggled to understand it.

"Soon they find Torchy, floating in the ocean," the clerk said, "Byrum Josephs charge this one white mon for shoot his black ass. Why in heaven's name the white mon kill some poor-ass launch-tender?"

Ward shrugged and before he could think of anything to say the clerk continued his castigation. "Besides, Torchy a bad-ass who make more enemies on this island than the seagrape tree have leaves. You has to take these papers over to the Courthouse on Halifax Street to register with Immigration."

\#   \#

Two

Ward exited the Customs Port Office to find the TV interviewers gone and the hoopla dissolved into the tropic-induced pokiness of the provincial city. Buildings weathered by centuries of colonization flanked the traffic that emitted fumes and filled the air with discordant horn blowing.

Because of the noontime August sun he crossed to the shady side, where the breeze off the ocean rendered the climate habitable. Locals trod along in both directions while tourists wandered in and out of shops displaying beach and leisure clothing as well as a variety of souvenirs. Some stores had porticos, others colorful awnings, all with gaudy signs promising bargains.

Street peddlers created a carnival atmosphere, hawking everything from fruits and vegetables to straw hats and decorative tee shirts to primitive paintings. Food vendors punctuated that clamor by huckstering native fare from crude but colorful carts.

Ward strode along, oblivious to peripheral activity, his gut roiled by memory of that encounter with Texas Jack Hower. Bigotry like that motivated his jaunt through the Caribbean, his destination South America, to countries of Latinos, where he'd be just another person, not some swarthy outcast with a Spanish name. He wanted to fit in, feel like every other human being, and no longer be demeaned as an inferior and condemned to have to prove himself as an equal to those descended from Northern Europeans.

Chingalo, the way that Customs clerk criticized the prosecutor suggested that Byrum Josephs didn't enjoy widespread support among his citizenry. And, hombre, those humps at World-Wide News 'dissed the man with rude interruptions and insinuations that the prosecutor didn't have a case. Obviously they intended to trip him up and embarrass him under the glare of international broadcasts.

Yep, in typical fashion, they endeavored to transform the American from the accused to the victim. Would Texas Jack and his bohunks go that mile for a Latino?

Turning onto Halifax Street he passed an open doorway from which wafted spicy fragrances that erased residual acrimony. He backpedaled to peer into the Pilgrim's Pride Café, where simplicity suggested economy, unlike some of the overpriced tourist traps he'd passed along the way.

Nobody said he had to go directly to Immigration without stopping for a bite and a beer. Hell, he had no intentions of immigrating, only to lay over as long as it took to repair his boat.

That open door and whirring ceiling fans obviated the place lacked air conditioning. Even so, the patrons at tables and booths didn't appear discomforted. Spotting a uniformed cop at one of the tables capped his decision to try the place.

So he sidled past chatting people seated at the tables lining the window wall. A white couple occupied the first booth along the opposite wall and two black couples filled up the third one.

He dropped into the empty second booth, doffing his cap while groaning delight at resting his wearies. Conyo, he yearned to lean back and snooze. Then he jerked to attentiveness at sight of the approaching waitress.

Ay caray! Believe that he dug those goodies, apparent in spite of her loose-fitting blouse and flowing skirt in a dazzling tropical design. Carefully coifed black hair piled atop her head framed the brownskin chica's pretty face. And those golden bangles dangling from her earlobes danced to her rhythmic walk that was saying something.

"Welcome to Pilgrim's Pride Café, sir. Care to slake you thirst with one of the rum punches we famous for?"

Oh yeah, he liked the impertinent way her dark eyes sparkled awareness of his admiration. This chica knew she stopped time. He endowed her with his killer smile, the one he believed chicas couldn't resist. "You don't mind, darlin', I'd just as soon have a cold beer."

"How you know me name? Me doesn't remember you bold face."

Trying not to reveal astonishment, Ward rolled his shoulders in the way he'd learned growing up in that Bronx barrio to respond to challenges or to flaunt his cool. A long-time fan of westerns, he'd taken to calling women darlin' when coming on to them, believing it sounded macho.

"Mon, how you know to call me Darla?" Hands on hips, she scanned his Latin good looks and his black hair brushed back into a short ponytail. "Take off you darkers so me better see if me knows you." Her gesture intimated she referred to his sunglasses.

Oh yeah, he'd play that misunderstanding for all it's worth. Believe that he considered this middle-thirties fox perfect for a fifty-one-year-old self-professed stud. "Fate, baby. Believe that I knew when I met my perfect lady she'd answer to Darla."

"Say what?" Waving a hand laden with bracelets and rings, she cut her dark eyes at him, then sucked her teeth to convey skepticism. "You jiving me, mon?"

"I'm laying truth on you, Darla."

She sucked her teeth again but failed to stifle the prideful smile that played at the corners of her full mouth. "You wish to order luncheon, bold face?"

"Sure. What's your special today?"

"For we plat du jour us has pan-fried shrimp with a mango sauce to make you jiving mouth water."

"Bring it to me, beautiful lady."

He grinned at the way she tossed her head, as if unaffected by the compliment. Then he watched her sashay off, her hips swaying like a salsa dancer's. No question where he'd focus his attention for this layover. Probably married though. Chicas that desirable don't run around unattached. She was single, every stud on the island would be chasing her. Yeah, but just maybe. . . .

Spicy aromas permeating the air induced him to gaze around, at the burly cop spooning in soup between bites on his roll, at two women feeding three kids at another table. The white couple sounded German, or Scandinavian, or something. Three old locals with raisin skin dunked chunks of bread in bowls of brown stew. A cocky young guy laid heavy jive on the chica across the table from him. Nothing different from what he'd see in any beanery in the world.

Darla returned to set a sweating bottle of beer and a glass in front of him. He took a long swig from the bottle, ignoring the glass. Sighing appreciation, he glanced at the label and frowned. "What the hell kind of beer is Hairoun?"

"It local, mon. You doesn't specify any brand so me serves we own beer brewed here in Saint Vincent."

Ward took another swallow. "Okay, good as any beer. But who in hell gave it a name like that?"

"The Carib Indians call this island Hairoun: home of the blessed. It the history of this place, mon."

"Okay, get yourself one and join me."

She cut her eyes and sucked her teeth at his audacity.

"Hey, it'll do you good to rest and have a little refreshment after a hectic lunch hour. C'mon, take a load off your feet."

She cocked her head and snickered, but caved to his persistent gesturing and slid down onto the bench across from him, exhaling relief. "Me rest for a small minute, bold face, but me want no beer." She rolled her eyes at the other waitress, a heavy gal.

"Afraid your husband will get pissed if he hears you sat with me?"

"Me no longer has no husband, mon."

"So what's the problem?" It took effort not to openly celebrate that revelation. Still, no husband didn't translate into untaken or available.

"This a small place, mon, and all that happen today be talk about tomorrow."

"You saying folks don't have anything better to do around here but gossip?"

"It typical, mon. You never before visit one of these islands?"

"Hell yeah, I've called at a whole string of them, sailing from Puerto Rico to Saint Lucia. Was on my way to Barbados when my destination got changed by a squall that damn near swamped my sailboat."

"Oh, for Lord's sake. You boat survive?"

"Yeah, I got battered but was lucky. That's why I'm going to hang around awhile and make necessary repairs. Sure hope it doesn't cost too damn much."

"Jesus Lord, all you rich Yankees sail down here in you big yachts, then too cheap to leave a few coins with we poor islanders."

"Hey, I'm just a Puerto Rican boy from the Bronx, not a rich Yankee. Retired, I'm on a jaunt through the Caribbean on a rebuilt sailboat."

"What kind of work you bold self retire from? You look to be a ball player or ring fighter."

He grinned and rolled his shoulders. "I boxed a little as a kid, a few times in the army. Light stuff. I worked as a New York City detective."

"So you rich now and doesn't work no more."

"I'm retired. Honest cops don't get rich."

"So how you have that boat to visit all these islands? You got you some obeah—some kind of Puerto Rican voodoo?"

"No magic. But it's a long story. Short story is: I underestimated the cost of cruising the Caribbean, even with the wind for free. Forget about it if I had to buy gasoline or diesel fuel. Fact is, I could use some extra bread. Maybe I can scare up a few bucks on the island by doing security work or something while my boat's being repaired."

"Best you had stopped some two weeks past. That fool prosecutor been wise to have an experienced investigator make his case before he victimize that Yankee mon."

"You mean the American yachtsman? I heard they don't have enough evidence to convict him."

"Lord, and that a good thing. The mon doesn't need to be punish for kill that scorpion. It amazing, mon, that no one do in Torchy long before that day."

"You saying the American killed the guy?"

"What difference it make? That fool prosecutor best to never hold Mister

Christopher in that dungeon."

"He must've had good reason to indict the guy."

"Byrum Josephs anxious to make his reputation. His pompous ass just appointed prosecutor not six months past. Best he learn to find evidence before he charge folks."

"Conviction record. We had a lot of that with the ADAs in New York who bull-headedly prosecuted cases to bolster their reputations."

"Arrogance, mon. Byrum Josephs think he God's gift to the world. The mon strut about trying to control everything and everybody meet his fancy. Damn stuff-shirt doesn't think he stink when he sweat."

"If the American killed the launch-man, it's only right he's convicted. Nobody should get away with murder."

"The white mon do the world a favor, ridding it of that animal."

"The clerk at Customs said the American had no reason to kill the guy."

"What that fool know?"

"How much do you know?"

Darla wrinkled her face in annoyance while rising and grumbling: "Bout time to fetch you food."

He grinned while watching her sashay off with sensual liquidity. Hell, she'd been real friendly—even volunteered that she didn't have a husband. Still, he found it hard to accept that the fox remained unattached. Hey, every once in a while a guy gets lucky.

The burly constable eyeballed him while sauntering past his booth, en route to the door. Ward figured the guy overheard him announce his having been a cop and decided to size up the New York variety.

Darla brought his plate of shrimp in mango sauce, along with an avocado salad and a bowl of steaming black-eyed peas. "Sit, and keep me company while I eat."

"Mon, me has other folks to tend to. You think a waitress free to spend the afternoon with any one customer?"

The tone of her rejection staggered him. Chingalo, he believed he had something going. Refusing to be brushed off, he said: "Okay, then have dinner with me tonight."

"Go 'bout you business and leave me be. Me has neither time nor desire to involve me'self with a foot-loose sailorman, here today and gone tomorrow."

#   #

Three

Ward glanced ahead to the governmental center, a confusion of aging Georgian-styled low-rise office buildings with an occasional mid-rise residential edifice, interspersed sporadically by austere church steeples. All types of vehicles and a conglomeration of pedestrians noisily interacted.

Entering the impressive structure that housed the Courthouse and Parliament he observed the locals greeting each other effusively, unlike taciturn New Yorkers. Females were as extroverted as the males. A couple of hotties reminded him of having struck out with Darla.

He snickered while searching for the Immigration Office, remembering those pouty lips that said no. Nobody wins them all. But that's one time he would have liked to score. Oh well, there's always mañana.

The clerk in the cage at Immigration stamped his visa and slid it back to him. "Enjoy you visit, sir."

"Thanks. Promise not to kill any launch-tenders during my stay."

"Mon, why you make light of so heinous a crime?"

"Sorry, didn't mean to rile you, bro'."

"You think you Yankee folk have God's right to kill Vincies at will?"

"Was only joking, man, with no intention of killing anybody." Ward hurried to exit into the concourse milling with people. Chingalo! That clerk's reaction attested that the prosecutor had supporters as well as critics.

But Texas Jack apparently intended to turn the trial into a circus, criticizing every phase of the proceedings by challenging that impressive mulatto to prove his case beyond any reasonable doubt. To his credit, the prosecutor had demonstrated intent to defend his integrity, in spite of Hower wounding him with acerbic taunts and questions.

However, it appears that Byrum Josephs needs to compile evidence that stands up to cross-examination, as well to media scrutiny. The defendant had been referred as a rich yachtsman, which meant high-priced lawyers capable of gouging holes in the prosecution.

He'd seen a lot of that in New York, and all too often suffered frustration. That's why the instructors and trainers dunned into them that you didn't bust anybody until you'd closed all the loopholes to prevent defense attorneys from confusing witnesses and confounding jurors.

Convictions required combing mountains of evidence for a few pebbles of

truth, to deny the skels beating the rap. A successful conclusion always justified the effort, besides rewarding him with pride.

But it grated in his gut that despite his high percentage of arrests, with proportionate convictions higher than most because of his dedication in wrapping cases up tightly before handing them to the DA's office, the hard-ass brass never promoted him to detective first grade. The humps deprived him of achieving that goal and earning the recognition he sought . . . and believed he deserved.

Sure the powers-that-be and self-righteous politicians claimed prejudice didn't exist in New York City. Shaking his head against that contention while loping down the hallway toward the exit he did a double-take at the plaque on one of the doors.

OFFICE OF THE HONORABLE PROSECUTOR

Considering that the prosecutor's case teetered on the brink of defeat because of criticism by the world press, that impressive mulatto might be receptive to the investigative skill Jack Hower disdained. Yep, an inquiry might be worth the effort, possibly resulting in his getting the chance to work a homicide again. Hey, he could use extra bread. And he'd love to stick it to Texas Jack

#　　#

Four

Ward sucked in resolve as he pushed open the door and ventured into a small anteroom crowded by three desks. Uniformed constables occupied two of them; one of them the burly guy he'd seen at the café. Recognition sparked in that man's eyes also.

"Any chance," Ward asked, "I can have a word with the prosecutor?"

The constable, with age etched in his chunky face, groaned as he pushed himself out of his chair and crossed to a paneled door. The other one, also mature, with a thin face and pencil mustache, scrutinized the visitor. After tapping on the door, the burly constable opened it sufficiently to stick his head in.

Ward couldn't hear what he said, but a moment later the constable waved him into the executive pomp of teak and gleaming steel. A bookcase with tiers of legal tomes back-dropped an impressive desk. The mulatto with full mustache postured importantly in his leather throne, his eyes questioning the intrusion.

Ward had removed his sunglasses and doffed his cap, and now extended his hand as he approached the desk. "How are you, sir? I'm Ward Perez, a retired New York City detective."

The prosecutor's annoyed expression partially receded into wrinkles of curiosity.

"Witnessed you holding your own against Jack Hower across from the Customs Port Office. The guy's arrogance must have irritated you. It sure rippled my gut."

"'T'is rather gratifying to hear all Americans are not insensitive," the prosecutor said as he rose to shake hands. "Jolly good to hear you do not subscribe to whitewashing the actions of your own, especially when the offense reprehensible." He waved Ward to one of the visitor's chairs before lowering himself into his throne.

Ward settled into the leather cushion of the sturdy teak chair. "I came here, sir, hoping we can make some arrangement for me to help you solidify your case."

The prosecutor studied the visitor, but didn't respond.

"Every case," Ward said, trying not to prattle nervously, "needs substantiation."

"Interesting, as well coincidental, having entertained employing an investigator to ensure the conviction. Understandably our chaps aren't trained with that sort of expertise, considering we have little capital crime in these small islands. When we do we know the perpetrators, therefore do not require investigators. But let us get to your qualifications."

"Twenty-eight years in the job, twenty-four as a detective, investigating every kind of case—more than eight with homicide. Check with NYPD."

"I most assuredly shall. May I assume you're familiar with our situation?"

Ward hunched his shoulders, unsure whether to admit he wasn't. But the prosecutor saved him by speaking. "One of our launch operators became the victim of a brutal homicide."

"From what I hear, you need to build a tighter case against the accused."

"Resulting from the critical press of your country, especially the scathing attacks by that indelicate person of World-Wide News. It leaves us without alternative but to enter court with an indisputable presentation, stifling criticism."

"I've got the experience and know-how, sir, to dig into crevices for evidence that'll help you build an air-tight case."

"T'would certainly be welcomed. We sorely lack that sort of expertise—rarely require it, actually. Nor does the budget allow for a proper homicide investigative unit."

"Can you stretch it for payment and expenses?"

"Just last evening I met with the prime minister, as well the home minister, to discuss this very matter. Those gentlemen supportive, though they limited me to a budget not to exceed ten thousand US dollars."

Ward winced, stung by the paucity of the offering. He'd heard of guys picking up five times that amount in capital cases. Okay, generally the defense rather than the prosecution retained them, and in big cosmopolitan centers, not in a dinky island most people never heard of.

He wondered if he shouldn't have approached the accused—a rich yachtsman. But then he'd be allied to Texas Jack. No thanks.

"Considering your level of expertise," the prosecutor said, "you'll quite likely earn that sum in rather a short time. What say we recompense you in the amount of one hundred dollars per day to allay whatever expenses—certainly far more than you are likely to require in our small island?"

Ward dipped his head side to side as he contemplated bickering for more.

"Upon presentation of conclusive evidence," the prosecutor said, "we shall release to you the balance. Rather a handsome reward, I'd say, for a few days work."

Those words: a few days seduced him. While he didn't consider it a fortune, no way he'd sneeze at ten thousand smackers. Hell, he'd probably spend the best part of a week before they got his boat repaired. So he might as well pick up those few bob during that layover to offset the cost of repairs, and still have a sock-full of greenbacks to spice up his life.

Best of all, he'd have the chance to work a homicide again—one getting worldwide exposure. Word of his involvement just might get back to The Apple. Chingalo! That'd be outasight!

"Well, what say you?"

"I'll need to be brought up to speed, considering it's a cold case."

"We shall most assuredly brief you quite adequately with every phase."

"Sounds good." Ward leaned across the desk to shake Joseph's hand, sealing the arrangement. Enthused and anxious to get to work, he asked: "Where are we presently?"

"Despite it being essentially circumstantial, we're confident we have a

convincing case. Here is a copy of the postmortem."

Ward accepted the folder but didn't bother to open and read it, since it only dealt with the cause of death. He'd bet a fin its findings qualified any number of people as suspects. "What's Christopher's arrest based on?"

"Local fishermen found the body of Torchy, the launch operator, floating in Bequia Channel, some eight to ten kilometers south of here. It contained ropes. Judging by the rust stains, he'd been tied to weights which broke away, allowing the body to surface—a rather certain indication of the work of an amateur. As the postmortem concludes, death resulted from three bullets fired from a thirty-two-caliber revolver."

"You recovered the weapon?"

"Unfortunately, not as yet."

Ward's brow arched as he wondered how they knew the weapon was a revolver rather than a semi-automatic pistol, or even a rifle, but he decided against questioning that for the present. "What specifically induced you to indict this Christopher guy?"

"A number of witnesses shall testify to his being the last person with the victim. He possesses a deep-sea yacht, the means to dispose of a body in the ocean. Word has it that he kept a snub-nosed thirty-two-caliber revolver aboard, ostensibly for shooting sharks."

Ward stifled a snicker at Josephs' presumption that those shots were fired by that particular yachtsman's revolver. Probably the owners of half of those boats moored in the area had weapons. Hell, predators were prevalent in the tropic waters of the Caribbean . . . as were incidents of piracy.

"The weapon is now missing," Josephs said, "and no one can account for its whereabouts."

"His defense attorney will have a dozen responses to that."

The prosecutor's scowl contorted his mustache, revealing that he didn't appreciate being disputed. "The morning of the murder, many witnessed Ogden Christopher and the launch-man engage in rather a row on the wharf of the Lagoon Hotel. Subsequently, those two departed in Torchy's launch, despite their heated differences, supposedly to convey Christopher to his yacht moored in the roadstead.

That indisputably makes Christopher the last person to have contact with the deceased."

Ward squelched retorting that if someone else killed the guy after the conclusion of that delivery Christopher didn't rate as the last person to see him. Others possessed .32s . . . may have stolen Christopher's. He hoped Josephs hadn't painted himself into a corner. Chingalo! Was he being hasty in jumping on this frustration in the making?

"We are convinced of Christopher's guilt," Josephs said as he sat back and puffed himself up. "We have associative evidence and can prove opportunity."

Ward wondered what <u>we</u> encompassed. They obviously didn't have much of a staff. But he steered away from that to concentrate on the case. "What about motive?"

"Anger, rather obviously."

"Induced by what?"

"Any number of possibilities." Vexation edged the prosecutor's voice. "It's not a bit unusual for the white wives of yachtsmen to have a go at a virile black man."

"You saying jealousy or race-hatred triggered the killing?"

"Any number of possibilities exist."

"Do you have witnesses—someone to point a finger at the perp?"

"Not as yet." Josephs handed him another file. "We haven't yet established motive, though there are any number of assumptions. Quite a few employees at the pier of the Lagoon Hotel witnessed them that morning exhibiting hostility. They are amenable to testifying that the accused and the victim went off together in Torchy's launch."

Ward squirmed, uncomfortable with suppositions to support circumstantial evidence. He really wanted this opportunity, yearned to dip his oar in again, could use the ten grand, but didn't want to end up looking like a chump. He blinked back a vision of Texas Jack on the tube questioning and ridiculing the Puerto Rican's expertise as a detective.

"Anyone accompany Christopher and Torchy on that launch?" he asked.

"Christopher's wife and a crewman of his yacht, according to employees at the wharf. Afraid you'll find those two rather uncooperative."

"I'm guessing you've already interviewed them."

"Quite so. His rather testy wife is cognizant she is not required to bear witness against her husband. The insolent deckhand claimed complete unawareness of any unpleasantness on the launch."

"Typical of skels and their cohorts."

"A circumstance that requires we obtain a bit more substantiation."

Ward had all he could do not to blurt out that they didn't need <u>a bit more</u>—but a <u>ton</u> more. Hell, they didn't have a bona-facie case yet. But the prosecutor continued to stare at him like he expected him to respond affirmatively. Carajo, Ward wished he'd been more discriminating before committing to a case with poor prospects of clearing, having pounded his head into enough dead-ends during his cop years. And he wasn't eager to be criticized on the tube by Texas Jack or some other race-baiting hump—having enough scars for one lifetime.

Okay, if he dug deep and found a starting point he might be able to follow it to a successful conclusion. "What evidence do you have from the launch, like fingerprints, blood or other bodily fluids, signs of a struggle, pieces of clothing—anything we can tie to the perp?"

"We haven't as yet recovered the launch. Quite likely Christopher sank it somewhere in the expanse of open sea."

Ward exhaled, daunted that they didn't even have a crime scene, a source of physical evidence and a place to theoretically reconstruct the events that led to the murder. Chingalo, they lacked the most rudimentary investigative direction.

"I assume you examined Christopher's hands for gunpowder residue." He gaped when Josephs stared blankly at him, obviously unfamiliar with the procedure. "It's to determine if he'd discharged a firearm recently."

"Actually, no. You see, we're not equipped for that sort of thing. Exactly why we welcome your expertise. Perhaps among these you'll discover direction." Josephs pushed a number of files to the front of his desk.

Ward glanced at them but didn't reach for them. "Two weeks. It's washed off by now. Do you have the clothing he wore at the time?"

"Never occurred to any of us to collect those. It's quite possible they remained on the yacht." Josephs tapped the files. "Something in this lot may prove enlightening."

Ward stared at them. Chingalo, he'd never heard of a police department that lacked investigative capability. He swiveled around to Constable Booker, who leaned against the doorjamb. "Beat cops always have the poop. What can you contribute?"

"No longer have a beat, sir, as you calls it, having been assigned to the prosecutor's office and no longer patrol the streets to hear rumors."

"Okay, based on your experience, what's your take on this?"

"As the honorable prosecutor informed you, we has no eyewitness to the murder."

Ward pondered whether Josephs realized one of his staff didn't make much of an effort to bolster the conviction. Then it occurred to him that Josephs engaged him without vetting his creds, raising concern for the level of the prosecutor's desperation.

Okay, in spite of the negatives, he'd shake the case until it yielded results. Hell, he yearned to do cop work again after a twelve-month hiatus . . . especially homicide investigating. So he'd damn well sift through everything and get to the bone of truth . . . prove himself as a crackerjack detective.

Rising, Ward picked up the files and ambled toward the door. "I'll study this stuff the rest of the afternoon so I'll be ready in the morning to probe in the right places for the evidence needed to bolster the conviction."

"Exactly why we are prepared to reward you, detective. We shall be banking rather heavily on you. National pride is at stake here."

So's a man's life, Ward wanted to say, but doubted that'd be bright . . . just might provoke the pompous prosecutor into rescinding the assignment. Dammit, he yearned for one last opportunity to solve a homicide. But he hoped he hadn't volunteered to perform mouth-to-mouth to resuscitate a horse that died two weeks ago.

#   #

Five

Ward headed for the Courthouse exit, eager to distance himself from that haughty prosecutor. Dios en cielo, was he an idiota for taking the case—considering the paucity of information?

"Why, sir, did you pop into the prosecutor's office?"

Startled by the Britishy voice, Ward snapped around to the two white guys poised with pads and pens—obviously reporters. Shaking off surprise, he chuckled and replied: "Just checking in with Immigration."

"Why then," the other one asked in an American voice, "were you in the prosecutor's office?"

"Social visit," Ward said, having no intention of satisfying their curiosity. All too often the media snoops prematurely publicized information that hindered investigations. And since he didn't see Kling, McVey or Texas Jack, he felt safe in not identifying himself, though he had little doubt they'd eventually learn his identity, as well as of his employment. Meanwhile he'd cling to anonymity.

So he strode away, ignoring their questions as he intermingled with tourists popping in and out of shops on Hillsboro Street. Grinding his teeth, he rehashed everything discussed with the prosecutor, rankled that none of it offered direction in taking the case apart. Man, it'd blow away his old buddies in blue if word got back to The Apple that he'd cracked a homicide in a remote waystation of Calypsoville.

But his optimism fizzled when he weighed the odds against clearing cold cases. They were, inarguably, difficult to solve, even in major metropolitan centers that enjoyed every forensic advantage. Evidence became tainted by time and incompetence. Too often witnesses had short memories, lost interest or changed their minds as to what they saw. Some moved away without leaving a forwarding address. Worse was when police files got lost in the shuffle, intentionally or by accident—or sheer ineptitude.

It perplexed him most that the prosecutor retained him without verifying his having been with NYPD. Okay, the guy was desperate, so Ward hunched dismissal of that and concentrated on formulating a direction. Generally he'd walk through the crime scene and try to conjure up the sequence of events. But here he was denied even that basic beginning.

Texas Jack's insinuations flashed in memory with implications of affirmative action and equal opportunity provisions being responsible for all he'd achieved. Bullshit! Nobody handed him success. He'd worked his ass off to earn recognition.

Not all that many Puerto Ricans made detective twenty-odd years ago. Pride dictated that he stand out in the job, inspiring him to apply diligence to produce sufficient evidence to assure convictions. That application resulted in his compiling an enviable arrest record.

Before that he spent a few years in uniform as a patrolman, until he'd earned promotion to serve as a plain-clothes cop. That was an exercise in frustration, searching for stolen cars that had probably been chopped into spare parts or shipped to Latin America by the time the owner reported the theft. Despite that, he persevered in compiling successes over the next few years, resulting in being awarded a gold shield—the credential of a detective.

However, the powers-that-be assigned him to pursue burglars in the ghetto . . . rascals who faded away as quickly as the loot they stole. Nevertheless, he made every effort to root them out, intent upon amassing an impressive arrest record.

He'd followed the lead of veteran detectives who'd established stables of confidential informants. Most squeals were gangbangers and small-time hoods that sold out their brethren for chump change, or to avenge a grievance, and many times to eliminate competition. Others were storekeepers and neighborhood people who wanted to rid their areas of bad guys, without divulging their identities.

Having eyes and ears on the street contributed to successes, which led to

assignment in Anti-Crime, a division devoted to combating organized criminals. In his case it amounted to taking down small-time wiseguys in Spanish Harlem. Finally the brass kicked him up to detective-second-grade in the homicide squad, but kept him uptown to take down the compatriotos and brothers.

Nevertheless, he continued to apply diligence, determined to prove himself deserving of that next promotion. But they never awarded him the designation of detective first-grade, a tag that said something about your abilities, besides carrying pay equal to lieutenants—the ticket to middle-class America.

Yeah, he knew his bosses denied him that accolade because he resisted going undercover for Narcotics, to spy on and betray people he'd grown up with in the 'hood. Prejudicial New Yorkers slammed doors in the faces of Puerto Ricans, dashing their hopes, and that intangible called pride . . . dissolving their compunctions about how they acquired money to survive.

Denied everything except menial jobs, they lost faith in the US society. Over time they evolved into full-time thugs. In many instances they reverted to barbarism in their zeal to savor the sweetness of payback. placing no more value on anybody else's life than they did on their own.

Fortunately, some persevered to overcome the roadblocks and made their way out of the ghetto. But too many fell through the cracks to wallow in self-pity. They sought to dispel the pain of defeat by hurting those who had systematically blocked their aspirations and punctured their dreams.

Ward knew vengeance didn't cure the pain. But how do you impress that on someone who's lost hope as well as respect for society's laws? They weren't about to listen to a cop, since they condemned the police as the handmaidens of the privileged, consequently their enemies. If they made him for an undercover narc they'd blow him away—along with his family.

Their disregard for authority created fear and, combined with their terrorism, convinced most people in the 'hood not to testify against them. That pervading dread rendered those miscreants untouchable in their slummy turfs.

But Ward had no reticence about marching into any barrio with a badge pinned to his chest, to invade the impoverished tenements and neglected hovels infested with vermin. All too often he'd tripped through trash-littered alleys where rodents scurried or tromped around in gutted buildings to bust wrongdoers. The inhabitants trapped there by economics concealed their gratitude for relieving their lives of the gangbangers. A whole lot of courage didn't exist in the ghetto.

Every kid who grew up in Spanish Harlem or the South Bronx knew about the <u>traficantes</u>, and cringed from their merciless manner of reprisal. Ward cared as much as anyone else about the area's children and shared the ardor of preventing them being turned into criminals by the dealers.

Yes, he yearned to help save them from sinking into the despair of narcotics dependency. But he'd long ago accepted the improbability of wiping out the drug trade as long as it continued to generate more money than most honest businesses and many major corporations. Fact is, marijuana rated as the most lucrative cash crop in the country.

Cops arrested scores of users and a few traffickers every day, only to be frustrated by seeing those mooks back on the street within a few hours after getting their wrists slapped by judges. Dishonest cops ignored the pushers as long as their pockets were stuffed with pay-offs. Politicians pontificated against the trade, but did little to stop it.

Consequently, he considered it pointless to risk life and limb in a futile effort. Besides, he wasn't about to put his family in jeopardy. The desperadoes considered themselves betrayed when a Puerto Rican fingered them . . . cop or no cop. Those bad-asses made their own rules, and didn't allow for exceptions.

So he did the best job he could, while steadfastly refusing to work Narcotics. His rat-bastard bosses expressed their resentment by denying him that desired promotion, the designation as supercop, regardless of the cases he brought to a successful conclusion.

If you didn't kowtow to those bullying deputy commissioners they'd stick it to you. They even denied him working in Manhattan, shunting him to Brooklyn. Still, he thanked God they hadn't exiled him to the boonies of Staten Island or the residential neighborhoods of Queens.

Born and bred in the crowded and bustling city, he needed its vibrancy to energize him.

He liked working homicide, where you dealt with forensic science, had a chance to solve a crime. You earned the respect, and even the envy, of other cops. You walked with your head high. But the last time he refused to go under as a narc, the humps reassigned him to burglary in Brooklyn. In spite of his record as a productive homicide detective, they stuck it to him, essentially demoting him.

Six

Ward jerked out of his abstraction to realize he'd wandered all the way to the Lagoon Hotel. Okay, why not capitalize on being where Christopher and the murdered launch-tender were last observed together? Just maybe he'd wheedle something useful out of those employees on the pier.

No doubt they've discussed the case with everyone, read about it in the newspaper and heard it talked to death on radio and TV; been coached by self-appointed authorities on how to describe what they saw. By now some have modified their stories, while others wrestled with second thoughts, besides being unsure of what they'd witnessed. Some had become hesitant of testifying. In contrast to those reluctant to come forward, or those who downplayed what they saw or heard, a few had a compulsion to boast of their importance by bragging having seen more than possible in a momentary glance.

But he determined to separate fact from mistaken belief, truth from exaggeration and actuality from fiction. Ward Perez had a date with destiny.

While approaching the pier he scanned the impressive hotel, stand-out amid a hodgepodge of aging two- and three-storied buildings that rambled around a wide bay and reached into craggy hills. Palm trees and leafy flora decorated rocky peaks that served as beacons for the sailing and motor yachts swaying to the tides, most with sea birds roosting in their rigging.

Clutching his files, he strode onto the wood-planked pier, passing an array of yachts that presented a dazzle of wealth, their mooring lines and dock fenders creaking and groaning. By peripheral vision he spotted a husky black guy skulking in the shade of a nearby verandah.

Ward surreptitiously assessed him, noting his bristly beard covering the lower part of a hard face with twisted features that made ugly sound complimentary. A multicolored skullcap crowned a tangle of snake-like dreadlocks—the hairdress of Rastas, the bad-asses of the Caribbean.

No denying that decent black nationalists wore that hairdo also, but this guy didn't impress him as a spokesman for upstanding citizens. A brightly printed shirt that Africans called a dashiki draped his broad shoulders and muscular torso, its tails hanging outside his baggy pants.

Why and who, Ward wondered, considered it important enough to stake out the dock? Did he surveil visitors or dockworkers, and for whom? If the mook's presence related at all to his case Ward conjectured that it just might not be a simple killing of rage, jealousy, self-defense or passion.

Hell, a rich, white yachtsman doesn't go around killing black launch tenders for kicks—not a sane one anyway. Yeah, he needed to learn the motive to confirm whether Christopher did the deed, assuming he wasn't off his rocker, or driven to a jealous rage by discovering his wife getting boffed by a black stud.

Nodding to those assumptions, he strode among employees lethargically trundling from boat to boat or shuffling to and from storage sheds, attending to repetitive tasks hour after hour and day after day. Sea birds hunkering on pilings appeared as sluggish as the dockworkers.

Ward approached two guys at the coffee station. "Hi, I'm Ward Perez, a special investigator for the prosecutor." Aroma from the coffee urn competed with the pungency of diesel oil and the acrid bite of gasoline. "Hoped you might fill me in on what occurred between Ogden Christopher and that launch-tender, Torchy."

The men exchanged glances, then stared blankly at the interloper. One hunched his shoulders while the other pretended interest in nearby gear. Ward suppressed sniggering at behavior typical of those reluctant to get involved.

"Any chance," Ward asked, "I can have some of that coffee?"

The one who'd hunched gestured toward the pot. Ward muttered gratitude while pouring himself a foam cupful. A few curious others sidled over, while remaining a short distance apart.

Wincing after sipping the strong and bitter coffee that had been brewing all day, Ward asked: "Are you all native to this island?"

Some arched their brows at the seeming insignificance of his inquiry. An older man snickered and said: "Me born and raised right here in Kingstown."

"Me also," a mature woman said.

"Me come up here from the Grenadines," a skinny fellow said.

Ward nodded as he placed those islands to the south. "Guess you're married and have kids to support," he said to no one in particular. "I sure know what it's like to pay rent and buy food, as well as shoes and such for the tykes. Fact is, I'm still burdened with money pressures."

"No different than all we," the woman said. And they nodded to each other.

"I'm inclined to believe," Ward said, "that most of you witnessed Mister

Christopher leave the wharf in Torchy's launch."

Yeah, he received a murmur, but couldn't decipher whether it indicated affirmation or denial. "Anyone mind telling me what occurred that fateful day?"

The older man pointed out to the bay and smacked his palms together. "Torchy go off to carry Mister Christopher to he yacht. That all us sees."

"Were they alone?" Ward asked.

"Mister Christopher have he wife and one he crewmon," the woman said.

"That Yankee mon a tightwad," the skinny fellow said, snickering. "Him moor he craft in the bay so him not pay to berth it here at the wharf."

"It cheaper," the woman said, "to pay water taxis to get back and forth."

The husky man beside her chuckled. "The mon tight, mon—more than the clam's ass, which waterproof." They all chuckled.

"Me find it strange," the woman said, "when the night-man say how him and he wife return to they yacht the night before those things happen, only to go ashore an hour or so later."

"Yes, Lord," the tall guy said, "it amaze me, mon, that the cheapskate pay for launches both ways when he spend nothing if he stay ashore."

"Anyone beside me wonder," another asked, "why they pays to stay in a hotel that night instead of sleep on they boat once they return to it?"

"Might be," the husky guy said, "they has fear of staying on they boat that night."

"Fear of what?" Ward asked.

"Lord knows," the man replied. The others hunched to indicate they were no better informed.

"I'd appreciate if you'd describe the encounter between Mister Christopher and Torchy that morning," Ward said.

A couple of them shrugged and glanced to others. The woman spoke up. "Mister Christopher purchase diving equipment from this chandlery, then hire a water taxi to carry it with he'self and he wife out to they yacht."

"T'wasn't no time a'tall," the older man said, "'fore Torchy arrive in he different launch."

"Lord, those folks blanches they fear on sight of Torchy," the skinny fellow said.

"Most in the island," the woman said, "fears that damn scorpion."

"You're saying the Christophers recognized that bad-ass?" Ward asked.

"No different than all us," the older man said. "All us quake we fear when us sees that bully."

"So you're saying Christopher knew Torchy?" Ward asked.

"Every soul on this island know the mon evil," the woman said.

"Him first show up most a year ago," the husky man said.

"It said him come from Cumberland Bay on the northwest coast," the woman said.

"That mon a menace the day him set foot in Kingstown," the older man said.

"But none expect more from a Black Carib," the skinny guy said.

Ward's brow arched. "I know about Caribs, the original Indian inhabitants, but don't understand the black part."

"Most three hundred years past," the husky one said, "a slave ship be sink off the coast of Bequia."

Ward noted that the guy pronounced the name of that island some eight or ten kilometers to the south as Bek-wah.

"Those Africans swims ashore," the heavy woman said, "and marry with the Caribs. Us calls they chil'rens black Caribs."

"They a fierce people," the skinny fellow added, "who kill and plunder, with no respect for authority."

"English soldiers," the older man said, "subdue the most of those barbarians more than a hundred years ago."

"Them round all them up," the woman added, "and ship most to the jungles of Central America."

"Some few escapes," the stocky man said, "and hides in the mountains of this main island."

"Torchy living proof," the woman said, "—well, a dead one now—that those savages survives to the present."

"Lord knows," the husky guy said, "how many run about and terrorize folks."

"What happened when Torchy arrived that day?" Ward asked, to prevent them going off on a tangent.

"The scorpion take it upon he'self," the woman said, "to take the diving equipment from the first water taxi to put in he own launch."

"Him ignore objections of Mister Christopher," the skinny fellow said."

"That first water taxi operator whimper," the woman said, "bout how Torchy bully him out the money him need to feed he family."

"But the mon show good sense to stay out of Torchy way," the skinny fellow said. "Torchy not one to mess with."

"Torchy surprise all we," the husky guy said, "by show a deaf ear to the American who beg he to leave that equipment alone."

"As it happen," the older man said, "a crewmon of that yacht happen along."

"But Torchy stand with he fists on he hips," the skinny fellow said, "and tell the Yankee yachtsman he doesn't take that oldster aboard he launch."

"That the first time," the husky guy said, "Mister Christopher stand fast and say he doesn't go on the launch of that bully without he deckhand."

"Lord, it surprise all we," the heavy woman said, "that Torchy give way to have that crewmon aboard."

"First time," the husky guy said, "any of we see that mean-ass back down."

"Seem to me," the skinny fellow said, "Torchy have more interest in Mister Christopher to board his launch than he do in carrying the equipment."

"Why?" Ward asked.

They shook their heads and shrugged.

"Surprise me, mon," the older man said, "when Torchy doesn't run off with they equipment. That he usual way."

"When Mister Christopher with he wife and crewmon go off with Torchy in he launch," the woman said, "that the last any of we see of the mon."

"And most us thanks God for that," the older man said.

"Did anyone hear gunshots?" Ward asked.

They shrugged. "Who know the sound of guns?" the older man replied. "The bay busy, mon, with boats of one type or another. Noise as common as these pesky flies."

"Besides," the husky guy said, "all us has things more important than watch boats come and go."

"I suppose you told all this to the prosecutor," Ward said.

A few averted their eyes. "Us grateful to Mister Christopher," the woman said, "for rid this island of that hoodlum. Why us speaks against that mon?"

"Torchy deserve shooting long before," the older man said.

"Maybe him disrespect Mrs. Christopher," the skinny fellow said, "which why that white mon shoot he ass."

"Torchy a scorpion," the woman said, "who force he'self on some few women."

"It why most folks fears he bad-ass," the older man said.

Ward grimaced at that information. It wasn't going to help the prosecutor win a conviction against the man who rid the island of that menace.

"Jus' might be," the older man said, "that the first water-taxi-driver wait for Torchy to take the Christophers to they yacht, then murders the brute for take he fare."

Others nodded to that. Ward hoped to hell the defense attorney didn't realize how good a case he had, with only circumstantial evidence to charge the yachtsman, but steadily increasing testimony to point elsewhere.

Too many times Ward heard ADAs worry whether the jurors found the defendant sympathetic. Worse was when any of those twelve people abhorred the victim and concluded that the world was better served without that hump.

He winced at the possibility that the prosecutor might not pay off if the investigation exonerated Christopher. He'd been counting on that ten grand to relieve the burden of another student loan. His son, Ramón, just graduated from Saint John's University with intent to start law school at New York University this fall . . . a formidable expense.

While thanking everyone and shaking their hands he spotted the bearded Rastaman with dreadlocks hanging from his wooly cap skulking nearby. Damn real it raised interest . . . and sparked hope.

#   #

Seven

Pretending unawareness of the husky black while strolling off the pier, Ward gazed at the variety of watercraft. Eager to learn whether the guy took an interest in him—and why—he sauntered along the seawall, feigning interest in the happenings on the bay. Sure enough the Rasta shadowed him, displaying experience by staying at a distance while keeping the mark in sight.

Ward stopped at a pebbly place on the bank, in the shade of a tree with smaller leaves than the seagrape but similar in shape, and its branches heavy with yellow-green apples. He skimmed stones across the surface of the bay, using that activity to surreptitiously glance around.

Disregarding the billowing cumulus clouds drifting out of the east, with dark undersides portending rain, Ward pondered the reason the Rasta kept an eye on things at the wharf and now shadowed him. Was there a bigger story here than either the prosecutor or Texas Jack contemplated? If so, he determined to pierce the veil and learn what it is.

An aging local in straggle-fringed straw hat loping past yelled to Ward while pointing to that accumulation of threatening clouds. "Rain come, mon. Rain come."

Ward waved gratefully to the guy and called back: "The tree'll shelter me."

"Lord, you Yankee never learn this land," the gnarled oldster scolded. "That a machineel tree, mon. When it rain, acid fall and blister you skin. Best you hie you Yankee self out from under there."

Carajo! He felt like an idiot for not recognizing the yellow apples. Yelling his thanks to the man, Ward darted out from under the tree just as the heavens deluged the earth. He pulled the visor of his cap down to shield his eyes while hurrying across the hardscrabble and weeds to Grenadines Wharf, a road flanked by shops shabbier than those on the streets frequented by tourists. Unconcerned for that, he took cover in the entrance of the closest.

Dammit, he'd lost sight of that Rasta—had hoped to pump information out of the bearded hump, maybe get a heads-up about a criminal conspiracy that the prosecutor had no knowledge of. One year out of harness and he'd gotten rusty, lost sight of the mook.

Berating himself for his goof, Ward watched the squall sweep past and the sun return to bathe the world. Grenadines Wharf returned to the carnival of merchants selling from crude stands to milling locals, and peddlers weaving among the multitudes, pushing carts or bent over with the weight of their burdens, all noisily hawking their wares.

Their voices along with those of babbling shoppers and tourists synthesized with traffic noises, to be punctured by the disharmony of squawking seabirds quarreling for scavenged food. Ward wandered up a side street away from the waterfront, in search of a place to crash after he took his boat to a boatyard for repairs.

He sure as hell didn't intend to get skinned by those pricey tourist hotels. Oh yeah, he exhilarated upon spotting the hand-painted legend, MANGO INN, on a stucco front in need of painting. But it suggested economy and prompted him to enter and check it out.

He found the inn small but clean, realized its low rates resulted from its simplicity and deficiency of amenities, specifically its lack of air conditioning. Obviously it catered to visiting islanders rather than Americans or Europeans. Okay by him since he wasn't all that fond of rabiblancos—a pejorative reference for white-asses who enjoy money and live in a totally different world than the poor asses exploited by the affluent.

He didn't have the luxury of air conditioning on his boat. They sure never had any when he grew up back in the South Bronx. Fact is, that apartment in Brooklyn when he first married, didn't enjoy it either. It wasn't like he needed to make sacrifices.

He selected one of the cheaper back rooms, with a small window looking out onto a mildew-streaked wall closing off a narrow patio overgrown with exotic plants—or weeds. The furniture he considered adequate, in spite of it looking like it survived the sailors of the Columbus voyages. At least the place appeared clean. Then a movement in the far corner caught his eye, but he didn't need to identify the scurrying thing.

Roaches were as common as flies in the South Bronx, and had required care and application to battle the infestations in his various Brooklyn apartments. Ay Dios, they run rife in Puerto Rico and every island he'd called at in the archipelago. Better than seeing spiders or centipedes, which he knew scampered through the islands, as did scorpions. So he wasn't about to complain if he occasionally encountered cucarachas.

#   #

Eight

Ward threw off the line of his sailboat bobbing at the mooring buoy, then motored it into a boatyard. A gruff guy assured him of attention just as soon as he finished with another yachtsman. Ward scoffed at that flattering inclusion—exaggerated in his case.

He packed clothing while waiting to hold him over during his sojourn ashore. All the while his mind swirled with uncertainty for having made that deal with the prosecutor. No denying the money became a factor in his decision to take the case. Yes, every buck counted when you lived on a pension, though other motives were equally compelling.

The misleading aspect of the case reminded him of that one in Crown Heights, Brooklyn some months after his transfer from homicide to burglary that brought about the closing stages of his police career. Responding to a burglary, he stumbled upon a dead body and dutifully called in the cocky bastards of Homicide, who never let you forget they rated as the elite of the police department . . . not that he didn't strut his stuff when he was in Homicide.

The West Indian kid next door to the victim admitted to having a lot of the victim's clothing and other possessions in his apartment, which he claimed he purchased from the deceased during weeks past, but had no receipts. Nor could he corroborate his alibi of having been studying in the park during the afternoon. He didn't have a steady job, spoke with that calypso accent and struck the two homicide dicks as desperate. Those honkies booked the kid without even considering any other perpetrator, and the ADA indicted.

Ward didn't believe the kid had done it, maybe because he admired the young guy for living on a shoestring, an ocean away from family and friends while attending Brooklyn College. Yeah, and also because the kid exhibited character by refusing to cop to a lesser plea . . . persisting his innocence.

Besides, Ward accepted as credible the kid's claim that he bought the clothing and stuff from the victim, since the dead guy turned out to be a user. Junkies will sell their belly buttons for a fix. Yes, and he responded to intuition, that analysis capability engendered by years of experience. Sure, he had to close the book on the burglary, but he refused to settle for Homicide's perp.

He leaned on his squeals, which resulted in turning up a few leads. One thing led to another, and before long he had the real culprit. The skel tried to stonewall him, but after a little persuasion confessed to the murder.

Boy, that pissed the ADA, since he'd bragged during a press conference about the swift and efficient work of both the DA's office and that of the Homicide Division. The two Homicide humps had steam coming out of their ears. They vociferously objected to Ward's booking the perp, yammering that he should have reported his findings to them and let it be their collar. They threatened payback.

A few days later the bastards stuck it to him by reassigning him to the South Bronx, to work in Anti-Crime again. You took your life in your hands in that precinct, referred to as Fort Apache—a battle-zone of gang wars and drive-by shootings, with the police generally in the crossfire. The place reeked with corruption, born of apathy. During his twenty-eight years he'd avoided being on anybody's pad. Nothing about that assignment qualified as duty a fifty-year-old cop wanted.

He'd broken up with Myrna the week before, ending a four-year alliance. So, unattached now and despondent because of that transfer, demotion and exile as it were, he opted for retirement. He had his belly full of New York, and of living as an alien in the city in which he'd been born. So he took the farm and sought a friendlier environment.

On this remote island he'd been handed one more chance to prove himself, though clearing the case was anything but promising. Ay Dios, he desperately wanted to cap off his career on an upbeat, not a sour note, to allow him to bask in the media light of supercop, with World-Wide News reporting his success to the whole goddam world . . . especially to all those hump-busting deputy-commissioners in The Apple.

\# \#

Nine

Ward yawned, wearied from a long day. Afternoon had waned by the time he finished negotiating the cost of repairs. Okay, he'd have to spend a few bob, but his baby would be in top shape in a couple of days, when he'd resume his journey to the fabled land of Spanish conquistadors.

Meanwhile he'd earn some bucks, a necessity considering the cost of cruising, plus the never-ending need for money to send home to his son. Not that Ward minded sacrificing to support Ramón. The kid earned his father's dedication, having graduated high in his class at Saint Johns University, therefore qualified to attend law school at NYU. Despite divorcing the boy's mother, Ward remained a father in fact, not only in name, supporting his son monetarily as well as inspirationally.

Orgullo simply translated means pride. To a Puerto Rican born in a New York barrio, it fulfilled every dream to have your son graduate as a lawyer. Believe that he bragged about Ramón to anyone who'd listen.

While dropping his duffel of clothing off at the hotel he noted the time as past six. Yeah, he'd goof for the rest of the day, to reinvigorate his brain so it'd be sharp in the morning. Then he'd shift the investigation into high gear.

His mouth watered for a beer, so he headed for the Pilgrim's Pride Café, even though that chica put a damper on his earlier overture. Hell, he'd had turndowns before that did miraculous flips and ended in bliss. Conyo, man, he'd talk some trash and just maybe inject a little passion in his life. A sailor's life is long days of aloneness. Believe he could do with a night of togetherness.

But he grimaced upon arriving at the café to find two other gals serving dinner. Oh, well, he'd catch up to her at lunch tomorrow. Wagging his head, he pondered whether to stay for a beer or go find a joint with a swinging ambiance.

"What you bold self doing back here?"

Startled by her voice, he swiveled around to see her with those bangles jiggling from her earlobes and a big straw-like pocketbook slung over her shoulder. "Hey there. You're all dressed up. Going somewhere special?"

"Home, mon. Time to be a family woman."

He gaped as she strode for the door, summarily abandoning him. Clenching his jaws in resolve, he pursued her to the sidewalk. "Guess your husband's waiting for you to bring home the groceries and cook his dinner."

"Mon, me not tell you me has no husband no more?"

He sputtered, lost for a reply. It did, however register that she remembered telling him that. But, just maybe, she told everybody.

"He be a policeman like you own self—'til that day those Rastas shoot the mon down in cold blood—four years past. Damn Trinidad dope dealers!"

"Hey, I'm sorry to hear that." Compassion etched Ward's face as he experienced the pain cops felt when hearing about other cops getting snuffed. It didn't surprise him that the man had been the victim of Rastas. He had a lot of experience with those bad-asses, who often wore their hair in long curls called dreadlocks—like that mook who'd stalked him at the pier.

Remembering the colorful cap that mook wore, he shook his head in wonderment at wearing something that wooly in the tropics. He accepted them in Brooklyn . . . in winter anyway. Matter of fact, Bed-Sty had the reputation as a breeding ground for those <u>natty dreads</u>, as African-Americans differentiated between the bad-asses and the decent adherents of that religious conviction.

A law-abiding Jamaican who subscribed to the Rastafarian philosophy preached to him years ago that they sought to raise the level of self-esteem among blacks. But they suffered the curse of gangbangers adopting the hairstyle and African garb, giving Rastamans a bad reputation.

"The pain fading," Darla said. "Me accustom me'self to be a widow."

"So what's your rush to get home?"

"Have me a daughter, mon."

"A little girl waiting for mommy to come home and prepare her dinner?"

"Thankfully she grown to a teenager."

"Hell, then she's able to feed herself. So relax and have a drink with me."

"This what you offer—to sit in this dismal place where me sweat and slave all day? Thank you, no."

"Hey, name the place."

"Mon, me hear you snivel 'bout spend money to repair you boat that you risks you life in. You doesn't sound like the mon can wine and dine this lady."

"Try me." He winced when she sucked her teeth. But, inhaling determination, he said: "Name your spot."

"All right, bold face, take me to the Lagoon, the luxury hotel where most you Yankee yachtsmen entertain you white ladies."

"You got it . . . though gringos don't consider Puerto Ricans Yankees . . . and wandering around in a rebuilt sailboat doesn't qualify me as a yachtsman."

"Whatever, mon. Just don't even think about anything beyond that one drink, after which me to get on home."

Ward grinned, amused by her declaration. Yeah, this chica had a right to be conceited. Okay, happy to have gotten the relationship off square one, he needed to plan square two, and hopefully three, following in progression.

Chasing chicas had a lot of similarities to clearing cases: one step at a time. Don't even think about making a collar until you've collected substantive evidence. And don't expect to cop some drawers until you have the chica cozying up to you.

#   #

Ten

He hailed a taxi, an economy hatchback barely large enough for both of them to squeeze into the back seat. That required he sit with his knees under his chin as they traversed streets swirling with pedestrians. Vehicles of every size and description competed for space, abrading each other with horns. Conyo, don't they have noise-abatement laws in this island?

Darla took a cellphone from her big straw bag and dialed, oblivious to that din. Then she spoke in a patois Ward didn't understand a word of, though he concluded she conversed with her daughter. He chuckled, remembering Jamaicans in New York supposedly speaking English, which he and most cops rarely understood. It reminded him of the expressions that clerk at Customs used, that he didn't understand.

So when Darla clicked off he asked her what they meant. She giggled. "Lord, you doesn't know long-head a compliment, mean he brainy. Gypsy-mouth say he talk to persuade, and not always truthful. Who use these words? And who they use them about?"

"The clerk at Customs when referring to Prosecutor Josephs."

Darla burst into laughter. "Lord, that the best description of that pompous fool me ever hear."

Ward speculated on what provoked that display. But as they swooshed past the sprawling fish market on Upper Bay Street his attention turned to shoppers milling around wooden stalls, as did flies swarming around seafood putrefying in the tropic sun. Its odor invaded the open windows of the taxi, since the zephyrs that rattled through the palm fronds comprised the vehicle's air conditioning.

Every jounce and turn brought their limbs into contact. Ward grinned when she damn near sprawled across him. "Lord, lord," she squealed, struggling to get upright, or push him off when the car's motion flung him across her. The taxi rounded a bend near the docks and pulled up to the impressive Lagoon Hotel, with its multi-storied façade and numerous verandahs.

She cut her eyes at Ward as he handed her out, criticizing him for his sneaky feels in the cab. He compressed his lips to suppress chuckling at her pretended modesty.

However, she mellowed as they strolled through the luxurious lobby to the bay side of the building, engulfed in that lavish environment and serenaded by a sultry calypso tune. Darla pointed to a table on the breezy verandah, with a view of the boats bobbing in the broad waterway.

A waiter in short white jacket served Darla a rum punch and Ward a cold beer. It didn't surprise him to receive Hairoun, since he hadn't specified any brand. Damned if he didn't admire the nationalistic attitudes of Vincentians.

Darla sipped her drink, then sighed and relaxed in the comfy rattan chair. Ward smiled, remembering that swelling of fulfillment when he'd gone to poshy places and felt like he'd arrived. Yeah, this chica deserved to be indulged. "Tell me, baby, that you're going to hang with me and have dinner."

"What else you bold self have in mind?" She sipped her drink, teasing him with her full lips caressing the rim of the glass and her dark eyes peering at him with feigned modesty. "You think to purchase this fine body with some plate of fancy food?"

"Hey, I'm inviting you to have dinner with me. Sure I'll try to get your gorgeous ass in bed. If I succeed, I want it to be because you want me as much as I want you."

She sniggered. "Most you braggarts falls short when it time to prove you'selves."

"Try me, baby. You with a world-class stud tonight."

She sucked her teeth. "Me may yet decide to take dinner with you bold self . . . but dinner only. Don't be thinking 'bout no other activities. Me just this day meet you bold self."

\#   \#

Eleven

"Want to stay here?" Ward asked after Darla caved to dine with him.

"This nice. Actually me prefers MATHILDA'S."

Ward shrugged and took her to that second floor saloon where they found the music scintillating. Seated at a table on the open terrace, and haloed by moonlight, they luxuriated in the evening breeze. Ward tapped his foot to the intoxicating calypso music wafting out from the interior room that induced the desire to dance to the rhythmic beats the locals referred to it as <u>jump-up</u>.

"Oo-ooh!" Ward approved the tasty calaloo soup, made from a green leaf as large as an elephant's ear, and cooked with chopped bacon and peeled shrimp. He considered ordering a second bowl, but the following course wiped out desire for more soup. They'd grilled dorado, as those islanders called mahi mahi, to perfection and served it with black-eyed peas and rice, along with golden fried plantain. Man, it didn't get any better, even in the best watering holes of Manhattan.

"Lord, me eat too much," Darla said, groaning and patting her stomach. "Me hang about with you bold self me soon become fat. Best us dance to help digestion."

Ward didn't need urging to get up on the floor and pull her fine body against his; to meld with her exciting curves while swaying to the intoxicating rhythm. Chingalo, she had his mercury bursting through the tube. When her blouse slipped off one shoulder he covered her satiny skin with soft kisses.

She cut her eyes to reprove him for his boldness. And while they stared at each other, she defiantly, he teasingly, their feet never lost the rhythm. He laid on her that cocky grin he'd adopted when a young buck in the barrio. Burying his face in her neck, he slowly gyrated his body against hers in mock copulation, having learned as a teenager that if a guy wants booty he has to press the advance. Ay conyo, this incredible chica ignited craving.

"Best you stop that foolishness. This gal doesn't going to jump in bed with some foot-loose sailorman because he buy her a few drinks and a plate of supper."

#

They lathered each other under the downrush of steaming water in the confines of the telephone-booth-sized metal stall shower in his hotel room. Her every touch sparked his sensual rush, inciting him to undulate against her while kissing her hungrily.

"Lord, mon, you one horny sailorman. Why you can't wait 'til us in the bed?"

"You turn me all the way on, chica. No way I can wait."

"And how you think me to enjoy having this fine body bumping against cold metal of this tin can? Come, towel off so we enjoy the bed."

He finished drying first and sat naked on the edge of the bed, adoring her as she toweled off. It took effort not to chuckle when she brushed out her hair. Two minutes in the sack and that black mane would be disheveled.

After dabbing herself with perfume from a small vial she carried in her big straw pocketbook, she sashayed toward him, with sensual syncopation. Ay chingalo! He gasped for breath when she took his face in her long fingers while bending to kiss his eyelids, then his cheeks. He cupped those gorgeous melons hanging in his face. And when she sucked at his mouth an electric rush pulsed through his being.

His temperature soared when she pushed him down on his back and straddled him. And he knew he'd visit every galaxy in the heavens.

#   #

Twelve

"Why don't you spend the night?" Ward said as he lay on his back watching her step into her flowery skirt.

Darla sucked her teeth. "You didn't get enough, damn animal?"

"Doubt I'd ever get enough of you, querida mia. Stay the night so we can start up again in the morning."

"Lord, mon, you leaves no encore in this chick." Then she chuckled. "Doubt you has any either."

"Stay and find out."

"Me doesn't dare. This a small place where if me seen leave you hotel room after the sun rise—every soul gossip about it."

"Big deal. You're a mature woman. They gotta' believe a good-looking chica like you is having sex."

"Not a time for bad examples with me daughter, Melissa, just turn seventeen."

"A seventeen year old daughter! How the hell old are you?"

"That you business, bold face? You doesn't like what you see, best you doesn't mess with this fine ass no more."

"Hey, I ain't chasing away a fox like you. What does your daughter do?"

"This autumn she leave for college." Darla had pulled on her clothes and slipped into sandals. After securing the straps she stood. "Melissa quite bright and a year ahead of she'self. Been saving every penny to send her to Jamaica to attend the University of the West Indies."

"Why not to a college in The States?"

"Lord God, mon, how me to afford those expensive schools in you country? Even in Jamaica me facing a financial strain."

"Tell me about it. Been there, done that. You must have been young when you had her."

"True, me but seventeen when me marry with Wilbur, a young constable—a good job in these islands. Us had a nice life and brought two chil'ren into this world."

"Two? What happened to the other one?"

"Dahlia die of some virus when she but nine. After me dear husband shot down by those damn Rastas, me had to waitress at the café. And me fortunate to raise me only daughter left so she a smart and decent young lady."

"Hey, that's super. You've gotta' be real proud."

"Sure, mon. Not all that many folks in Saint Vincent and the Grenadines been to college, or send they chil'ren." She pulled her loose-fitting blouse over her head, careful not to muss her upswept crown of hair, having just groomed it. "You mention how you aware of the cost of education. Does you have you own."

"Yeah, I got a twenty-two year old starting law school. That's why I'm strapped for money. I always took care of my son and always will."

"And what happened to the boy's mama?"

"We've been divorced nearly fifteen years now. Probably the dumbest mistake I ever made. I didn't realize what I'd lost until after she remarried."

"How long you'all was married?" She inserted one of her dangling earrings.

"Ten years. Don't ask why it ended. Don't know myself. Part of it I attribute to being a cop on the streets, which made me vulnerable to all the available broads. Needed to mature to realize I lost something special."

She inserted the other earring and both danced to the rhythm of her movements. "You never marry again?"

"Yeah, like a dope I married a sexy showgirl—a big-time mistake. I'd reached that stage where I wanted to settle down and have a family—and stupidly married a chica too preoccupied with preserving her figure to have children. That ended four years later."

"How long you doesn't be married now?"

He turned his eyes ceiling-ward as he calculated it in his head. "Eight, but I lived with a chica in Manhattan for almost three."

"You never thought to marry she?"

"Naw, too many differences between us, the least being she was Jewish. Myrna's an executive with a major retailer in New York and lived in a different world than I did. But I learned a lot from her. Come to think of it, Myrna introduced me to sailing."

"Interesting as you history be, mon, me needs to tend to me sweet daughter. Good thing me call she and tell she to feed she'self. See you tomorrow."

"What convinced you to have sex with me?"

Ward's question froze her with her hand on the doorknob. "What wrong with you, fool? You doesn't think women becomes horny?"

He sputtered—didn't manage a response.

"Lord, me been yearning for a strong bull like you bold self."

"You saying there are no strong bulls on this island."

"Mon, the island run with bulls. But they possessive and demanding. Me has no desire to be servant to some bossy fool. Had me a husband—a good man—may he rest in peace."

"And how do I fit in?"

"You perfect, mon, because me needs to have me itches scratched and you soon be gone from this island to save me from clutter me life."

"You're widowed four years and never had a fling?"

"Me not say me such. But that affair exactly that which me wish to avoid hereafter. It end bitterly. Good night."

He missed her the moment the door clicked shut. She'd mixed affection with passion, satisfying him totally. Closing his eyes, he conjured up her pretty face and that sexy and self-possessed walk, her incredible frankness. Yes, and he grinned at her insolence.

Damned if he didn't desire to have that warm and affectionate woman at his side through the night. Even after both marriages and his alliance with Myrna ending badly, he yearned for a soul mate, to share his life, to console and be consoled by, to share joys with, to love tenderly as well as passionately.

\#   \#

Thirteen

Ward squinted, annoyed by the morning sun shafting through his small window. He shielded his eyes to read the time on his watch. The low-end hotel provided neither a clock, a radio nor a television set.

Groaning, he struggled to a sitting position, then threw one leg after the other out of bed. He shook his head to dispel the grogginess resulting from a fitful sleep. The disjointed pieces of the case had tumbled around in his cerebral mazes all night.

Unable to sleep he'd turned on the lamp and read much of the data in the files given him by the prosecutor. And after rehashing a lot of it he found himself at a loss to make sense of what in hell Josephs based his indictment on. Probable cause paled against reasonable doubt. No ADA in New York dared to file an indictment on such stingy evidence—all of it circumstantial. Chingalo, every judge in The Apple would toss it.

Maybe this Christopher guy didn't do the deed. Ward sure as hell didn't want to send an innocent to a long term in the slammer . . . especially an American in a foreign country. Then he snickered at the irony. In the US the rich, white yachtsman probably would not have been incarcerated for killing a lowly launch-tender—of any color. His high-priced lawyer would arrange for him to be out on bail until the trial, then finagle a verdict of justifiable homicide and get the client set free without spending an hour in stir.

Here in these British West Indies he ended up the victim of vindictiveness. People who've suffered centuries of ethnic persecution had their souls scarred by bigotry and intolerance that fueled desire for vengeance. Besides that they'd had to suffer the arrogance of those superior Yankees who exploited them, purchasing the meager products they grew or produced at below world-prices. No way they'd let this rich, white American walk free and flaunt supremacy.

Shaking his head to dispel negativity, he accepted that only by applying a positive attitude had he any chance of clearing the case. And he damned well intended to learn whether that rich guy was guilty or innocent. Get ready, world, to score one for the Puerto Rican.

He'd learned from veteran cops that investigative work required a meticulous combing of clues, followed by careful analysis. But with a lack of physical or forensic evidence he needed to mine nuggets of information from interrogation. Ask any question and listen carefully to the answer. Then use snippets elicited as a guide to subsequent questions. The most obscure thing broke cases and assured convictions. All he had to do was figure out where to start and who to interrogate . . . in pursuing leads for a two-week-old crime.

Based on what he culled from those dockworkers any number of people qualified as the perp. And that Rasta remained a mystery. No doubt the hump figured in the thing somewhere. But where? Yep, he needed to find that hard-face with his wiry beard and pump answers out of his ugly ass.

After showering and shaving, he donned faded jeans, deciding that long pants gave a better cop-appearance than shorts. He topped it with a short-sleeve shirt that could only be described as a multi-colored statement in large paisley prints. His off-duty drinking buddies always kidded him about his Puerto Rican shirts.

After slipping bare feet into once-white sneakers, he grabbed his baseball cap and sunglasses before heading for the courthouse, determined to talk to the prosecutor and everyone else associated with the case in his quest for useful information. Screw breakfast, it being more important to get there before they got too busy with court business to give him time and attention. He needed to understand what motivated Josephs to indict that particular yachtsman.

His mind buzzed with doubts as he strode up Bedford Street, oblivious to vehicles and humans. The rain startled him—sheeting down without warning. He hunched into his shoulders against the cold shower while searching for shelter. The Courthouse was more than a block away. Rather than compete with others dashing for refuge in the entrances of the closest stores, he hunkered under the narrow overhang of a magazines and newspaper stand. Holy shit! He gawked at the headline in the local paper.

SPECIAL INVESTIGATOR ASSIGNED TO CHRISTOPHER CASE.

Publicity was the last thing he wanted this early in the investigation. It pissed him that Josephs denied him freedom to investigate without being pestered by meddlesome reporters.

Sure he expected that stuffed shirt to claim it had somehow been leaked. Amazing how many leaks occurred in New York, with everybody wide-eyed and questioning how it happened. He'd often told his sidekicks that there couldn't be a leak if an insider didn't crack the faucet.

Gritting his teeth he nodded to his conclusion that the cagey prosecutor covered his ass by setting the stage to shirk off responsibility if he failed to win a conviction. Despite not having considered that when he solicited the opportunity to work the case, he now accepted it as the reason that haughty sonofabitch engaged him without a background check. Having a New York City detective in the media glare created a scapegoat to sluff blame onto.

He'd hoped to conduct the investigation unencumbered by news-hounds. Nope, he didn't doubt those snoops would quickly learn the identity of the ex-New York cop. They had a reputation for voracious pursuit of material to fill up their newspaper columns and nightly TV reports—turning the smallest item into sensationalism to attract readers and viewers. Hell, their bosses only concerned themselves with obtaining the statistical ammo of legions of subscribers to justify their socking it to the purchasers of commercial space and time.

Kling, McVey and Texas Jack will see the headline and deduce the identity of the investigator. Okay, so no way he'd enjoy anonymity. Nope, you rarely got it your way in this life.

The media-hawks always had their sensors flapping in the wind and occasionally came up with information before the police, though cops rarely admitted that. Perhaps he'd be able to turn that intrusiveness to his advantage by convincing one or more of them to share what they knew.

Yeah right, reporters were going to relinquish the advantage derived from

knowing something you didn't. He had a better chance of winning the Powerball Lottery.

#   #

Fourteen

Impatient to get to the courthouse and rip into that prosecutor, Ward trotted up Halifax Street, with his head and shoulders pelted by rain. Pushing into the ante-office he growled to Constable Booker: "Need to talk to the man—now!"

The constable groaned as he struggled out of his creaky swivel chair to cross to the prosecutor's office door, rap on it and stick his head in. After a moment he withdrew and held the door open.

"You're a member of the staff," Josephs greeted in his resonant voice, "therefore welcome at any time to report progress."

It irked Ward that the guy didn't bother to glance up from the files he perused. However, he harnessed his emotions, accepting the wisdom of not butting heads with his employer. So he removed his cap while taking the seat gestured to by Byrum Josephs.

"Happened on a Rasta hanging around the docks. Am hoping he'll give us insight on that murder."

"Surely you don't believe the American yachtsman is mixed up with Rastamans."

Ward clenched his teeth, irked by Josephs' scoffing response. Hell, he believed he deserved support rather than pessimistic scorn after that newspaper cop-out. No, he wasn't ready to breach that subject yet. Damned right he intended to when he considered the timing diplomatic.

"Any other business?" Josephs sounded bored, propped regally in his leather throne.

Ward compressed his lips to conceal resentment of being addressed as an intellectual inferior. However, he wasn't comfortable word-dueling with the snooty bastard who looked like he'd emerged from Savile Row. No denying the man looked executive in his dark blue pinstriped suit, white on white shirt, and gold and blue necktie.

He grimaced as he compared that ensemble to his yellow and blue Puerto Rican shirt with faded dungarees. Fuck 'em all. Anybody doesn't like it can. . . .

"I'm told," Byrum Josephs said as he cleaned his horn-rimmed glasses with a white linen handkerchief, "that Christopher has hired security people to guard his wife. Perhaps the chap you noticed serves in that capacity."

"Doubtful. But that's why I need to learn why he haunts the pier, and who he reports to. It just might open some doors to support your case."

"Is that a presumption or a supportable conclusion?"

Ward gnashed his teeth to suppress exposing indignation. Years in the bureaucratic harness inured him to kowtow to superiors.

"Did you, perchance," Josephs questioned in his superior manner, "interview Mrs. Christopher and that deckhand while at the Lagoon Hotel Pier?"

"Wasn't ready to traipse around the bay in a water taxi."

"Their yacht is berthed at the pier."

"Thought they moored the damn thing in the bay."

"I rather believed we'd informed you of that change— taken by his wife after his incarceration."

"Not a problem, sir. I can get back there later. It's that Rasta that's on my mind at the moment. His presence interests me more now that I know Christopher's yacht is docked there."

"I'm sure I don't know any more than you do why the chap loiters about."

Josephs rolled a cigar in his palms, snipped off the end with a shiny little gadget, then lit it with a fancy-looking lighter.

"Next time I run into that hump," Ward said, "I'll beat some answers out of his scruffy ass."

"For heaven's sake, be discreet. Avoid criticism by the bloody media. Don't want to be accused of bad form, do we? Actually, I'd rather not be apprised."

Ward grinned understanding. "My gut feeling is that whoever hired the Rasta to keep an eye on the dockworkers, or on Christopher's wife, can give us positive direction as to who murdered Torchy and why."

"We know full well by whom. Don't confuse the issue." Josephs blew a

plume of smoke in Ward's direction. "Any other matters?"

Ward made a face as he drew away from the acrid cloud. "Why was my taking on this investigation leaked?"

Josephs calmly pulled on the cigar and blew out another cloud. "We enjoy a free society here, exactly as you do in your country, keeping the public abreast of the mechanisms of government. Surely you don't object to transparency."

"Only when it sets me up as the fall-guy."

"Whatever does that mean?"

"That the ex-New York dick becomes the goat if you fail to convict Christopher."

"Rubbish! This is a joint effort, not a one-man show. And you certainly aren't the main focus in this office."

"Tell me you didn't jump at my offer to work the case because it gave you somebody to shuck off failure on if a jury refuses to convict, claiming that the professional detective failed to provide sufficient evidence."

"Ridiculous. I welcome your involvement because your expertise far exceeds anything enjoyed by law enforcement personnel on this island. Frankly, I'm rather gratified to enlist your service with so little reward, considering the government budgeted stringently."

Ward winced, stung by being reminded he'd caved to a meager amount.

"Had I lacked confidence in you, detective, I'd not have retained you." Josephs blew out another plume of smoke.

Ward rose to escape it. "Just like to know I'm not being set up as the fall guy."

"Procuring the necessary evidence rather likely will eradicate that psychotic fear of failure."

Ward inhaled a long breath of self-control to refrain from retorting and pissing off the guy. True, essentially he free-lanced the case, but he knew damned well since the stuffed shirt hired—or retained him, in his lingo—he therefore could dismiss him. The benefits from obtaining ten grand swayed him to contain negative emotions. So he asked: "Why was Christopher remanded rather than released on bail?"

Josephs expelled a puff of smoke. "The bloke's a flight risk."

"Amazing," Ward said, "that the American Legation hasn't gotten him sprung on bail."

"They attempted to. Consequently continuing to hold him may depend on the evidence you provide—which at the moment is all mouth and trousers."

Ward had never heard that one, though he interpreted it as maligning his success to date. It took effort but he refrained from reminding that this is his first day on a cold case, two weeks old and yesterday's news.

"When, pray tell, do you expect to present encouraging results?"

"After I interview Christopher I'll have a better idea how to proceed."

"Assuming, of course, that you fare better than we, considering his evasive responses. I'll have Constable Bivens motor you to where he's incarcerated at Fort Charlotte."

#   #

Fifteen

Constable Bivens clutched the wheel with both hands while motoring the official vehicle, a compact with stick shift. A middle-aged man with a pencil mustache, he looked spit and polish in his crisply laundered uniform. And he remained stiffly erect and attentive as they passed through town, then into the suburban hills where a variety of flora separated attractive homes.

Ward took in his surroundings while passing out of the immediate suburbs then into an area of smaller homes, then into a wooded copse dotted with shanties. The few locals they passed paid little heed to the police vehicle, while a few sneered at it. Ward learned years ago that poor folks had run-ins with the law and retained grievances. Too few liked cops.

Shrugging that off, he noted that most dwellings they passed needed repairs and painting. Hardscrabble and weeds surrounded those shacks. Occasional vehicles, most aged and battered, sat out front where a lawn ought to be. Birds of different sizes and colors flitted about scavenging scattered trash. An occasional small animal slinked from bushy clump to bushy clump, while beetles and other crawlies scurried across open areas.

Then they entered an area of better houses with gardens bristling with colorful flora, from blazing red bougainvillea to yellow and purple bugles of allemandes.

"Rather populated here," Bivens said as he gestured toward clusters of houses lorded over by giant ferns growing amidst palms and bamboo trees. "At least t'is for those of us from Bequia, where we are less than five thousand souls scattered about, while this island has a bit more than one hundred thousand residents."

Ward nodded, while concentrating on the upscale neighborhood with streets shaded by towering breadfruit trees, interspersed with slightly shorter mango trees, their elongated leaves fluttering in the breeze.

An occasional flamboyant tree dazzled with scarlet brilliance as the road climbed into forested hills dotted with larger and more impressive homes, enhanced by plantings of blossoming frangipani as well as flowering heliconia and hibiscus.

"Who belongs to the super digs?" Ward asked.

"We have our wealthy, sir . . . our professionals and successful businessmen. However, many of those residences belong to foreigners, from England and other European places, as well your own country. It often amaze me how many of your countrymen seek residence here, while more than a few of ours emigrate to your country."

Ward hunched indifference to that irony, focusing on the steep incline they labored up to reach the promontory Bivens called Berkshire Hill. From there, they enjoyed a panoramic view of Kingstown and the surrounding countryside where lush vegetation punctuated the sprawl of buildings.

Beyond that, the bay sparkled with reflections of the tropic sun that melted into the Caribbean Sea, trafficked by sailboats and motoryachts of every size. Sea birds glided above the chop, intermittently alighting on vessels, channel markers, and pilings.

A fort loomed ahead, its weathered blocks evidence of its having sustained long years of tropic erosion. "Constructed a bit more than two centuries past," Bivens lectured, "during the reign of George the Third and named for his queen."

"And now," Ward said, "that chunk of antiquity is a habitat for low-lifes."

"Actually, sir, t'is a women's penal facility with a bakery that makes bread for themselves as well the hospital and other public institutions. T'is also a museum displaying Black Carib art."

Ward shrugged, then asked: "Why is Christopher held in a women's prison?"

"T'was decided a better option than subjecting him to the brutality that occurs occasionally in the men's facility. Rather expect we'd be scathed by the American press should the mon suffer anything untoward . . . most assuredly should he not be convicted."

"Think they'd be justified?"

"Would those same critics react thusly, sir, to a black man victimized in your country?"

Ward didn't bother to pursue a moot point. Race relations still remained a problem in the good old US of A, in spite of the populace having elected an African American president. And Puerto Ricans still bore their exclusive disdain. Gracias a Dios that things had improved and his people were climbing the middle-class ladder.

Shrugging to dismiss memory of suffering as the butt of prejudice through so many years of his life, he scanned the massive arch they passed under. It occurred to him that most of the array of ancient cannons atop the fort pointed inland. That suggested the colonist had more problems with islanders than with raiders from the sea. He stifled a chuckle as he wondered if Christopher rated as the first sea-borne predator.

#   #

Sixteen

Ward left Bivens chatting with prison personnel in an office near the entrance. An official ushered him to a stark and dusty interview room barely large enough for a small metal table and two straight-back metal chairs with plywood seats. All had scratches and dents from long use and abuse. The dank air hung heavy, reminiscent of a cavern where the moisture never evaporated.

Two jailers brought in a gaunt man in faded coveralls two sizes too large. Ogden Christopher peered quizzically at Ward while sitting dutifully across the table. His eyes narrowed with questioning as he watched the two guards leave and clunk the door closed behind them. Concern fazed his eyes as he turned to the stranger in casual civilian attire.

Ward recalled his paper work detailing the tall and lean prisoner with his pallid complexion as fifty-two, a year older than himself, though the man looked ten or fifteen years older. Ward ascribed that to the conditions the guy had been condemned to suffer these past two weeks. Rich yachtsmen weren't conditioned by any experiences in their pampered lives to languish in tropic dungeons.

Sandy brown hair speckled with gray receded from his forehead, topping a gaunt face with trauma lines etched in it. Both his nose and ears were prominent. He continually blinked gray-green eyes while scanning the stranger across the small table.

"I'm Ward Perez, an ex-New York City detective retained by the Prosecutor's office to investigate the killing of that launch-man."

The forlorn prisoner's eyes fluttered confusion. "Perhaps I should have my lawyer present." The nervous quaver in his voice rang with the trace of southern accent. His mannerisms evolved from insecure to haughty—the rich guy enduring an interview by the state-employee, a few pegs below his social level.

"That's up to you, sir. My intent is for us to have an informal talk, precluding any need for you to pay your attorney to hang around. But do whatever makes you happy."

"What exactly have you in mind to discuss?"

"Your theory of how that launch-man was killed."

"Are you saying you people are beginning to realize I might be innocent?"

"I'm saying I'd like to hear your side of it and make a report based on my own findings."

"My lawyer—solicitor—barrister—whatever—assures me I'll be exonerated, especially considering the world-wide publicity."

"Be that as it may, sir. Right now I'd appreciate if you answered a few questions."

"You obviously aren't a Vincentian—sound American, though you appear to be Mexican or something." He looked askance at Ward's raucous shirt.

Ward suppressed letting those remarks intimidate him. Nor had he intentions of satisfying the hump's ethnic supposition, or let the guy's superior attitude irritate him. "Let's get down to business, sir, such as discussing that trip on the deceased's launch."

"I've told all that to both the police and that pompous prosecutor. Consult their records."

"Done that. Now I'd like to hear it from your lips."

"Why would it be any different?"

"Humor me. I'm one of those who'd rather build a case from evidence I personally gather, rather than that contaminated by the prejudicial attitudes of others."

"That's admirable, but surely you don't expect me to incriminate myself?"

"Of course not, sir. I'm only asking that you relate what transpired between you and the launch-man on that fateful day."

Christopher pursed his lips, exposing stubbornness.

"Trust me, sir, that I don't have any grievances, like being incensed by the killing of a fellow islander—being I'm American, as you discerned."

When Christopher wagged his head indecisively, Ward said: "Since I'm free-lance and not officially with the local police, I don't have to worry about arrest and conviction records. My job, pure and simple, is to make an objective report."

Ward inhaled patience as he watched Christopher wring his hands, his pained expression suggesting mental conflict of whether to cooperate or stonewall the inquirer.

Christopher's tenseness dissolved and his resentful scowl diminished. "That Torchy person conveyed us in his launch to our vessel, along with the diving gear we'd purchased at the chandlery of the Lagoon Hotel Pier. What more is there to say?"

"You saying nothing occurred on that launch?"

"Once my wife and I, as well as my crewman, were aboard with our air tanks and other equipment, that Torchy person left in his launch. Haven't idea one where he went after that."

Ward employed silence as his next question.

Christopher stared expectantly at the interrogator, then blurted: "Perhaps you need to interview some of those locals, such as other launch operators and people of that ilk. They'd certainly know more than I about how those people spend their time and with whom they associate."

"Why, sir, did you allow Torchy to chase off the initial launch tender?"

Christopher sputtered, wrung his hands and averted his eyes.

"According to dock workers," Ward said, "you didn't oppose his taking possession of your equipment."

"Haven't you been informed of the reputation of that bully? What choice had I? If I'd been ten or so years younger. . . ." He continued to wring his hands.

"Had you been previously intimidated by said launch-man?"

Christopher flinched, then glanced away. After a moment he shook his head.

"Then why," Ward asked, "did you shrink when Torchy arrived?"

"Everyone around the docks regarded that bully as someone to be avoided."

"But how, sir, did you recognize that particular launch-man as the reputed bully?"

"The man probably had been described to me. Perhaps one of the dockworkers mentioned him by name. Yes, of course, one of them must have identified the ruffian and probably referred to him by name when he approached that day. Or, perhaps, the other launch operator did."

"Those dockworkers at the Lagoon Hotel Pier testified that you exhibited fear upon sight of Torchy . . . before anyone spoke his name."

Christopher flailed his hands. "I certainly can't say for sure who described the man and warned me to be wary of him. At any rate, I reacted to widely known information about that brute with a reputation for—"

"You saying you show fear every time you encounter someone reputed to be a bully?"

"I'd merely been prudent. Why take chances instead of sidestepping trouble? If that's all you have to discuss then—"

"Perhaps that launch-man said something that morning that suggested concern—even something that might have sounded inconsequential at the time."

Christopher laughed, a humorless rattle that rose from deep within him. "Have you any idea, detective, of the ordeal I've suffered subsequent to that morning, incarcerated in this moldy stone fort the past two weeks, forced to suffer appalling conditions and denied contact with the outside world? Consequently, I've had to leave my wife alone on the yacht with no one to protect her."

Ward wondered if the woman was in any peril—especially from that Rasta at the dock. Nevertheless, he wasn't anxious to hear of the man's travails and end up feeling sorry for him. During his years as a cop he'd listened to the woes and complaints of countless perps who tried to elicit sympathy, despite having committed despicable crimes.

"Haven't thought anything at all about whatever that Torchy person might have said," Christopher grumbled. "Besides, I doubt that under the best of circumstances I'd remember any unimportant banter of a launch-tender."

Ward again utilized silence to induce admittances from the perp.

His eyes cast downward, Christopher looked and sounded morose while muttering: "I've been forced to spend a small fortune bringing a lawyer in from Jamaica to represent me because I couldn't expect fairness in this island."

Ward's brow furrowed, since everything he'd heard suggested that the locals commended the American for ridding their island of the despised bully. And he again suppressed a snicker as he replayed in his mind the guy's concern for legal expenses. The dockworkers had inferred that the rich guy was a cheapskate.

Or did he have legitimate financial concerns? In his time Ward had come across a few supposedly wealthy people who'd fallen on hard times, but persistently acted like they belonged to the elite.

"During that launch trip," Ward said, changing tack, "were you incensed by Torchy ogling your wife?"

"That never happened!"

"People at the wharf remember Torchy ogling your wife."

"My wife is quite attractive—has more than likely drawn the admiring glances of many men. That launch person, or others of his ilk, may have ogled her, but it would not have provoked me, even had I been aware of it—though I doubt people of that station have the audacity to be seen doing it."

Ward recalled that earlier remark Christopher made about her being alone on the yacht with no one to protect her. He wondered if there were others like that Rasta who threatened the lady? Was there a much larger picture than a simple murder fused by sudden anger?

Had Christopher's wife given him reason to suspect something between her and the husky black? Had she had flings with black dudes in other islands? Rumors abounded about white chicas who succumbed to that enticement.

Maybe he could get Byrum Josephs to inquire in the other islands about the behavior of the Christophers. Scandalous stories never died. If she'd bedded a black man, or even cheated with a white one, the word would be out.

"Okay," he said, "then you're telling me that your wife never had any involvement with other men—of whatever social level."

"Are you demeaning my wife? This interview is terminated. I demand to be returned to my cell—with nothing more to say without my lawyer present."

"I apologize, sir. Never meant to insult—"

"Apology not accepted. Have me returned to my cell."

"Last question, sir: Were you involved with this Torchy in some nefarious undertaking?"

Christopher gasped—then sputtered: "I remind you, investigator, I am from a wealthy and highly respected family of Virginia, not one to be maligned as a criminal."

"Why would you kill him then?"

Christopher jerked back against the seatback and gawked. "Why in hell would I kill some—some launch-tender?"

"Who's the bearded Rasta hanging around the Lagoon Hotel Pier?"

Christopher tensed. "He hangs around there?"

"Obviously you know him."

"No! No, I have no idea who he is?"

"Then why are you upset at mention of his hanging out at that pier?"

Christopher shrunk into his shoulders and turned away. "I have nothing more to discuss with you, investigator."

"Need to ask you before I leave, sir, about your pistol."

Christopher drew into his shoulders and shrunk to the back of his chair. His eyes glinted resentment.

"Have it from dependable sources, sir, that you keep a thirty-two revolver aboard your yacht for shooting sharks."

Christopher paled as he stammered: "Haven't been aware of it for some months."

"How is that possible?"

"Might have misplaced it. Rarely had use for it. Maybe one of the many deckhands I've employed over the years stole the damn thing."

Ward snickered at the guy's concocting excuses rather than fess up to having it, much less to using it on Torchy. Damned if the guy didn't demonstrate the capability to stonewall examinations. His demeanor indicated he had little fear of conviction. Hell, he probably had a high-priced lawyer advising him, as well as reminding him that the world press trumpets his cause.

"One last question, sir. Why do you claim innocence instead of pleading justifiable homicide?"

"How does that affect your investigation?"

"Mystifies me since juries rarely convict a guy for defending himself or anyone in his family, especially a wife, from a brutal rapist with the reputation Torchy had."

"I'll take my chances in court." Christopher turned away, lines of stubbornness in his long face. "No more questions without my lawyer present."

Ward nodded to that as he rose to leave. Unfamiliar with the laws in this island, he abided by those back in The States, requiring he cease grilling a skel when he asked for a lawyer. His cop's intuition convinced him that Christopher did the deed, based on Christopher's attitude, expressions and evasiveness.

But why? Yeah, he needed motive to prove it. Nothing about the man suggested that he acted as a psychotic racist. Fact is he exhibited a high degree of intelligence and certainly of education. Maybe he couldn't be labeled a liberal, but he sure didn't peek out of the eyeholes of a white sheet. And how does the Rasta fit into the picture.

# #

Seventeen

Ward leaned back in the police car, closed his eyes, and scowled at his lack of success in eliciting answers. Nothing Christopher had divulged, nor anything from the dockworkers, served as incriminating. Yeah, Christopher was probably guilty, but he hadn't acquired evidence to support that assertion.

Christopher impressed him as smart enough to know he'd get a walk if he copped to justifiable homicide. His lawyer sure as hell realized it and more than likely advised it. Okay, then why did the guy persist in a long and involved trial when he could bail out the easy way . . . get his ass out of that dungeon?

Did it have anything to do with that Rasta skulking around the docks? Mention of that mook sure sent a shudder through the guy. Yes, Ward knew he needed to learn more about that ugly brute, with hopes of that leading to discovery of the motive for why Torchy got iced . . . and why Christopher didn't cop a plea.

Ward glanced out the car window while cruising along a cliff with a vista of boats in the nearby sea. Funny, when he thought about it, how he had no affinity for seafaring in his younger years. He'd been flown to Korea when a young man in the army, and back across the Pacific one-year later.

At those altitudes he hadn't connected with the watery world below.

Growing up in the South Bronx, he knew the turgid river as a dismal place where barges docked and garbage floated on the surface. He'd watched guys dive into that muck on a steamy summer day and swim around, but he never shared that urge; didn't need the experience of surfacing with a condom or toilet paper hanging from his nose.

In the army they crossed rivers in trucks, but he'd always been more concerned that the structures sustained the weight and vibration of those vehicles . . . and hadn't been booby-trapped.

Chingalo, he dreaded wading through muddy streams in the Carolinas during training exercises—those areas rife with water moccasins and occasional alligators. Besides, even with warfare simulated, you didn't enjoy having live ammo whizzing above your head while struggling to wade to shore . He still had nightmares from that shit.

There were occasions when he'd been around lakes with boats on them, but hadn't been enticed to go boating, satisfied to relax in a waterside café sipping beer. Fact is he enjoyed sipping beer with or without a water view. Water never fascinated him.

. . . Not until Myrna took him sailing one Sunday morning, renting a little sloop from a boatyard in City Island, an upscale peninsula in the Bronx that jutted into Long Island Sound. He chuckled, remembering his reluctance to venture out there in that cockleshell.

Bouncing on the chop and wallowing in the swells didn't qualify as his idea of fun, especially since he didn't have a lot of confidence that they had the ability to control it. But he didn't want Myrna to suspect him of being chicken. Macho served as a necessary characteristic to survive in the barrio.

Chingalo, it had shaken him up to see that gal adeptly handle the perky vessel. He never thought of females as sailors, it being a male thing in his mindset. But this chica had the thing standing on end, racing across the choppy bay, completely in her control. She didn't even look like she applied a lot of effort. Fact is she beamed her pleasure. And it fascinated and excited him.

Reluctance converted to interest, leading to participation. She instructed him in the art of sailing, beginning a lasting fascination. Hell yeah, he'd yearned to own a sailboat, despite his realization that he lacked the wherewithal. Cops earned a good living, but not sufficient to become yachtsmen—if they weren't corrupted. Ward had too much pride to go on anybody's pad. Orgullo guided his decisions.

Besides, he had to keep Ramón in college. He didn't want his son to be distracted by the need to earn a living. Sure, the boy worked odd jobs to pick up small change for personal things. But Ward took care of the necessities, negating any chance of owning a boat, of any size.

Still, he enjoyed the occasional Sunday sailings with Myrna. When he retired on a pension he abandoned all hope of buying a boat, especially with Ramón on the verge of graduating Saint John's and aspiring to attend law school . . . at NYU no less.

No longer anchored to a job, Ward visited his brother in Mayaguez. Leon had retired from the railroad and relocated to Puerto Rico the year before. He sang the praises of living in a Latino society so ardently that Ward couldn't resist checking it out.

A chica named Lupita introduced him to La Parguera, the seashore Mecca on the south coast where professionals from the cities erupted in weekend debauchery. Having no to return to a job on Monday, he sent Lupita back to Mayaguez on a bus.

He'd been entranced after happening on that derelict sailboat in the mudflats of the delta. Careful examination increased assurance that it could be refurbished. And he'd double-checked the law to verify that since it had been abandoned, it became free for the taking. He assumed it hadn't attracted anyone else's attention because boaters now wanted fiberglass hulls, not wood planking. Hell, what mattered most to him was that it didn't cost him a dime . . . to purchase at least. So he hired laborers and the use of a tow truck, applying a mighty effort to extricate it from the mud and load it onto a boat trailer.

Taking it to a boat yard, he hosed it down to remove muck and vegetation, allowing him to replace rotted planking and some structural parts. It began four months of labor that resulted in his finally owning a sailboat: a thirty-two-foot sloop with a wide hull, perfect for cruising.

\#   \#

Eighteen

"He not in," Booker grumbled.

Ward paused in mid-stride, halfway across the ante office while headed for the prosecutor's door. Shrugging acceptance, he went to his desk. As he sat he checked his watch and grimaced; still an hour before lunch. He chortled at rutting like a young buck, after romping like a bull last night. Okay, he needed to contain patience to go to the Pilgrim's Pride Café and be with Darla.

Conyo, he could almost inhale her essence, feel her naked flesh against his, revisit the scintillation of their melding. Chingalo, you'd think he had enough booty to last him a week. Hell, at fifty-one you shouldn't need poon every damn night. But he yearned to be with her.

Sitting on the wooden chair at the small desk they gave him to work at, a few feet from the abutting desks of the two constables, he scratched his head and stared at the stack of stuffed file folders he assumed the prosecutor left for him.

Over the years he'd accustomed himself to accumulating information relative to a case, even if most of it lacked connection. It took studying it long and hard from different angles to cull out a few relevant facts. Old-timers instilled in him the need for objectivity. Yes, and they impressed on him that detachment is healthy, especially when emotionally involved, as one is when determined to earn kudos. Most important is to gather all of the facts while recognizing that everything has limitations.

So he grudgingly accepted that he had to sift through that pile of confusion for the nugget that might lead to proof-positive that Christopher killed the launch-man. More importantly, he needed to uncover a motive that negated the kind of justification that had any chance of denying Josephs getting a conviction.

He caved to the drudgery of sifting through that jumble for something that opened a door to the next level. Yes, he had to secure a conviction to earn praise as a supercop, alleviating the pain in his heart for not achieving that accolade in The Apple.

Everything pertinent to the case had endless pages. Yet even with every facet of the investigation covered, in duplicate at times, as well as triplicate on occasion, he failed to encounter anything that bolstered the indictment. He found it all too goddamned circumstantial to convince a jury to convict. Fact is, it mystified him that Josephs indicted the guy on such flimsy evidence . . . especially since Josephs had to realize Christopher had that justifiable homicide cop-out.

"Hopefully we are making progress?" Ward didn't need to glance up to identify the resonant voice. However, respect dictated that he acknowledge Byrum Josephs' follow-up question. "Your interview of Ogden Christopher illuminate anything?"

"The guy's too smart to incriminate himself. Nope, still on square-one, sifting through everything for that passage to square-two."

"Dig a bit deeper. Roil the surface if you must. We can't very well enter court with our knickers in a twist."

Ward's brow arched at that one. But he refrained from responding or remarking.

"Your American press is blistering us with adverse publicity," Josephs said, "and damned well having a field day with this, as if it's an absurdity to accuse a rich, white American of stooping to kill a poor black Vincentian."

Ward decided against irritating the stuffed-shirt by admitting that while his gut-feeling convinced him of Christopher's guilt, he doubted they'd uncover enough substantive evidence to convict the guy. No question the guy gets a walk when he pleads justifiable homicide . . . frustrating Josephs.

True, he felt as compelled as the prosecutor to win the case, believing Christopher had ulterior motives since he danced around grasping the one plea that'd likely get his ass off that hook . . . and out of that dungeon. Besides, Ward, like most detectives, enjoyed shaking the trees for incriminating fruit.

"To avoid world-wide condemnation," Josephs said, "we shall require a rather dramatic bit of discovery."

Ward averted his eyes, unsympathetic to his whining. The New York police had dealt with an antagonistic press more times than he cared to remember. At least the precinct captains and deputy commissioners had. At his level they stonewalled the fourth estate, leaving public relations to the bosses and the politician.

But courtesy required he reply. So he forced himself to hold the gaze of the prosecutor. "We'll have a case by the time we go to court." Twenty-eight years of bureaucracy had taught him how to play the bosses.

"I'm bloody well relying on you for exactly that."

Ward watched Josephs stride into his office and swing the door closed behind him. Snickering, he returned his attention to the documents on his desk, determined to find the trip-wire to launch him on the road to discovery.

#   #

## Nineteen

Basic investigating demanded he answer six questions: who, what, where, when, why and how. Ward had little doubt that Christopher qualified as <u>who</u>. <u>What</u> depended on whether the evidence he turned up indicated malice aforethought or an unintentional act of passion. <u>Where</u> he presumed as somewhere in Blue Lagoon or on the seaway to Bequia Channel, at the confluence of the Atlantic and the eastern Caribbean.

<u>When</u> had to be two weeks ago, based on the testimony of the dockworkers as far as the last time they or anybody else had seen Torchy. <u>How</u> was by three bullets from a .32 according to the medical examiner; delivered by a revolver according to the prosecutor . . . and denied possession of by the perp. If he could answer <u>why</u> he'd have motive, and possibly the element needed to pin the tail on Christopher.

In New York they assigned homicide detectives a bevy of personnel to work cases. The cocky elitists enjoyed a crime-scene-unit consisting of techies, criminalists, a medical examiner, crime scene artist, photographers, videotaping specialist, fingerprint people, every kind of forensic specialists and behavioral experts. Oh yeah, and he had direction and advice from the legal beagles of the DA's office. Here, they didn't even have a crime lab—not that he had any evidence that needed processing.

Glancing to Constables Bivens and Booker, both intent on paper work at abutting desks, he'd bet a cee-note they had sources they guarded jealously.

Neither had a guarantee he'd remain assigned to the prosecutor's office to sit on his ass for the remainder of his law enforcement career. That served as a damned good reason for both to retain connections on the streets. Believe that cops had a full awareness of the value of information.

"Who was Christopher's arresting officer?" he asked—neither in particular.

"Actually, we were," Bivens replied, quivering his thin head.

"We went together," Booker said in his gruff way, "in the Coast Patrol boat to Union Island and took the mon in custody."

"He wasn't here in Kingstown," Ward asked, "or on this island?"

"His fleeing in he yacht," Bivens said, "serve as reason enough for Prosecutor Josephs to convince the judge to detain the mon while awaiting trial."

"In spite of the pleading of his lawyer and the US legate," Booker added.

"Why would a man on the run," Ward asked, "go to Union Island, one of the Grenadines, part of this country, instead of fleeing this jurisdiction?"

"By Prosecutor Joseph's orders," Bivens said, "the Coast Patrol intercepted the mon and his big yacht and escorted it there."

"Intercepted it where?" Ward asked. "If it was in the Grenadines, he wasn't fleeing the country. Somebody booking would head for Cuba or Venezuela."

"Quite right, sir," Bivens said, "but almost without exception yachtsmen sail in the Caribbean, enjoying the protection of the leeward side of the islands. The Coast

Patrol intercepted Christopher in the Atlantic, off the windward coast of the island of Canouan, suggesting flight, most probably to Granada or Barbados."

"Part of the British Commonwealth," Ward reminded, "where he'd easily be extradited from."

"Curiously," Bivens said, "the vessel at anchor and the mon with one of his deckhands scuba diving off those reefs."

"Which struck us," Booker added, "as more than a bit arrogant. But you have all that information in the files on you desk. You need only to read it, rather than interrupt our work."

"You have an objection to my questioning you?"

"What in hell to be gained, mon?" Booker grouched. Then he lowered his voice to add: "No jury going to punish that mon for rid this island of Torchy."

"That's the consensus I've encountered," Ward admitted, "but I've been engaged to provide grist for the conviction mill. To do that, I need some heads-ups, and you guys know more about what happens in the streets of Kingstown than anyone else."

"We not on the street any longer," Booker grumbled.

"However," Bivens said, "we're aware of many in these islands with cause to kill Torchy. The mon make more enemies than the forest have calabash trees."

"Damn scamp respect no one," Booker grumbled. "He have the gall to impose he'self on any woman, when he have a mind to."

"With no concern," Bivens added, "whether they have husbands or gentleman friends. You don't mess with a mon's lady without expecting to feel the lash of that mon's anger."

"The scamp brash," Booker said, "and have a way of borrow things without first asking. If he need a paddle, some rope or other equipment he simply take it from the closest unattended boat, then laugh when that person demand it returned."

"When us confront he one time," Bivens said, "for take equipment from a chandler's wharf, the cheeky bully grin and insist he borrow it."

"Didn't you arrest him?" Ward asked.

"The chandler refuse to press charges," Booker said, "fearful that Torchy be release in a few months and seek him out."

"All on the island hesitate to file charges against he," Bivens said, "fearful that him retaliate by bash they face."

"The mon a scorpion," Booker said, "and most worry that he bite they ass if not taken off the streets permanently."

"So why is this prosecutor so adamant about pinning this thing on Christopher," Ward asked, "when any number of people might have done the deed?"

"The evidence point to Christopher," Booker said, "above all others."

"All of it circumstantial," Ward reminded.

"The prosecutor may well have acted a bit impetuous," Bivens conceded.

"But had he not acted at all," Booker said, "folks sure to criticize him for denying protection to Vincies from callous and ruthless offenses by white yachtsmen with their superior airs."

Ward flinched at that, aware of his inclusion in that aspersion, in spite of owning a refurbished sailboat . . . and being Puerto Rican.

"He has stated in unyielding terms," Booker grumbled, "that we will not suffer victimization by foreigners . . . not even Americans."

"That kind of rhetoric," Ward said, "has a way of making people feel good, but it doesn't sway a jury. You need substantive evidence to convict someone for murder."

"It never occur in you country?" Bivens asked, "that a prosecutor indict someone without proper documentation?"

Ward almost snapped back how they trained detectives to acquire rock-solid evidence. Then memory convinced him not to defend a losing argument. "What is it," he asked instead, "that's driving the prosecutor to pin this thing on Christopher?"

Bivens glanced toward the paneled door to the prosecutor's office and spoke in lowered voice. "Ambition, mon. This trial have world-wide publicity and conviction sure to catapult Byrum Josephs to consideration for the next Prime Minister."

"Few have he grit," Booker added. "Fewer performs as he have, starting life in a small town up the leeward coast called Wallilabou Bay."

"He father," Bivens said, "operate a parlor—what you calls in you country a convenience store. In that small place it barely earn enough for the family to survive."

"The youngest of three," Booker added, "the mon have two sisters, who marry and migrate with they husbands to other islands."

"Byrum Josephs escape that place," Bivens said, "by earn a scholarship at the age of seventeen to the University of London in England."

"Not that many young men of Saint Vincent and the Grenadines," Booker added, "accomplish such."

"Few visit England," Bivens said.

"Fewer been to university," Booker added, "there or anywhere else."

"The mon bright," Bivens said, puffing out his chest, "and earn a degree in finance by the age of twenty-one."

"Then him remain in London," Booker added, "to work for a bank while he study law at night."

"Upon passing the bar," Bivens said, "a London firm recruit him in a position few black men attained in those years.

"So he returned home and became a hero in a robe," Ward quipped.

"Not immediately," Bivens said. "The mon remain in London for some years."

"Married there," Booker said, "to an English woman."

"Blessed with two sons," Bivens added. "Conlan now twenty-eight and Justin twenty-three, both quite nicely established in London; Conlan with an investment firm, while Justin is finishing his second year of law school to follow in he father's footsteps."

"All Vincies," Booker boasted, "be proud of the boys."

"Though we sees little of them," Bivens said. "They rarely visits. Doubtful they considers themselves Vincies."

"Does Josephs' wife live on the island?" Ward asked.

Bivens glanced furtively to Josephs' office door, and lowered his voice another notch before informing: "The lady pass away when the youngest but sixteen."

"The mon put them in boarding school in London," Booker added, "before returning to practice law in Saint Vincent and the Grenadines.

"Quite wealthy by then," Bivens said.

"A bit more than a year after settling in Kingstown," Booker said, "the mon marry with Velva Parham, the law clerk and a special friend of Judge Alva Boteen."

"However," Bivens said, "Judge Boteen pass away five years later, leaving Josephs without a political benefactor in an island where influence and standing are inherited.

It surprise no one that their marriage sour soon after—no longer having value."

"The mon cause it to happen," Booker whispered, "by he blatant chase after women. For a time, everyone talk about how he create scandal by carouse with those below he station."

"My belief," Bivens said, "is that the lady had no more value to him once the judge pass on. So, to rid himself of she, he openly commit infidelity to make the woman so angry she walk out his house and slam the door."

"Putting the onus on she ass for cause the rift in their marriage," Booker added, "therefore relinquish any claim on the mon's wealth."

All three tensed at the clicking sound of the door to the prosecutor's office. It swung open and Byrum Josephs strode out. "Can one of you motor me to attend a luncheon at The Valley, a restaurant at the Emerald Valley Resort?"

"Most assuredly, sir," Bivens replied, rising.

\#   \#

Twenty

Ward hummed to the melody in his head as he sauntered out of the courthouse, throbbing with anticipation of seeing Darla.

"Why did you visit the prosecutor's office again?"

He spun about to the unexpected voice to face two reporters. The skinnier one said: "I'm guessing you're the American detective investigating the Christopher case."

"I'm an American sailor visiting the various islands of the archipelago."

"Yeah, right," the other one said, a chunky guy with a thick neck and the wide shoulders of a football linebacker.

"It's a simple question," the thin guy with glasses commented acerbically.

But Ward just rolled his shoulders as he sniggered and strode away, scoffing at the guy's bravado because of proximity to his muscular companion. He'd learned as a kid to never back down from anyone. Get your ass whipped, even stomped, but don't let a living ass treat you like a punk.

He clicked his mind back to the case, determined to understand Byrum Josephs' obsession. Dammit, if he didn't succeed in digging up the needed evidence, thereby satisfying the prosecutor's fixation, he just might forfeit the balance of the ten thousand—money to ease his financial burden. Suing the guy's ass figured to prove as productive as pissing up a rope. Foreign courts rarely ruled in favor of American litigants.

Hombre, he yearned to clear this case, considering the improbability of ever again working a homicide. This could be that apex in a man's life when he earns his fifteen minutes of fame. And he'd like to get that money in one chunk, not spread out. Besides, he doubted his ability to put up with his fucking lordship too long. Sure, he'd subjugated himself to overbearing superiors for a whole lot longer. But retirement got him out from under those thumbs, so he didn't have to cave to a lot of shit anymore.

Arriving at the Pilgrim's Pride Café he dropped into the one empty booth and searched around. He grinned upon spotting Darla gliding from one table to another, like an exotic butterfly in her pale yellow and white tunic over a flowing skirt decorated with a typical West Indian motif in more colors than a flower show. Yeah, he needed a one-more-once of last night's passionate escapade, if for no other reason than to clarify whether the rush he felt resulted from explosive sex or infatuation.

"You wish to order, sir?"

"It's me, babe. Ward. You forget me—the Puerto Rican stud?"

"T'is you done the forgetting, mon. Why me not hear word one from you jiving ass all this day?"

He winced as it dawned on him that women get edgy when they don't hear from the guy the morning after—especially when the guy scored on the first date. Ay chingalo, he should have called and stroked her . . . not that he had her phone number. But he could have called the café.

Okay, he'd lay some jive on her. "Went real early to interview Ogden Christopher in the prison. Didn't call and awaken you at that hour, concerned that you get sufficient sleep after that exhaustive night."

She cut her eyes at him and sucked her teeth.

"Once inside the fort I couldn't contact anyone on the outside. Spent the rest of the morning back at the courthouse reviewing everything, digging through the files and into every record."

"You Gypsy-mouth like you employer. Word is, you with his lordship at the courthouse first thing this morning."

He winced again, then sought words to talk himself out of that box.

"Admit, mon, you have you fill of me last night."

"You serious? Why do you think I rushed here soon as I was free?"

"Why you lie so, Yankee sailorman? No need to keep on with you bullshit."

"I really was busy, darlin'. So I got my schedule mixed—"

"Darlin'? What this darlin'? You jiving yesterday when you say you know me name?"

He groaned—could only grimace his stupidity for exposing that subterfuge.

"You not just a jive-cat—you a damn liar." And she pranced off.

"Hey, what about my lunch?"

"Molly, you mind tending to that sailor'mon?" she called to the other waitress, the heavy woman.

Ward groaned when Molly shuffled to his table. "Great, now I have to order from her stonewalling buddy. Boy, this is some kettle of fish."

"We has no kettle of fish, sir, but has lambi—barbecued fish and conch."

When he grimaced acceptance, she announced that they served it with fried plantain and cassava.

"Whatever. Just get me a bottle of cold beer."

Okay, he'd wait her out. Women generally relented and gave a guy a chance to bail out. So he picked at the lambi, not particularly relishing it, and nursed his beer, enjoying it little more than he did the food.

He followed Darla with his eyes, while wondering how long before she softened up. Women! Finally, she passed close to him.

"Talk to me, for Christ's sake!"

"Why? So you jive me again?"

"Don't be a hard-ass, Darla. I've yearned for you all morning—unable to concentrate on work."

"That a pile of dog doo, mon. You no different than all other heartless brutes. You have you booty you finish with the woman."

"Why are you so bitter? Did some guy put a hurting on you?"

"Worse than that, Yankee mon. Him threw me in the dust bin when him had he fill, same as you doing."

"How can you say that? I'm here, ain't I?"

"Why? You get you bold self horny and think to cop booty again from that same gullible fool who fall for you jive?"

"Not true, Darla. Memory of last night haunted me all morning. It's a miracle I got my reports filed. Tomorrow I'll probably find a dozen errors because I couldn't shake you out of my head and concentrate on my work."

"But not enough to make one small phone call."

"Didn't see any reason to call, having planned all along to be in for lunch."

She sucked her teeth.

"Querida, you turned me on last night, and I can't wash your essence off my body or purge the memory of you from my mind. Dios en cielo, I yearn for you . . . remember the feel of your nakedness against mine . . . your intoxicating aura that invades my brain."

"You think me to ever again believe you lying ass?"

"Truth, Darla. Can't wait to have you in my arms again, my mouth on yours, tasting the nectar that lingered all night."

"Lord, you bold ass has talent to charm a woman."

"No jive. I spent the day anxious for lunchtime so I could come here and be with you. I fantasized how we'd go to some romantic place for supper."

"Shoo-oot! You think me bother to take supper with you lying ass?"

"C'mon, you must, Darla! We'll have wine and all, get woozy and recline naked in each others arms—kiss each other all the way to heaven."

She turned her head to conceal it quivering while trying to suppress the smile that broke at the corners of her mouth.

"C'mon, Darla, we'll have a helluva supper, then a repeat of last night."

"Where it written us must first have supper?"

"What time do you finish?"

"Usually 'bout six o'clock. You can wait that long?"

"Not really, but I got no choices."

She tried but failed to stifle her grin. And he beamed as she sashayed off.

#   #

Twenty-One

Exultant from having effected reconciliation, he considered having another beer to celebrate his success. So he searched around for Darla. His head jerked back when he spotted that hard-faced Rastaman with the bristly beard, partially blocked from view by a white guy in the aisle seat of their booth. Conyo, how could he have sat there in proximity to the guy without noticing him? Sure as hell the hump was aware of him.

Another white guy with a round face sat across from them and focused his owlish eyes on whichever of the two he addressed or spoke to him. Ward figured him for Middle Eastern or Turkish, based on his features and complexion. The guy combed long strands of dark hair crossways over his expanding baldness and plastered it down with hair spray. Having every hair meticulously in place said volumes for narcissism.

The thin guy, half blocking the Rasta wore a once-white nautical cap, now sweat-stained and scarred where the insignia had been. His pallid complexion reminded Ward of wiseguys he'd known who slept all day and emerged only at night, denying their skin contact with sunlight.

The husky black guy with his wiry beard looked like every other mean-assed natty dread he'd taken into custody. He couldn't remember a docile one, or one not snarling and resentful, consequently a handful for any cop. Arrests generally required back-up.

The guy's red, black and green woolly tam reminded Ward of the Rastafarian in Brooklyn who explained that those were the colors of the Marcus Garvey movement. Red represented the blood of Jamaican martyrs, black the color of African skin, green for Caribbean vegetation and the hope of winning out over oppression, deprivation and denigration.

The pallid-complexioned twerp halfway blocking out the Rasta ground out his cigarette in one of the dirty bowls that cluttered their table while bobbing his head in concession to whatever the Turk or Arab said. His scowl suggested reluctance as he clambered to his feet and clomped over to Ward's table.

Deducing that they sent an emissary, Ward accepted that those humps were as interested in him as he was in them.

The twerp appeared to have one eye glazed over. He motioned with his skinny head toward where he'd come from. "Mister Ajakian want to have one word with you." He had a French accent.

Ward assumed he referred to the narcissistic Turk or Arab, doubting the Rasta had that Asiatic-sounding name. "He wants to chat, tell him to shuffle his ass over here."

The twerp sneered at Ward, his glazed eye staring into space. "It better you show respect by go to Mister Ajakian, so bad thing no happen."

"Scram, you scruffy bastard, before I get up and throw you through a wall."

The gutter-rat snarled at him but retreated to his table. He flailed his arms while conversing excitedly with the other two. Forcing a smile, the swarthy pudge-ball with his hair

103

plastered across his bald spot, rose and waddled over to Ward.

"I am Bajuk Ajakian. We might chat for a bit, yes?" His Mid-Eastern accent, as well as his name bolstered Ward's assumption of his being an Arab or Turk. But he sounded like he'd learned English from Brits as opposed to Americans. Ward gestured him to sit while appraising the vain bastard, decked out in oyster-colored slacks with light teal shirt open at the neck, along with brown and bone saddle shoes . . . all expensive.

"Am I correct that your name is Perez?" He didn't wait for a reply as he sat, an oily grin on his round face. He folded his hands on the table, displaying a large gold ring set with a diamond embedded in onyx. "You are Puerto Rican, no?"

"That bother you?"

"I mention it that you realize I am quite informed. Example: you served as a detective of police in the city of New York. I am correct, no?"

Ward concluded the pudge-ball read that article in the newspaper and deduced Ward's identity, unless he had a pipe into the prosecutor's office, or a connection with Texas Jack or one of those other peeping Toms. Whatever, Ward decided to rattle the guy by being obnoxious. "You got a problem with that?"

"Impressed actually. Let us discuss your investigation of the murder of Torchy."

"Why? You did it?"

The man blinked, stunned. Instantly recovering, he laughed—but his eyes didn't. "I have curiosity why you investigate so ardently to prosecute Ogden Christopher, a fellow American?"

"I'm getting paid to do it. And you damn sure know who's paying me, considering you made it your business to learn that I'm Puerto Rican and a retired New York dick."

Ajakian laughed again, and again his eyes didn't. "Actually my curiosity is more in what you have discovered thus far, or have not, though I doubt you collect much in the way of evidence. You see, I am convinced of Christopher's innocence."

"Why? Because you and your cruddy cohorts killed Torchy?"

His oily grin shrunk to an oily smile. "I assure you I had no part in that. Perhaps you consider earning a perquisite by keeping me informed of your progress?"

"Forget it. I took a job and those are the people I work for."

"An opportunity to avail yourself of considerable extra dollars."

"Stuff your extra dollars. I've never been on anybody's pad."

"Do not posture so defiantly, Detective Perez. You are quite vulnerable—no longer enjoying the shield of New York policemen."

"Let me give you some advice, Bajuk Ajakian. One: I'm accustomed to dealing with all kinds of skels and badasses that make you and your bozos look like Sunday school brats. Two: I don't scare easily, having been threatened by the ugliest asses in one of the most-bad towns in the world. Three: I'm a product of the Bronx barrios and more of a badass than you or those two mooks you pal out with. Four: I'd take pleasure in kicking your collective asses. You want to hear number five?"

"Four are quite sufficient." Ajakian feigned a smile as he rose and shuffled back to his table.

"You lose you mind, mon, by anger those folks?" Darla scolded him. "They bad, mon. They murders and rapes."

"They rape you?" When she winced, then grimaced annoyance and shook her head, he asked: "Who'd they murder?"

"Why you stubborn, mon and doesn't believe they evil?"

"Okay, I believe you. But I need to know more about them."

"How me know about them . . . except the gossip me hears?"

"Maybe you overheard something when serving them."

"How, when they wizzy-wizzy so no one able to hear what said. Besides, you think me stand here and prattle about them, while they eyeballing me?"

"Okay, tell me about them when we meet at my hotel later." He paid his check and sauntered out of the café, rolling his shoulders to send a message of fearlessness to those skels.

#

"That one will be a problem," the skinny Frenchman said, as he and his grim-faced companions watched Ward exit.

The Rastaman sniggered. "Only should the mon live."

The Frenchman ran his thumb over the blade of the knife at the side of his plate. "I carve this one as one does the ham at Christmas."

Bajuk Ajakian shook his head. "Murdering him is quite likely to attract unwanted attention, even to alerting Interpol of our presence here and jeopardize our remaining on the island until Christopher is released."

"Mon, us hang about too long," the Rastaman said, "these police learn of a warrant for me and send me ass back to Jamaica."

"No police have yet approached you," Ajakian said. "So for the moment that which is important is to dissuade that detective from uncovering evidence damaging to Christopher and possibly resulting in his long-term incarceration, preventing us from gleaning that needed information."

"What you suggest we do then?" the Frenchman asked.

"You will accompany Gallyvan," Ajakian said to the twerp while gesturing to the Rastaman. "Convince that cheeky snoop to abandon the investigation. No additional evidence, no conviction."

The Frenchman ran his finger over the edge of the knife again. "I carve him so he have no nose to stick into things again."

"I want him beaten and convinced, not killed," Ajakian said. "Nor do I want

Facial disfigurement to bring attention to his having been coerced."

"Then why do I must be there?" the twerp asked. "The job is for Gallyvan, a brute who enjoy to beat people."

Gallyvan fell against the back of the booth, laughing. "You hear bad-ass Bonbieu, who talk some shit about jug folks but shrink away when it time for fight with he fist. Best he stay and suckle he mama. Me doesn't need help to whip that Puerto Rican."

"It is better," Ajakian said, "if Bonbieu holds his hands behind him, allowing you to beat only his body. Leave no marks on his face to publicize efforts to discourage his investigating."

"I cut off only one ear," Bonbieu said, fingering the knife again.

"For the moment," Ajakian said, "let us inflict on him a beating. Should he learn nothing from that message, then shall we consider selective surgery."

#   #

Twenty-Two

Ward breathed heavily, expelling residual vexation while striding away from the café. He yanked the visor of his cap down to shade his face. Interaction with skels always riled him up. Okay, he had players now that figured in the killing of Torchy. But he still needed to tie Christopher to that Turk, then pin some shit on him and his thugs.

"Mind if I walk along? Need to talk with you."

Ward flexed defensively as he glanced at a tall white man approaching him. Then he relaxed when he saw it was an old guy with his square face peppered with liver spots. But the codger wore a really mod collarless knit shirt with subdued stripes.

"I'm Harry Gundersen." He thrust out a wrinkled hand. "Was a reporter in the old days for the Cleveland Plain Dealer. Am now pursuing the Christopher story."

"Was a reporter?" Ward asked.

"Retired, but trying hard as hell to make a one-time free-lance come-back, with the Christopher story."

Ward continued striding, unreceptive to the intrusion of a news-hawk. Nor was he sympathetic to the oldster's panting while persistently hobbling along.

"Can we slow down," the old man gasped, "and chat for a minute?"

When Ward didn't respond, he said: "Give me a break, detective. After reading that article in the paper, I hung out at the courthouse and spotted you visiting the prosecutor's office, so know you're working on the Christopher case."

"Slick, Pops. Can't believe I didn't peg you shadowing me." He slowed a little, sympathetic to the oldster's excessive puffing.

"I just might be able to help you solve your case—in return for an exclusive."

"That why you came to this island—to scoop this case?"

"Been here most three years now. Another couple years and I'll be considered a local." He labored to keep pace, breathing heavily, with perspiration speckling his face.

"Wrong flavor for a local, Pops. So what's your story: you married or living with one of the island's waheenies, or what?"

"Widowed. Josephine died six years ago. Wasn't long after that I started roaming the islands to dispel loneliness, and ended up here."

"From Cleveland, right . . . home of the Indians?" Ward slowed a bit more while pointing to his cap. "I'm the enemy."

"Don't live in Cleveland any more. Josephine and I retired to Winter Haven in Florida some nine years before she died." He leaned forward, panting.

"And I suppose you worked for a local newspaper."

"Did for a bit, but they didn't pay a decent price to free-lancers. Needed to supplement my pension. Besides, like most writers, I like to see my name in print."

Feeling guilty because of the oldster's panting, Ward again reduced his gait.

Poet sighed audibly as he mopped perspiration from his face. "Hoping to get published by the syndicated press . . .

less concerned for the money than seeing my name on an important by-line in different cities in The States . . . just once before I die."

Ward nodded, impressed by the oldster pursuing his dream.

"We got a deal?" the oldster asked, his eyes pleading.

"Depends on what you've got." The guy didn't impress him as a hotshot newspaperman, but if he had something.
. . .

Ward learned in his cop days to value informers. So Ward caved to accompany the oldster to a nearby sidewalk café him to seats shaded by an awning.

The oldster plopped onto the metal chair, sprawled his legs out and mopped his brow with a soiled handkerchief. "Figure what I've got is worth the price of a beer."

Ward chuckled, amused by the oldster's chutzpah. Shrugging concession, he ordered two beers. While waiting he noted that the oldster's chinos showed wear, as did his sneakers, despite the modish shirt being a winner.

"Talk to me, Harry."

"Most everybody on the island calls me Poet because I write poetry that the local paper publishes. I've tried to write serious stuff but it doesn't always issue from this muddled old brain."

"You got your problems and I got mine. What makes you think I'm interested in anything you have to say?" It didn't surprise him to be served Hairoun.

"Hope you're ready, Mister Detective, for a story about Ogden Christopher."

#   #

Twenty-Three

Poet took a long swig of beer before speaking—punctuated by heavy breathing. "Made a trip some three weeks past to Union Island, one of the Grenadines about thirty miles to the south. Clifton Harbor is one of the prettiest roadsteads in the Caribbean, with its variety of yachts anchored in the lee of rugged mountains. Went there hoping for that venue to uncork a wellspring of creativity."

Ward shifted on the hard seat, hoping the oldster had something relevant to impart, a justification for this sit-down. Too many times he'd been promised diamonds only to receive coal.

Poet took another swig of beer before continuing. "Been having a brew on the verandah of the Anchorage Yacht Club when I overheard a trio of yachtsman at a nearby table. One of them brought the attention of his drinking buddies to a good-sized sailboat approaching the hotel pier jutting into the bay. He said the Ole Virginny was Ogden Christopher's sixty-six-foot motorsailer."

Ward perked to attentiveness.

"Then the guy snickered," Poet went on, "and remarked that Christopher qualified as the worst navigator in the Caribbean. The others joined him in reviling the man. One of them cackled that Christopher couldn't find his way to the head without the aid of satellite navigation. Their talkfest degenerated into each outdoing the other in demeaning Christopher's navigating ability."

Ward rolled his head around, wondering how much credence he could apply to whatever the oldster said. He remembered Christopher as intelligent. Still, despite skepticism, he remained attentive hopeful of the oldster disclosing something useful.

"Had no familiarity with them or the subject of their verbal assault," Poet said, "but I listened—not only to what they said but how they said it. Hoped to devise a story situation I could build around. Really opened my eyes when Christopher and his attractive wife joined the hypocrites— all part of the fraternity of rich yachtsmen who roam the Caribbean. She's one good-looking woman. The blond guy with a handlebar mustache asked Christopher about the hullabaloo in Curaçao a few days earlier.

"Christopher replied that around the time Handlebar Mustache departed Curaçao, a diamond cutter had been found murdered. According to rumors, the man had contracted to cut stones stolen from the robbery of a diamond center in Rotterdam."

Ward's eyes narrowed as he wondered if what he heard related to Christopher. What the hell could a diamond robbery in Holland have to do with killing a launch-tender on this island?

"He went on to relate," Poet rattled on, "how Interpol somehow learned of the intentions of that jeweler to cut those diamonds and recruited him to help them trap the jewel thieves—probably by offering immunity to prosecution. However, that jeweler ended up with his throat cut, inducing a swarm of police to comb the island for his murderer . . . and the diamonds."

Ward grimaced impatience when Poet took a swig before continuing. "That's all Christopher said he knew since he departed Curaçao the following day. When Handlebar Mustache asked Christopher if his boat had been stopped and searched, Christopher stared wide-eyed at him and shook his head. Handlebar Mustache explained how his boat had been stopped when he rounded Palm Island. Christopher gawked, looked like he'd chuck his lunch."

"What's all that got to do with Christopher killing Torchy?

Poet held up a hand. "Handlebar Mustache informed that the Coast Guarders who boarded and searched his vessel told him that the Joint Interagency Task Forces, a group of US agencies headed up by them and in concert with the Coast Patrols of the various Caribbean governments, boarded and searched all vessels recently departed Curaçao to prevent any of them smuggling out the stolen diamonds or the suspected perpetrators."

When Ward shifted restlessly, Poet again raised his hand and said: "Handlebar Mustache said he'd learned they had a dragnet out for three men who disappeared and are believed to have been involved in both the diamond robbery in Rotterdam and the killing of the jeweler in Curaçao."

Ward's eyes narrowed as he digested that bit of information.

Poet took a big breath, then another long swig. "Looked to me like Christopher blanched. However, his wife remarked with an air of unconcern that they could search their boat any time. More than likely would, the blond yachtsman said, since they had a list of all vessels that called at Curaçao during the past week."

Ward waved that off as irrelevant, so Poet jabbered: "One of the others said the patrol boat probably was busy in other parts of the Grenadines but is expected it to return by nightfall, at which time the Christophers need to prepare to be boarded. Christopher shrugged to imply that he had no problem with that and nothing to hide."

Ward swirled his eyes impatiently, then half-grinned when Poet belched. The oldster took a swig of beer before continuing. "Something about the edginess of Christopher and his wife made me wonder if I'd stumbled onto a sensational story."

"That's all you've got?" Ward asked.

"After the better part of an hour," Poet jabbered, "the Christophers claimed they needed to take their boat out to the anchorage. Don't mind telling you I wanted to keep on eyeballing Christopher's wife. Damned handsome woman who made me yearn to be twenty years younger—maybe thirty."

"Yeah, yeah, a hottie. You've spouted lots of speculations without a dime's worth of affirmation."

Poet sputtered, but before he managed to object, Ward said: "Gotta' go.

We'll talk again another time."

"There's more." Ward had started to lift himself out of his chair, then rethought his impatience, sighed concession and settled back down. Poet signaled the waitress for another round of beers.

Ward started to object, then reconsidered in hopes the codger spouted something worth the price of that suds. But he signaled the waitress for only one bottle, indicating he didn't want more.

#   #

## Twenty-Four

Poet chuckled self-consciously. "Bleary-eyed from guzzling too much suds, went to my room to snooze. But I returned to the bar that evening to have one before dinner. A rotund fellow waddled in and struck up a conversation with a yachtsmen alongside me. Said he'd heard uncomplimentary things about Ogden Christopher as a tightwad as well about his navigating ability. But he'd seen it all a bit ago. Crossing from Barbados, he skirted the windward side of Canouan Island, and saw the Ole Virginny, anchored off those reefs not that much north of Friendship Point."

Ward sat erect.

"Whyever, the other guy asked," Poet continued, "would Christopher risk his boat like that? He'd be a sight better off anchoring on the leeward side of Canouan, preferably in Charlestown Bay . . . whatever the cost."

When Ward nodded, indicating attentiveness, Poet continued. "That other fellow said he'd expected Christopher to spend the night in Clifton Harbor, rather than make the passage north late in the afternoon, after having just arrived."

"Second time I've heard of Christopher being off Canouan Island," Ward said. "But on different dates."

"Then my information is valid. You interested now?"

"Problem is that everything you've said doesn't conclusively link Christopher to any wrongdoing. Even if it did it's hearsay and can't be used in court. Okay, it suggests avenues of investigation, but before it has value, conjecture has to be converted to fact."

"I can get more." Excitement fluttered Poet's voice. "I have contacts from the old days. One of my old buddies, now with the Washington Post, has agreed to get me a rundown on Christopher's financial situation."

"Why? He lollygags around the Caribbean in a sixty-six foot motorsailer."

"Suppose he doesn't have the wealth he's reputed to have. Wouldn't that lead to speculation that he'd be amenable to diamond smuggling?"

"Where the hell you get that idea?"

"Weren't you listening? There's a dragnet out for whoever is smuggling those diamonds out of Curaçao."

"Yeah, but it doesn't light up any buttons for me. I'm searching for the killer of that launch-tender."

"One thing can lead to another. You need a motive. Maybe it has something to do with smuggled diamonds."

"Okay, I'm beginning to see a light blinking in that direction, considering the interest those mooks at the Pilgrim's Pride Café expressed in Christopher."

Poet's rheumy eyes glimmered. "Another buddy from the old days is poking around in Curaçao for info about that diamond business."

"That might have value."

"They'll also inform me if Christopher consorted with any criminal types like that bunch you had words with in that café."

"Pathetic bunch of small-time hoods."

"Bigger-time than you give them credit for. Anyway, what would you say if my contacts place that Armenian in Curaçao at the time the diamond cutter got murdered?"

"Do it. Then we'll talk about it. I'll also be interested in whatever you have on the two skels he pals around with."

"So you ready to work together?"

"Why do you need to team up with me, or anybody else?"

"Worked human interest stories, never covered crime. You're a professional cop, experienced in gathering and analyzing evidence. Frankly, I need you, or someone with your expertise, to qualify my pieces. And you can profit by my sources of information for background checks, et cetera. Okay?"

"Give me time to think about it."

"Think about what? I can be a valuable asset to you. What do you need to convince you to let me work with you?"

"Can't hang around and chew the rag with you now. Am on my way to interview Christopher's wife."

"Great! I'll tag along—maybe get an exclusive."

"Not a good idea. A reporter might spook her. If you have a car you can drop me off at the Lagoon Hotel pier."

"Sorry. Had used Chevys when I worked in Cleveland and a rebuilt beetle in Florida. Always wanted a Chrysler. Never could afford—"

"No problem. I'll hoof it. Why don't we meet for lunch tomorrow and rap some more?"

"We can meet for dinner tonight. I have nothing special to do."

"I have—a date with Darla, that foxy waitresses at the Pilgrim's Pride Café."

"You serious? Don't you know Darla is Byrum Joseph's girlfriend?"

BEN CERO

Ward gawked.

"Was, anyway," Poet rambled on. "They broke up when he married the Braithwaite woman. Rumor has it they mended their fences—may be sneaking around together."

Ward blinked—lost for words.

"I'm sure Josephs takes care that his jealous wife doesn't learn of any tête-à-têtes," Poet said. "That old gal has the political influence in the family, and Josephs isn't about to jeopardize that."

Ward shook his head, despondent as he strode away.

#   #

Twenty-Five

His head hung, Ward tromped onto the Lagoon Hotel Pier, still simmering from that blockbuster. Incredible that Josephs never mentioned it. And Darla! Ay chingalo, probably his lordship isn't aware that he and Darla tumbled in the sheets. How will the stuffed-shirt react when he finds out? Will he revoke the contract?

Why in hell didn't Darla warn him after learning he went to work for the that haughty hump? His eyes narrowed as he replayed that conversation of her badmouthing Josephs for jailing Christopher. Maybe that old coot confused it. Writers!

He wiped his face to clear away all unrelated matters, needing to concentrate on his purpose for being on the pier. He'd clarify the Darla business later—skeptical of its validity.

"Chingalo!" burst from him as he scanned the array of luxury boats. How much did it cost per day to dock a fifty, sixty, or seventy-foot yacht? And how about those of a hundred feet or more? Who the hell could afford to tie up there day after day? No question that he gazed at a mega-bucks industry—in one tiny and remote waystation in the Caribbean—with countless more around the world.

Besides the dozen or so at the wharf, others bobbed and weaved at offshore moorings. The seabirds sure liked to roost on them. Doubtful the owners enjoyed cleaning off that guano every day.

He read the nameplates on the sterns of sailing craft, unsure how else to distinguish a motorsailer from any other sailing vessel. He'd always been confused whether a yawl or a ketch has the mizzen mast abaft the cockpit.

Spotting the nameplate of the designated vessel, he glanced up to the rigging to be surprised that Ole Virginny, like his sloop, had only one mast, but a helluva lot taller than his, and stepped atop a full cabin above the deck. The housing in his sloop might better described as a cavern recessed into the boat's bowels. This vessel offered all the amenities of a cabin cruiser while enjoying the attributes of a sailboat.

He snickered upon detecting movement in his peripheral vision, but didn't reveal his awareness. Rolling his shoulders in that pugnacious way he learned to as a kid in the barrio, he strode to the two burly guards at the gangplank of the motorsailer. While introducing himself and informing them that the prosecutor's office had arranged for him to interview Mrs. Christopher, he glanced over their shoulders. He stifled a smile upon glimpsing the bearded Rastaman in his colorful dashiki and woolly tam.

Why, he wondered, did that dapper Turk and his scruffy cohorts take so much interest in him? What made that Rasta think he wouldn't be recognized—or did he want to be?

He hunched concession that Poet may have value. Sure, the oldster gave erroneous information. Nobody's perfect. Yep, he needed to cultivate the guy, as well as others, as local informants.

Hopefully Poet really had the sources he claimed, and succeeded in getting a line on Bajuk Ajakian. The answers to the puzzle probably centered on that vain pudgeball. It didn't strain his credulity to assume that Ajakian had a hand in that diamond robbery in Holland. Nor did the probability that Christopher smuggled those diamonds out of Curaçao. But why was Torchy killed? <u>Why</u> leads to <u>who</u> and a conviction . . . earning him that ten grand and kudos as a supercop.

And why did the Christophers employ this kind of muscle in a tranquil harbor like Kingstown? The populace didn't threaten her, or her husband. Actually, most locals were grateful to Christopher for exterminating a menace.

However, as peaceful as everything appeared, he knew from experience that crime in one form or another existed everywhere. These islands served as waystations for South American drugs. You trafficked in narcotics, you dealt in mayhem. And only the naïve and the foolhardy disregarded the possibility of criminals lurking in every shadow . . . in every part of the world.

Receiving permission to board, he gripped the rope handrail and climbed the gangplank to the motorsailer's deck—all the while impressed by the vessel and the wealth it represented. It refuted suspicion of Christopher needing to smuggle diamonds out of Curaçao. But, assuming he had, why'd he have the bad judgment to double-cross the pudge—an Armenian according to Poet? Why else did they employ guards around the clock?

Vicki Christopher awaited him, standing stiffly under a striped awning in the open well aft of the cockpit. Ward tried not to be obvious eyeballing that mature blonde who'd retained her beauty and incited ogling in spite of her stern demeanor. Sky blue eyes enhanced her creamy complexion burnished by the sun.

She'd cloaked her desirable parts in stylish culottes and a colorful sequined tee-shirt—wore sparse jewelry: a necklace, a few bracelets, earrings, two rings—all striking. No doubt she obtained them from one of those snobby salons he lacked the financial capability to venture into. Designer sunglasses dangled from manicured fingers.

"You're the interviewer from the prosecutor's office?" Her question bristled with impatience and condescension, in a discernible southern drawl and the diction of the educated. Unfriendliness sparked in blue eyes that critically examined his raucous shirt.

"Yes, ma'am. I've been retained to investigate the murder your husband is accused of."

"Wouldn't it have been prudent to investigate before incarcerating him?"

"That wasn't my call, ma'am."

"What exactly is your call?"

"To get pertinent answers, ma'am." He tried to conceal resenting her staring hard-eyed and down her nose at him. He'd suffered that before, by the offspring of European immigrants who regarded Caribbeanos as inferiors.

Generally, he'd prattle about inconsequential things to relax the subject. But her attitude incited meanness. "How well did you know Torchy, ma'am?"

Her head jerked back and her eyes sparked resentment. He suppressed sniggering, having interpreted the stubborn crease-lines in her face as defiance to dignifying his audacious question. But he held her stare, letting silence intensify the inquiry.

After a moment she retorted: "Why ever would I have any familiarity with a launch operator?"

"Rumor has it, ma'am, that you had some sort of relationship with Torchy."

"How dare you!"

"Just a rumor, ma'am, but I have to check it out."

"Is that your reason for coming here—to insult me?"

"There are those who say you and the launch-man had a mutual attraction."

"That's a damned lie! I despised that disgusting brute. Who exactly—"

"That's a very strong emotion, ma'am. What caused it?"

She clasped her hands and trembled. Then she shook her head in umbrage and turned away from his demanding stare. "Ask anyone on the island: he was despicable."

"I'm asking you. I'd very much like to know why you personally disliked him so intensely, which suggests your association with him was more than casual."

"How dare you?" She turned back to him, twirling her sunglasses, her eyes ablaze with blue fire.

"Then why are you so emotional about the mention of him?"

"He was abominable."

"Is that why you killed him?"

"What? First you arraign my husband for murdering that no'count launch-man, and now accuse me of killing him. What sort of game are you people playing? No wonder the media condemns your practices."

"Was it because Torchy made passes at you?"

"I certainly would hope not. He was despicable."

"So you killed him."

"No! I did not!"

"Then who did, Mrs. Christopher—your husband?"

"Get off my vessel!"

"I remind you, ma'am, that your husband's case will soon go to court. If you want to help him, you have to be candid with me."

"How can anything discussed with you possibly help Ogden?"

"Trust me, ma'am. You need to answer whether your husband killed Torchy."

She glared at him, her lips parted, her eyes blazing with hostility.

"Please answer, ma'am. Did your husband kill Torchy?"

"Ogden did not kill that person." Her head quivered. Averting her eyes she added: "Nor did I."

She squared her shoulders, assumed a stubborn stance. "That's as much as I want to talk about it. This interview is terminated."

She spun away from him and stared out at the seaway, her posture stiffly erect. The dazzle of sun in her face prompted her to don her dark glasses. "I'd appreciate your leaving my vessel."

He smirked, offended by her speaking with her back to him. "As you wish, ma'am. One last question. In what way are you and your husband involved with

Bajuk Ajakian?"

Her shoulders stiffened. She turned back to him, glaring through those smoky lenses. "Why would you suggest that we're at all involved with him?"

"It's obvious that you're acquainted with him." He watched her blink, sensed that he'd struck a nerve with that flyer. He'd learned a long time ago to cast a fishhook and see what it snags. Having hooked a minnow he'd continue fishing for a lunker, eager to learn what kind of connection with Ajakian existed. "Well, ma'am?"

"We're acquainted with lots of people. We sail around the Caribbean, meet all sorts of different people."

The slight tremor in her voice encouraged him that he'd opened a crack in her hard-ass reserve. "How particularly with Bajuk Ajakian? He's not a yachtsman."

"Mister Ajakian frequents the right places, dresses correctly, has polished manners, apparently is cultured."

"Did your husband have business dealings with Bajuk Ajakian?"

"Absolutely not!"

Ay chico, she answered that one too quickly—and emotionally—with a nervous tremor in her voice. She turned away from him again, still wringing her hands.

"I don't know what folks have been telling you, detective, but they're all lies."

"How did you come to know Bajuk Ajakian, ma'am?"

She sputtered, spun back to him. "Why? What has that to do with Ogden

being incarcerated?"

"It may prove extenuating for your husband. So tell me how you came to be acquainted with Bajuk Ajakian, ma'am, unless you have something to hide."

She clenched her jaws and glowered at him. He glared back. And after a

moment she pursed her lips and rolled her eyes back to search memory. "In Martinique, if I remember correctly— some three months ago."

"Tell me about it—all of it."

"What is there to tell? We called on Martinique, met some people at a marina bar—struck up a conversation, with him and his wife, though her name doesn't come to mind at the moment."

"Anyone else at that encounter?"

She rolled her eyes back again. "Oh, another couple accompanied them—Mustafa something—with a delightful French thing."

"Was this Mustafa with Ajakian when you met him in Curaçao?"

She gasped. "Never said I encountered Mister Ajakian in Curaçao. You're trying to trick me into saying something incriminating. We've talked enough. From now on, play your games with my lawyer." She turned her back to him.

He smarted at being dismissed like that. Dammit, he'd have liked to pursue the subject but wasn't certain what he searched for or where to probe. And he wasn't sure if he violated her rights in this country by continuing to interrogate after she'd asked for a lawyer. True, she hadn't been arrested, and they just might not have that law here.

Shaking off those thoughts, he said: "I'm told one of your crewmen accompanied you on that launch the day Torchy was killed. I'd like to interview him."

"Why?" She kept her back to him. "He'll tell you exactly what I have. We all boarded this yacht and the launch left. None of us know how that belligerent person ended up getting killed. Why don't you ask those launch people, his type?"

"In what way was he belligerent?"

She fluttered her hands about. "Belligerent. Just belligerent."

"Perhaps your crewman can explain it, ma'am. I'd like a word with him."

She spun around and blistered him with those glowering blue eyes. Ward held her stare. She blinked first and called to someone to fetch Caleb. Removing her sunglasses, she stared forward, unspeaking.

Ward shuffled about for two uncomfortable minutes staring at her back and the rigid set of her shoulders before the leathery old guy trundled over to them. A small black man with thin but ropy arms, he wore shorts cut down from dungarees, with a sweat-soiled tanktop. A religious medal mounted on a round piece of leather dangled from a leather thong around his neck. It swayed with the rhythm of his lope.

"I need to ask you about the day Torchy was killed," Ward said to him.

"I've answered that," Mrs. Christopher said, wringing her hands.

"If you don't mind, ma'am, I'd like this man's version."

"T'is word for word the very same," Caleb said, a slight tremor in his calypso brogue. "All we together in that launch, and then all we come aboard this vessel the same time. And that launch go off somewhere." He slapped his palms together and gestured out toward the bay.

"There are witnesses," Ward said, "that place you on that launch when Torchy was killed, leading to suppositions that you killed him out of loyalty to your employers."

Caleb gasped. His eyes flicked to Mrs. Christopher, then back to the interrogator. He clutched his religious medal and moaned.

"That's a lie!" Mrs. Christopher blurted out, her sunglasses dangling from balled fists. "Caleb had nothing to do with the murder of Torchy."

"Why are you upset and praying?" Ward asked Caleb.

"He prays often," Mrs. Christopher said. "Caleb is quite religious . . . a good Christian man and valued employee, very loyal to our family."

"Loyal enough to take the rap for that murder," Ward asked, "and be the only one punished?"

Caleb stumbled two steps back and gawked at the inquisitor.

"Time to get the truth out," Ward said to him. "Get in front of these charges so you can get a break and not be punished too severely."

Dios, he hoped the old guy didn't cry. Sure looked like he was about to. Then his face stiffened with resolution and he announced: "My punishment be in the next life—to burn in hell if it the will of God."

"Let's talk about this life," Ward said. "I know you believe in God and in telling the truth. Tell me what happened that morning."

"Me have swear me loyalty to this family, who take care of me now me grow old. Beat me with you hose, sir, but me still has no information for you."

The conviction in the deckhand's voice convinced Ward that the guy had toughened up. There had been that instance of weakness, but Mrs. Christopher plugged the dike. Dammit, that's why they interrogated witnesses separately, to prevent them from influencing each other. Goddammit, he'd goofed by letting her stem the flow of confession. Que bobo! He knew better. Old cops never die, they just violate procedure.

#   #

Twenty-Six

Gallyvan kicked at a patch of weeds and loose pebbles. He shuffled about, venting frustration while watching the detective boarded the motorsailer. Ras'mon, how long need he wait before that damn snoop come back down the gangplank?

No way he and Bonbieu dared assault the cheeky copper when they left the café, with the street full of folks to witness against them. So they trailed the mon, hoping to catch him alone. But the damn spic join up with some old whitey and go sit with he in a sidewalk café to swill beer.

He and that fey-assed Frenchman lacked alternatives but hunker in a shady spot to wait, then tail his ass when he leave that oldster. But they failed to get his strutting ass alone, with all them folks fill the damn street the whole way to the Lagoon pier. And once that Puerto Rican arrive at the gangplank of Christopher's vessel they have no choice but hang about 'til him disembark.

Gallyvan sniggered, at Bonbieu when him shuffle he skinny ass out the sun by scurry across the hardscrabble to a grungy café. Not he, mon. Him doesn't scamper like a slug to hide from the light, like that fey-assed motherfucker.

However, with that Puerto Rican aboard the motorsailer, and sure to be there most a half hour, he have no reason to tarry. Nor did he fear that spic cop getting anything out of

Christopher's wife, having put too much fear in that fine bitch for she to blabber and have them come after she ass.

But him doesn't feel as confident about that old deckhand. Mon, best they'd let Bonbieu jug that old coot to eliminate that concern. But chickenshit Ajakian have concern of such drawing attention to them.

Ras'mon, best you let every living ass on the island know how bad you is and no living ass best mess with you. However, he resisted overriding Ajakian's decisions . . . for now.

With no reason to continue surveilling the yacht until the copper disembarked, Gallyvan trundled across the hardscrabble to join the Frenchman in that weather-beaten café. Bonbieu had ordered a cold soda for both of them, along with a small plate of mangoes, banana, paw paw, guava, and pineapple.

"How long you think we wait for that one?" Bonbieu asked while chewing open-mouthed.

Gallyvan dropped into a chair and balled his fists. "Mon, me hope it soon—me anxious to whip he Puerto Rican ass."

"If he live." Bonbieu brandished a stiletto and ran his thumb along its blade.

"Ras'mon, you too eager to jug folks. How many you kill in that fashion?"

Bonbieu grinned, exposing broken teeth engulfed in the concoction of chewed fruit.

"Us has no choice," Gallyvan said while selecting a few pieces of guava and paw paw, "but bide we time until him leaves the yacht."

#   #

Twenty-Seven

Ward scowled his disappointment for failing to spot the Rastaman while jouncing across the gangway. He'd hoped to shake some answers out of the hump. Seguro, it would require application, considering the guy's bulk. Nevertheless, he believed himself capable; had whupped on some heavy bad-asses during his cop years. Maybe the mook fled to the shade, too much of a candy-ass to remain in the sun. So he'd give him a few minutes to show his ugly puss.

Donning his sunglasses and pulling his cap down to shade his face, he strolled off the pier and along the waterfront, where the screeching of birds competed with the brupping of boats. Every once in a while he stopped to pick up a stone and skim it out on the water, and watched it ripple distorted reflections of the setting sun on the light chop.

The exercise permitted him to search around without making it apparent. It didn't take long before he saw the natty dread crossing the hardscrabble toward him. Surprised at the boldness of the guy's approach, he skimmed another stone while trying to determine whether the hump intended an encounter.

Then he noticed the skinny Frenchman tagging along. Two presented a problem. Okay, he wouldn't beat on the Rasta today—would, in fact, be too busy talking himself out of a confrontation.

Christopher's remark about leaving his wife unprotected echoed in memory. This figured to be a lot more than animosity between a white yachtsman and a black launch-tender, or a low-ass boatman ogling the wife of a rich American. But how did a low-ass launch-tender like Torchy get involved with Christopher and Ajakian? And how did it all relate to Torchy getting whacked?

If diamonds had been smuggled on that motorsailer, Ajakian could have gained possession of them even with Christopher in custody, unless Christopher was running a game at the Armenian. Then why put Torchy on Christopher instead of employing one of his thugs? Confusing.

Rolling his shoulders to project audacity, he turned to face the approaching Rastaman and the glazed-eye punk. In the South Bronx they called guys with eyes like that Tuerto. The skinny little bastard, with a cigarette dangling from his lips, separated from the Rasta as they advanced. Ward suppressed smiling at the attempt to be cunning, presuming that Tuerto intended to flank him, Ward steeled himself for the encounter.

Okay, he needed to take one of them out quickly so he'd only have to tangle with the other. That required a split-second decision as to which of them he found most vulnerable at that precise moment. Size and strength would not be the deciding factor. He'd eliminate the one least prepared by laying a lightning strike in his vital area so he'd only confront the other.

The Frenchman blinked continually because of smoke curling into his good eye from the cigarette dangling from the corner of his sneering mouth. "Mister Ajakian," he said to Ward as they neared, "send us to influence that you no more interfere in this business." A cocky smirk twisted his pasty face.

"Hear what this mon tell you," Gallyvan said, grinning anticipation of the intended engagement. "Us needs to convince you to stop messing with things can delay Mister Christopher be release from that gaol."

Ward wondered why that was important, then dismissed that and all other distracting concerns. He held both hands palms out in a submissive gesture as he addressed the Jamaican. "Your mission is accomplished, brother man. I just quit investigating."

He knew his disclaimer didn't dissuade them but hoped for it to dilute their vigilance, a better defense than challenging them. Watching them part as they closed on him, he surmised Tuerto intended to slip behind him to pin his arms while the black pounded on him. At least he hoped that's what they planned instead of the other way.

The Jamaican's coarse curls hung out of his woolly cap like a tangle of snakes. Despite his loose-fitting clothes, Ward saw he rippled with muscles. Survival required exacting application. Okay, he preferred the brute in front rather than behind him.

Focusing on the Jamaican, he pretended unconcern for the Frenchman, who sidled around him. Yes, he had misgiving, fearing Tuerto might shank him. Meanwhile he sought to dilute their vigil. "I'm convinced to change my evil ways, brother man. Tell you boss he doesn't have to worry about me any more."

Gallyvan opened his mouth wide to expel a high-pitch laugh, exposing gold teeth. "Ras'mon, you show a fresh mouth in that café, and fancy you dumb self a bad-ass. Me not believe you drop this investigation without a hard lesson—hard, mon—one you doesn't forget."

Ward focused on the eyes of the Rasta, as the brute strutted toward him, grinning. They telegraphed that the gutter-rat circled him, so he poised for the encounter.

"Best you flee this island when us finish whipping you ass," Gallyvan said.

The tensing of his shoulders and the balling of his fists in preparation of throwing his first punch telegraphed that the Frenchman had gotten into place. "Or get you ass kicked one more once," Gallyvan added, grinning cockily.

Ward felt Tuerto grasp his right arm a second before the other hand clamped on his left arm; positioning himself. Ward thrust one flexed arm backward, burying his elbow in the guy's gut. He heard the gasp and the expulsion of air, felt the grip released, heard the scuffling of tripping feet. Ward didn't turn, didn't take his eyes off the cocky Jamaican who had his fist in motion, arrogance radiating from his bearded face.

Gallyvan's eyes widened with disbelief when the Frenchman stumbled backwards. He suspended his intended punch in mid-swing for a fraction of a second. When he resumed the motion, with reduced velocity, Ward threw out one arm to deflect the blow. At the same time, Ward buried his other fist in the Jamaican's solar plexus. The baboon gasped and buckled to his knees, sucking for air.

Swinging around to the Frenchman, Ward found him sitting on the ground, dazed and clutching his stomach. He scurried backwards on the seat of his pants when Ward raised a foot.

Scoffing disdain for the frog-eater, Ward spun about to see the Jamaican arching his back while struggling to regain his footing. So he swiveled away from the dummy who didn't know when to quit and lashed backwards with a karate kick that caught the guy square in the face, knocking him asshole over teakettles. While pirouetting full around, he watched the Rasta collapse in a heap by the side of the seawall, part of his head and one arm dangling over it.

Adjusting his cap and darkers, which had been cast askew by his vigorous motion, Ward glared at the sitting Frenchman. "Next time, I really kick your ass, Tuerto. Tell that brainless Rasta when he comes to he oughtta' learn how to fight, before somebody kills him. And warn your slimy boss I'm going to beat on his pudgy ass too. He started some shit with a bad-ass Puerto Rican."

#   #

Twenty-Eight

Ward strode up Halifax Street hyperventilating to blow off residual anger. His inner turmoil rendered him oblivious to the locals and tourists, and unresponsive to the late afternoon cacophony of peddlers.

Damned if it wasn't a throwback to his cop days. His adrenaline always pumped after battering some unruly skel. It had been like that in the barrio when he was a kid. He'd get into a fight and be wired for a long time.

Funny how most of those slugfests occurred when a guy called him out over some chica, like she was a madonna or something. You had to respond to the challenge if you wanted to walk the streets.

Man, you had better be bad; roll your shoulders and swagger like you dared any living ass to get in your face—or get tagged as a punk. Being big-boned and strong, Ward rarely got called out. Bullies avoided taking on someone that might put a hurting on their ass.

It still amazed him how many times he'd had woofing sessions with dudes because he walked up the street with a certain chica. They ignored the fact that you chatted with a neighbor or classmate—resented your association with her.

Ward never understood that kind of possessiveness and jealousy. Hell, there were chicas to spare. Snap your fingers, man, you had a chica's attention. But when you

CALYPSO

scored, hombre, you better do a good job. Count on her bad-mouthing you if you didn't ring that muchacha's bell. Thereafter all the other chicas snickered when you passed. And the guys treated you as a punk—might try to score on your ass.

When he rumbled downtown on the subway his eyes always wandered to that different environment, inducing him to aspire for that way of life. It began when he was in the army, then intensified, influenced by what he came in contact with after being assigned to a beat in Borough Hall, Brooklyn.

That area exposed him to gentler women, the kind he wanted for the mother of his children. No way he'd let his kids be born, much less grow up, in that barrio.

He grinned as he recalled that day he'd been walking his Brooklyn beat and happened on that derelict annoying a young lady. After chasing the bum off, he escorted the pretty lady a block to the brownstone building where she lived.

Her being Hispanic and arresting as hell made him wonder how to turn the thing personal. She'd damn sure enthralled him by the educated way she talked, pronouncing her words succinctly, and not contracting them nor slurring over the consonants. Nor did she use any of the gutter vernaculars of the hip cats in the 'hood.

It shook him up to learn that she lived alone in the boarding house. She explained that her father sold his tailor shop on Fulton Street and moved the family to Mount Vernon in Westchester County to escape the urban perils. She returned to attend Brooklyn College because of it being less expensive than anything in that county north of New York City.

That beautiful Puertoriqueña enthralled him—the exception in the world almost thirty years ago. Damned few Puerto Rican guys got to go to college in those days, much less the girls.

Ward told her his name and asked hers. Rosalía Catanía pealed like a church bell. He watched her climb the concrete steps to the front entrance, and anguished that he might never see her again. She pulled the door open and as she stepped in he called to her. "Rosalía!"

Even in memory it resonated. When she paused, he'd asked: "Think we can go for a pizza sometime?" Because of her expression of uncertainty, he laid a persistent gaze on her, to which she responded by smiling demurely.

Apparently his blue uniform dispelled reluctance and gave her confidence that she'd be safe with him. Okay, he could dig that. Hell, whatever it took.

That chance meeting began a delightful succession of pizzas on Friday nights, and soon after movies on Saturday nights. Eventually their relationship escalated to taking the subway to Spanish Harlem, to Latino restaurants and dance clubs. On occasional Sundays they picnicked in Prospect Park.

She always brought books to study, which impressed him. It took three months for them to concur that they went steady. Rosalía, then only eighteen, resisted sex, adamant she wait to be certain before she succumbed to a man. He respected that—admired her—adored her.

Rosalía represented everything he wanted in his wife and the mother of his children. Some months later he moved to Brooklyn to be closer to her. In that transition he separated himself from the 'hood, the brothers, and barrio life. He earned enough as a cop to graduate to the mainstream.

Three years later, when Rosalía finished college and got a job as a substitute teacher, they married. Two years after that the birth of Ramón filled their hearts with joy. When

Ramón reached six, they entered him in after-school day-care so Rosalía could resume her career.

They planned to save for a nice little house in the suburbs of Queens and the kind of life-style they had until then only dared to dream about . . . aspirations beyond the scope of most Hispanics of those times. However, both worked long hours, then pursued individual interests, she with educators, he with cops. Togetherness faded and they lost the bond of common interest.

Rosalía attended graduate school two nights a week, widening their gap. He flopped by himself in front of the tube those nights; occasionally propped himself on a bar stool in a local pub and swilled beer, where he became susceptible to side stuff.

When she earned her masters he rejoiced with her. But he secretly resented the degree to which she surpassed him in education. Her appointment to assistant principle underscored their cerebral and professional differences.

He not only liked being a cop but considered it the best job available to him. The majority of Puerto Ricans poked along in menial labor, with most doors to upper level employment closed to them. You were an outcast unless your antecedents originated in Europe. Unbelievably those offspring of threadbare immigrants had the gall to tell you that you didn't belong in America.

His dad worked as a janitor in a building in Washington Heights, riding the subway to and from work, which kept him away from their little apartment much of the time. Papá became an old man with a lot of ailments and one day he just faded away. Mamá did maid work in Riverdale, an exhausting trip to that enclave of the wealthy and privileged.

She died of pneumonia one winter at the age of fifty-five—young for Middle Americans but normal for indigent

Puerto Ricans. By then he'd already served in the army, returned home and become a cop. He accepted the loss of his parents with the equanimity of people condemned to be disadvantaged.

Jeremiah Ward, an African-American social worker had helped his father and mother settle in the Bronx slum upon their arrival from Puerto Rico, then spent time teaching them to survive in that mean world. He'd gotten Papá the job as janitor. In gratitude, they named their first-born on the mainland after him.

Years later, when Jeremiah Ward became a ward heeler, he wielded the influence that got Ward onto the police force. The homeboys regarded cops as the enemy, but Ward didn't want to work on the railroad like his brother, Leon, freezing in winter and broiling in summer, bending his back with heavy steel rails and bulky wooden ties to repair the endless miles of tracks.

Working after school during his high school years exhausted his desire to buss tables, mop floors, bust his ass with deliveries from a truck, push around those wagons loaded with garments through the midtown streets. Those and other menial job were what was available to Puerto Ricans and blacks. You had a dark cast and a Spanish name you weren't shit.

Having graduated high school close to the top of his class, as well as having served in the army, got him accepted on the force, then under pressure to hire more minorities. But getting through the academy presented another challenge.

Some of the trainers practiced a subtle bigotry that weeded out many of the blacks and Hispanics. Aware of that device, Ward blocked out their connivances intended to intimidate and discourage—determination his guide to survive his rookie probation. He doubted he'd have other comparable opportunities to escape the barrio and integrate into the middle class.

True to form, the whiz-bang decision-makers assigned him to a beat in Spanish Harlem, as opposed to an Anglo area. Okay, he had a job, earned more than most people he knew, enjoyed perks they never dreamed of, like health care and paid vacations, with the prospect of a pension to reward him for twenty or more years of service.

With no end of temptations, the toughest part became staying clean. It took discipline to disassociate himself from the dirty cops and steer clear of the corruption. At the same time you had to remain one of the boys, not isolate yourself and be ignored by your brothers in blue when trouble went down. Cops had to stick together to survive in those streets, where mortality had too little value. It helped that the majority of cops stayed clean, dedicated to their jobs.

#   #

Twenty-Nine

Ward sniggered at memory of the brass transferring him to Brooklyn. After three years of refusing to succumb to their badgering to go undercover, they punished him in their peevish way by isolating him from the heart of the city. He considered it a benediction, preferable to Spanish Harlem, and the first time in his life that he mixed with a variety of people, not only Hispanics. Chingalo, he felt like an American.

While he never condoned the proliferation of dope, he refused narc duty. Of course he realized how much it hurt the neighborhood and would have liked it cleaned up as much as the next guy, as eager as anyone to relieve the kids of the peer-pressure of using. But he considered going under to spy on traffickers anathema to a homey.

His boyhood oath to the gang still had significance, though he never ran with them to the extent that it got him in trouble. God blessed him with more smarts than most of the homeboys. His prowess as a stickball player and with a basketball exempted him from many criminal and gang activities.

The guys wanted him to practice, be prepared to compete, make the 'hood proud. Having the winningest teams in the Bronx rated among the most important things in each 'hood, which encompassed specific streets. They had too few things to be proud about.

As a result, he enjoyed the good luck to avoid being arrested as a teenager, as most of the homies had. A guy's name on the blotter served as one of the excuses to deny admission to the police universe.

No, he never denied how much pressure there had been on the kids who stayed in school. Street people envied them and wanted them in the gutter. Addicts and dealers sought to hook them and bleed away their money to support that habit. Gangbangers wanted them involved in crime, therefore controlled and exploited. It took a miracle to grow up clean in the South Bronx.

They barely got by in his home, eliminating any prospects of going to college when he graduated high school. With few better options, he enlisted in the army.

After that tour of duty in Korea he ended up at Fort Bragg in North Carolina, where he got a refresher course in racial and ethnic aversion. Despite the percentage of blacks and Hispanics, bigotry ran rampant in the army. A lot of Anglos were skinheads and Nazis—in the US Army! Those bigots disliked somebody named Perez no less than they did those with surnames like Washington or Goldberg.

He knew he couldn't spend the rest of his life sharing close quarters with bastards like that, pretending unawareness of their repugnancy. It really grated in his gut to be pandered to by guys he knew wished they didn't have to share close quarters with him. Sure he heard all the diatribes about equality in the armed forces. But every day he experienced bigotry, in spite of being Caucasian—Hispanics weren't regarded as regular whites. How in hell did those black guys deal with it?

\#   \#

Thirty

Bajuk Ajakian paced the cobblestones in front of TARTERBULL'S, a waterfront café on Upper Bay Street, where pedestrian and vehicle traffic choked the thoroughfare. He gritted his teeth while impatiently scanning the sidewalk for Gallyvan and Bonbieu. Snorting, he refused to accept the remotest possibility of that detective from New York emerging victorious over Gallyvan, convinced of the African's physical incomparability.

But in spite of the loyalty and support he'd received from the African so much had gone wrong. He cursed himself for having gotten involved in that violent enterprise of those damnable diamonds? Cunning had heretofore served him well, provided him with a comfortable existence.

True, he'd suffered setbacks, but nothing to compare with this succession of frustrations. During childhood, in that suburb of Yerevan, he became adept at coaxing the things he wanted out of his parents, and of wheedling out of chores so he could romp in the high plateaus of Armenia.

Boyhood ended when he left home, having earned a scholarship to attend college in Moscow. In that sprawling and bustling capital of the Soviet Republics he first tasted the female fruit and had his initiation in alcoholic intoxication. Thereafter vodka and women became compelling. But it required money, a commodity he and his family had too little of. So he wheedled alcohol and sex out of older and less attractive females.

That ploy also served to allow him to apply the majority of his attention to his studies. Fascinated by financial subjects, he graduated close to the top in his class. That achievement led to his being recruited as a clerk by the Vneshtorgbank, the Foreign Trade Bank, where the Union of Soviet Socialists Republics processed international transactions.

While delving into voluminous files to evaluate exchanges of funds, he discovered laxities resulting from poor accounting practices. Untold millions of rubles moved about without proper oversight.

When he suggested to his superiors the need for improved supervision, it shocked him to earn their enmity for threatening to rock the bureaucratic ark. They preferred to be ostriches and expected others to suffer self-inflicted blindness rather that draw attention to problems. Those in charge imposed the burden of correcting problems on those that exposed them. Better to pretend unawareness.

Intrigued by that sanctioning of inaccuracies, he tested the system by availing himself of small amounts of money. Amazed by how easily he buried it with paper work, he increased the amounts, capping off the first year with an amount equal to three thousands of US dollars—a fortune to a lowly paid clerk.

That lucre permitted him to lure attractive females. He soon became a party animal at the cafés he frequented, which required he increase his illicit income. Utilizing information acquired from earlier withdrawals and transfers, and the ease of obscuring everything, he embezzled amounts over a number of months that totaled ten thousands of US dollars. Confusion in the records buried the transactions.

But as time passed he yearned for more than the restricted pastimes in the Soviet Union; desired to taste the sophisticated pleasures of the west. To afford it he siphoned off, over a period of months, an amount equal to one hundred thousands of US dollars, a veritable fortune in those years. Obtaining the exit visa and a leave of absence proved more difficult than acquiring the money. Having accomplished that he flew to Paris to wallow in Western decadence.

Soon after arriving he fell madly in love with Sophie Leferve, a blonde hedonist who immersed him in the most voluptuous experiences of his life. It stung and sobered him how quickly he frittered away money in the City of Light. He never deluded himself that when he ran out of money he forfeited Sophie, as well as all other sybarites who exploited money-dispensers to indulge their epicurean lifestyles.

Disinclined to return to the sterile world of Moscow, he searched for an opportunity to finance continuance in the West. He had little doubt that if he returned to the Vneshtorgbank he'd easily embezzle amounts equivalent to hundreds of thousands of US dollars, but had less confidence he'd wheedle his way out of the Soviet Union having overstayed his visa.

So he inveigled one of his new acquaintances into helping him land a position as an account executive for a British investment firm that sought additional representation on the Continent. He'd studied English in college and spoke it well, read and wrote it fluently, besides speaking Russian and French, and of course Armenian.

He concentrated on privately financed trusts in various parts of Europe, especially those large and cumbersome accounts that other account executives avoided because of the burden of detail. Debonair and personable, he gained the confidence of many wealthy investors, who appreciated his dedicating endless hours studying, analyzing, and assessing their various investments.

Unbeknownst to them, he highlighted accounts that hadn't had activity in years. During discussions with them he discerned whether they appreciated the growth of those investments over the years. To his delight, funds existed where neither investors nor accountants were aware of.

He drained off a little here and a little there, gaining confidence over time to manipulate those accounts to his advantage. Thereafter, over a period of three years, he siphoned off the equivalent of more than four million US dollars, transferring it to banks in Switzerland and Monaco.

A Bavarian client discovered irregularities which led to investigation that exposed misappropriation. The resultant publicity incited others to institute examinations, concluding with charges filed against Bajuk in a number of countries. He shrugged off as meaningless his being discharged by the British firm, too occupied with defending against those indictments, desperate to avoid imprisonment. Legal fees and graft amounted to more than two million US dollars.

Surviving the litigious assaults, he resettled in Monaco, where he married Naja, a handsome Syrian woman. Through her he met other Semitics, among them Mustafa Erkaban, a personable Turk who spent like a man contemptuous of money. They vacationed together in Martinique, and during a conversation there Bajuk confessed to his friend his inability to spend as freely as did Mustafa.

The sallow-faced Turk admonished him for such concerns. So much of money existed in the world. It took only daring to thrust in the hand and take for yourself the share of a lion. Then Mustafa revealed that he dealt in stolen diamonds, with little or no risk. Yes, he promised to introduce Bajuk to that lucrative trade.

Soon after returning to Monaco, Mustafa divulged his plan to steal a bag of uncut diamonds from Rotterdam and send them to a diamond cutter he worked with in South Africa, to render them unidentifiable, consequently untraceable. Then he'd sell them in Europe where they'd have a value equivalent to two or three millions of US dollars.

Seduced by the prospect of obtaining a share of that windfall, Bajuk accompanied his friend to Rotterdam to survey the situation and to learn that man's proficiency. There they discovered that five bags of uncut diamonds existed, not simply one. However, security had also been increased.

To accomplish the robbery, Mustafa enlisted another Turk, Ismet Okyar, with his accomplice, a French gutter-rat named Bonbieu. While assessing his hastily organized gang as well as the security systems of the diamond center, Mustafa felt they needed additional muscle, someone dependable, capable, and fearless. But they needed to find that cohort quickly, with the diamonds due to be shipped within a day or two.

#   #

Thirty-One

Ajakian gaped upon spotting Gallyvan, trailed by Bonbieu. Both lurched up the road, battered and forlorn. Shaking his head in dejection, he turned and plodded into the waterfront saloon, to drop onto a chair at a small round table.

When Gallyvan tromped in a moment later, Ajakian saw the purple welt on his black face. Coagulated blood formed a scabby bubble on his split lip, with a trail of dried blood staining his wiry beard.

"Say nothing!" Ajakian admonished when Gallyvan trundled to the side of the table, his eyes downcast in contrition. "I've no patience for excuses."

"This chicken-shit Frenchman," Gallyvan whined, "sit on he ass and let that copper kick me face."

"I do not sit," Bonbieu protested, circling the table to keep it between himself and the brutish Jamaican. "The cop, he knock me down."

"You grab he hands proper the mon never knock down you skinny ass, and then me beat that spic senseless."

"I never have the chance. Poof! I am sitting—with much pain in stomach."

Ajakian contained his frustration while signaling the waitress to bring coffee. Then, unable to contain his frustration, he growled: "This episode quite likely will motivate that detective to search harder for evidence to condemn Christopher. Therefore is it essential we communicate with that bumbling yachtsman to learn the location of the diamonds . . . if indeed he cached them on that reef."

"He wife on that yacht," Gallyvan said. "Those guards doesn't protect that fine bitch if me have a mind to root some information from she fine ass."

"I truly doubt she knows the location," Ajakian said. "She would have broken and told us when we questioned them—too frightened not to be truthful."

"When we demand of Christopher, with my knife at his throat," Bonbieu said, "to know where those gems, he tell us he hide them in the reef on the ocean side of the island of Canouan. Why not we rent a boat and search that reef? We need only to hire a diver."

"Me a diver, mon," Gallyvan said. "Me one damned good diver. Mon, me born to fish and such."

"There is more than one reef," Ajakian said. "Both are quite large. Even if we knew which to search it is unlikely we will find them without knowing their approximate location and in what manner the cache is marked."

"Why not we visit him in that prison to obtain that information?" Bonbieu asked.

"We dare not, needing to register, perhaps produce passports," Ajakian said. "Such might alert Interpol of our presence on this island—forcing us to flee without gaining possession of the diamonds."

Gallyvan snapped his fingers, his eyes sparking revelation. "Why us not send a copper to talk to the mon?"

Ajakian scoffed. "Where do we find such a copper?"

The waitress served their order, which suspended conversation. Gallyvan waited until she left, though his covetous eyes followed her until she rounded a different table. "The last few nights me with a whore who complain how she and other gals be shake down by Constable Booker before he transfer to the prosecutor's office. On occasion now the mon drop by for free booty."

When Ajakian brightened Gallyvan suggested: "Us needs only threaten that copper with exposure to convince he to visit Christopher in the prison and obtain the location on the reef."

Ajakian's owl eyes glistened. "Why did you not tell me of this before?"

"I only just learn of it last night, mon."

"Arrange the meeting. Remind said constable of our knowledge of his iniquity, but also offer him sufficient incentive to encourage his performance."

"Why we must pay his crooked ass?" Gallyvan asked.

"To assure his compliance," Ajakian responded. "Go! Offer the man more than he can ignore, convincing him to obtain for us that vital information."

"Us still has money sufficient to bribe a copper?" Gallyvan asked.

"Offering and paying are unrelated functions," Ajakian said.

#　　#

Thirty-Two

Bonbieu sneered as Gallyvan swaggered off. "A brute with much arrogance, that African."

"I admire him," Ajakian said.

"But why? What is special about one of those?"

"He impressed me from the first moment I saw him." Ajakian rolled his eyes back to recapture the memory of that encounter with a muscle-bound black topped by that tangle of straw-like curls, who neither looked, acted nor spoke in a gentle manner. Incredible how fortunate it had been to encounter him at that precise juncture.

He'd returned to his hotel room after that meeting when Mustafa Erkaban decided they needed more muscle. It shocked him to interrupt a burglary—of his room. The brash African exposed not an ounce of timidity upon being caught in the act.

Mustafa Erkaban had that day provided Bajuk with a three-fifty-seven magnum semi-automatic pistol, which Bajuk aimed at the savage. "Back against the wall, or I blow a hole through your head."

"Careful, mon, you doesn't accidentally wound me."

"Be assured it will not be by accident." Ajakian thrust the pistol out with both hands—apprehensive—having little familiarity with blacks.

"Say what? Call the damn po-lice, mon, and end this foolishness."

"What is your name?"

"What difference it make, mon?"

"I demand your name. Provoke me and I kill you."

"Fuck you, motherfucker! Me damn name Gallyvan. Now go ahead and pull you damn trigger if you think it that easy to kill a human being. Or maybe you get you kicks from kill a black man."

"You are amazingly without concern for someone facing death. Gallyvan is your sur name or given name?"

"Say what? What you damn game, mon? You plan to kill me ass or write a damn book?"

"I demand to know your full name."

"Fuck you, motherfucker. It bother you that me has no second name like some honky."

"You amaze me. Have you no fear?"

"Fear of what, mon? Fear to die?"

"It is what most people dread most."

"Ras'mon, me mama tell me when me naught but a tyke running wild on the streets of Kingston that me end up dead. It surprise me to live this long. So what you can do? Pull you trigger. Don't miss or me mess up you white ass."

"I have for you a proposition, to allow you to graduate from a petty thief to a person of means. Have you interest in making considerable money?"

"Me robbing you hotel room. You think it for naught?"

"Rather for petty income. My confederates and I plan to purloin diamonds valued at several millions of dollars. Because we have need for an additional man, I tested you to see if you had the courage to impress me to enlist you."

"Ras'mon, you threaten to kill me ass in some kind of fucking game?"

"Your choice, of course, is to continue stealing piddling amounts from hotel rooms until you are caught and imprisoned, or join us in one robbery that will earn you a quarter of one millions of dollars."

"Say what?"

"Two hundred and fifty thousands of US dollars. Do you wish to join us?"

"Damn straight, mon!"

#

"Incredible how he impressed me." Ajakian's eyes sparkled from memory.

"And me, mon ami. Did I impress you also?"

"Actually, no. Through intermediaries Mustafa Erkaban contacted Ismet Okyar, your partner in Rotterdam. Precisely because we were not impressed by either of you did we seek a fifth person."

Ajakian rose and dropped a few Saint Vincent dollars on the table. "I walk and deliberate, with hopes of finding a solution to our dilemma." He left Bonbieu sulkily glaring after him.

#   #

Thirty-Three

"Kindly enlighten me as to how your violent encounter advanced the case."

Ward clenched his teeth, uncertain how to respond.

"I rather thought by this time you'd have uncovered at least a number of clues regarding the murder of Torchy—have bolstered the case somewhat."

Ward didn't reply, cowed by that overbearing stare as well as diminished being in that teak and stainless steel ambiance.

"Do you have any actual progress to report," Josephs asked.

"You knew this case was cold when you engaged me to tighten the noose around Christopher's neck."

"Hopefully you have a definitive direction to accomplish that."

"I'm beginning to put some pieces together."

"What pieces, precisely?"

"I need to connect the dots before elaborating on it." Chingalo, Ward realized he wasn't equipped to play this mind-game with a dude that had a lot more smarts than he did, plus three times the education.

Josephs lifted a cigar from the humidor and rolled it between his palms. "You'd do better to apply more energy to pursuing the case preferable to peripheral matters."

When Ward wrinkled his face—confused, Josephs said: "Rumor has it that you spend a goodly amount of time doting on a particular waitress—as opposed to utilizing that concentration on the case."

Ward gulped. "Heard you had a thing with Darla, but that it ended. Tell me she's still your squeeze and I'll back off."

"She is not my squeeze, as you indelicately characterize it. My dalliance with her ended quite a bit before I remarried. Be assured, investigator, that I am not in the least bothered by your association with her."

Ward swallowed the urge to retort to the prosecutor's condescending tone. But prudence restrained him from butting heads. He turned to exit the office.

"Don't fancy yourself some sort of lothario," Josephs called after him, "since you're not the only chap on the island enjoying the company of said waitress."

Ward spun back. "You saying she's the town pump?"

"I'm not at all critical of her. I simply suggest you apply more effort to pursuing the case, rather than relishing bedding her as an accomplishment."

"Let's change the subject before we bruise each other's egos."

"As you wish. What would you prefer to discuss?"

"What can you tell me about Bajuk Ajakian?"

Josephs knit his brows while expertly rolling the Corona-Corona between his palms. "The chap arrived on the island rather recently and has done nothing in Saint Vincent to attract attention. Does something about the man provide you with some investigative insight—some direction in your floundering about for clues?"

"I'm working on connecting Ajakian and Christopher."

"In what way, pray tell?"

"It deals with motive, the ingredient you need most when you present your case to prevent him walking on a plea of justified homicide."

"Jolly good. Exactly what's required. Be kind enough to amplify that assertion."

"Nothing specific yet, but I'm searching for an avenue of discovery."

"Frankly, I find it difficult to imagine any sort of connection between those two. Are you certain you have basis to deduce some sort of alliance?"

"I'll fill you in as soon as I have something substantial."

Josephs sniffed the cigar with the proficiency of an aficionado. "Keep me informed of your progress, investigator."

Ward accepted the dismissal and flipped on his Yankee baseball cap as he pulled the door closed behind him. He exhaled, relieved for having avoided being caught in a bluff. But he was still incensed and wondered why he didn't tell the arrogant hump to stuff his case. But that ten grand, while not a fortune, sure as hell felt like a windfall with Ramón's law school tuition impending.

Besides, he had a compulsion to work the homicide. Doubtful he'd get another shot at one—especially a case with all that international media coverage. It'd be a kick if word got back to The Apple about his success here.

\#   \#

Thirty-Four

"Back again?"

Startled, Ward paused momentarily while pushing through the door to exit the courthouse. He sneered upon recognizing the two reporters, then strode away.

No way he'd chat with those nosy humps with speculations about Darla monopolizing his concerns. How do you fall for someone you don't know? He felt like an asshole.

Passing a café with a canopy shading its sidewalk tables, he decided to stop for a beer while he sat and pondered that situation. He needed to kill the half hour anyway before they met at his hotel. So he wrestled with whether to keep the rendezvous. Believe that he had no intention of becoming emotionally involved with some street mutt.

He nursed the Hairoun while rehashing all the upsetting things he'd heard. Ay Dios, it'd diminish his pride as a Latin lover if Darla jumped into bed with every guy tipped his hat to her, as Josephs intimated.

Biggest goddam problem for Puerto Ricans had to be sus orgullos—their pride. Deny them employment, decent housing and sufficient food—beat them—throw their asses in jail—but don't mess with their pride.

Poet said that she and Josephs had started seeing each other on the sly. Gnashing his teeth, he recalled the resonance of jealousy in Josephs' voice. Then a voice duplicator among his memory synapses replayed Darla scathing the prosecutor for his indictment of Christopher. Damn sure didn't sound like a love affair.

Considering those two came from different worlds, in an environment that perpetuated social caste, it took effort putting them on the same page. All of the progress of the twentieth century hadn't erased British mores and the social differences deeply ingrained in these islands between born-withs and born-withouts. True, Josephs wasn't to the manor born, but he'd risen mega-degrees since his humble beginnings. Darla never climbed above the status of waitress in a hash-house . . . A dump that didn't even have air conditioning.

He grunted acceptance that loneliness initiated his union with her. Long days at sea affected him differently than bumming around in a city bustling with females. But even there a man needs to bond, as opposed to bouncing from one chica to another.

Memory clicked of Constable Bivens's whispered confidentiality about how Josephs had carried on with a woman below his station to provoke his wife into shedding him, consequently denying her sharing his wealth. Chingalo, he hadn't realized who the constable alluded to. Usually when personages of Josephs' social strata amused themselves with inferiors they restricted that activity to the shadows.

Dios en cielo, did Darla realize at some point that Josephs used her to provoke his wife into divorcing him, that she'd been the pawn in that game? Sure, that's why she lashed out with such vitriol about the conniver.

Dammit, he needed to settle this thing in his mind before meeting Darla at the hotel. Draining the bottle, he dropped a couple of bills on the table and ambled along the sidewalk, those concerns tumbling around in his head.

That carnival of peddlers hawking their wares confused his thinking and amplified his frustration, as did the blaring horns of traffic. Conyo, if motorists in New York made that kind of racket, cops would run out of noise abatement tickets.

Dammit, without that squall, he'd have crossed that stretch of ocean to Barbados and never called at Kingstown, not be here confused and taunted by this shit. But he couldn't undo what occurred—couldn't change history.

Incidents in his past flashed into mind, as did the realization that he rarely learned by mistakes. His life had been a crazy quilt of dumb decisions. Didn't he end up marrying Delores Rey—the marquis queen in a boisterous club in midtown Manhattan?

Even back then, when blinded by infatuation, he'd have been wise to associate her with that environment—two degrees above a strip joint—rather than elevating her to a Broadway star or something.

Thirty-nine at the time, and divorced for some years from Rosalía, he became infatuated with that twenty-seven-year-old voluptuary who thrived on being the half-naked temptress every horny guy hooted at. Damn real it rankled him after marrying her to see those hard-ons hanging out with her at the bar and treating her to pricey drinks. It didn't matter that she didn't bed with any of them; just letting them rub against her gouged his Puerto Rican pride. No way he was able to stay married to a woman who diminished his ego. Still, it took four years to accept he'd made a mistake and divorce her.

Myrna Goldberg became his next fascination. A stylish and foxy divorcee who'd risen to a business executive, she really looked super-good for forty. Within a few months he moved into her trendy Soho apartment.

A new life began, with an introduction to theater and museums, as well as sailboating out of City Island. The downer was people looking askance at them—some of them sneering disapproval. He stuck out like a channel marker in the mid-town places they frequented, and suffered ostracism he'd never experienced among Latinos.

From his family's Mediterranean origins he inherited black hair and eyes, and a heavy beard that accentuated his swarthiness. No, it wouldn't surprise him to learn that the tar had been brushed on antecedents somewhere along the line back in the island. Not that it mattered in Puerto Rico. You were considered white among Caribbean Hispanics if you looked predominantly Caucasian, and negrito if you had color, features, and hair typical of that race.

True, no one considered him black or mulatto, but rather referred to him as Puerto Rican or Hispanic, a designation bestowed on them by pretentious superiors—even by Italians and Jews, who had their own ethnic baggage.

Things like that fester in a man's soul. He may refuse to accept he is inferior to anyone, but he has to continually convince himself that he can walk as tall as they do.

Coincidentally, he and Myrna broke up a week before he retired . . . not that one thing influenced the other. Too many incidents contributed to the evaporation of their enchantment to pinpoint specifics. Both accepted that the time had come to move on, without histrionics or recriminations.

Okay, maybe his break-up contributed to his decision to pack it in. As a cop he'd swallowed his bile of discontent one time too many. Since he'd earned eligibility to retire he didn't have to take any more shit. And he didn't want to stay in New York.

His big brother, Leon, who retired a year before and moved to Puerto Rico touted life there as a hell of a lot more pleasant and more affordable than anything in The States. Leon raved about how it pleasured him to live among his own in a decent neighborhood, not in a ghetto. So Ward joined his big brother to be among his own kind.

Funny how life takes all those turns. While visiting with Leon and weighing the pros and cons of whether to move to the island he happened on that derelict vessel that resulted in his wandering around the Caribbean. Life had a way of surprising him. He just never knew what to expect around the next corner.

Agh, what the hell good is rehashing all that shit? He had to face Darla to decide whether to condemn her as a loose bitch or accept her as someone he could care for.

#   #

Thirty-Five

"Why didn't you tell me?"

Darla paused in pulling her blouse over her head. "What is it me not tell you?"

Ward sat on the bed in his skivvies, watching her slip out of the blouse then remove her brassiere. Chingalo, he tried not to be vamped by that fine body. If she failed to relieve his angst, he didn't want to prolong the infatuation. "Byrum Josephs. You had a fling with him."

"T'wasn't important," she muttered, averting her eyes as she dropped both garments on a chair.

"How can it not be important? I'm working for him."

"The thing between we happen before you bold self visit this island, mon. How it now can be you business?" She slithered out of her skirt and kicked it aside with a show of exasperation.

"I need to know whether it's still going on between you two."

Her eyes jerked around to him, glowering with resentment. "Hell no! But why it you business?"

"I care for you."

She tensed and stared at him—confusion phasing her pupils. Her eyes narrowed as she searched his face. "This jive?"

When he shook his head, she said: "Mon, you know not how much me share that sentiment, but hesitate to let me'self have affection for a mon me know so short a time."

"Let's start out by telling me what's going on between you two."

"Not one damn thing. All we had ended before you bold self arrive."

"Explain it to me . . . how you had a romance with him . . . how you broke up . . . when you broke up . . . why you broke up."

"Me doesn't enjoy to rehash how the mon threw me over after us date and grow close for most a year. Lord, me was living in a fairy tale—so never believe, even when jolted to reality, that he marry with that snooty Braithwaite bitch."

"Without any hint of it happening?"

"Nary a peep. Afterward me realize him attach he ambitious ass with her highfalutin family because they have influence."

"Considering you live in different worlds, I have a problem putting you two together."

"Actually me never think to have an affair with the mon, though me admire he for achieving as him did and because him strikingly handsome."

"So one day out of the blue he just pranced into the café and you two got struck by the lightning bolt."

"Oh, stop you foolishness, mon. Yes, one day him stop for lunch. Soon after him stop often."

"Were you married then?"

"Jesus sakes, no. Me widow nearly two years. You think—"

"And he?"

"The mon tell me he separated and in the throes of divorcing Velva Parham. He visit often and us chats and becomes friendly."

"Just friendly?"

"The first time him invite me to dinner, me decline, fearful me let me'self be suck into a back-street affair. But the mon convince me him want only me company so him doesn't eat alone. He tell me that him lonely and how him appreciate to have a friendly face across the table."

"Oh, there's a line."

"Yes, t'is, but me lonely as well, and he also have a face to gaze upon."

"You believed he was getting divorced?"

"Me believe every damn word from the mon's mouth. Me foolish eyes filled with stars. Yes, me believe him God's gift." She shuffled about, waving her arms in front of her, discomforted by being naked except for panties.

"So you two became a thing, and you figured you owed him some booty, or did he demand you put out?"

"T'wasn't like that. Stop you foolishness, mon. You knew me not then and have no right to criticize that which happen." She crossed her arms across her breast.

"You're right. But I'm curious. How did you two get so thick?"

Her head quivered with annoyance as she turned away from him. The small room restricted her prancing. "The mon take me to expensive places me never before visits, and us enjoy meals together like me never know exist."

"The prelude to seduction."

"Yes, t'was. One such night him surprise me by invite me to a weekend in Bequia. Before me have a chance to refuse, him assure me we to have separate rooms."

"And you believed he didn't want to bounce on your bones."

"Mon, me not the fool. Me see the mon have yearning in he eyes. And, yes, mon, me flattered."

"You mean you fell for his line."

"Me alone, mon, a widow, and have yearnings also. Surely you know me have passion in this soul."

Ward glanced away, regretting having egged her into sharing intimacies he really didn't want to hear.

"Yes, after dinner, him make he play. Me doesn't going to deny me old enough to know one doesn't simply receive without give."

"Okay. Okay, so he scored, because you felt obligated."

"No, mon, because me kitten purring. Me human." She dropped her arms from shielding her breasts and leaned belligerently toward him. "Truth be told, me need he much as him want me. Did you think me a virgin when you first start you jive?"

Ward winced, stung by that verbal jab. And he rued having provoked her confession.

"Me mistake be that me fall hard—hard, mon. Thereafter it become a steady affair."

His ears buzzed with confusion and he barely heard her utter: "Me never know he use me to discard Velva Parham."

Ward sought words to divert her from reliving the agony of having been deceived. "Bet he showered you with expensive gifts, like a lotta' rich guys."

"Most these fine togs you see me in be from he. But t'wasn't that him need to buy me body. Us having the affair, and me truly affectionate toward the mon. It tore out me heart when me learn, without one bit of warning, that him gone and marry that dragon."

Ward leaned his head to the side as he realized he'd never seen the prosecutor's wife, so couldn't visualize her.

"Lord, me never even know him finalize he divorce with Velva Parham. Nor have me one clue that the mon woo another woman." Darla scowled and shook her head. "That Braithwaite cow not his type, but the widow rich and influential, a member of the right family. And him one ambitious bastard."

"I though he had money, didn't need to marry her for that."

"No, mon, him seek influence. Him have money but lack position. She family among those that governs here. Four months after him marry gargantua, the old prosecutor retire and Byrum appointed to succeed him. Believe he never get that position without taking that cow to wife."

"I assume he didn't come around again after the wedding." Ward held his breath, waiting and hoping for reassurance.

"Some months pass before him strut him haughty self into the café. T'was before him appointed prosecutor. The mon have the gall to come by to jive me how he marry her only to further he career, and say him love only me."

She snickered. "Me send he packing, with he damn gypsy-mouth. Lord, believe me curse he ass proper." She moved to the wicker chair near the dresser and sat, her head bowed and her face drawn and distraught.

"There's a rumor around," Ward said, "that he's trying to resurrect the affair."

She sucked her teeth. "Maybe me more woman than any mon can forget."

"I'll attest to that. But I've heard that the two of you are still a thing."

"Damn lie! It end bitterly, but, yes, him try to make it begin again."

"What the hell does that mean?"

"Him start visiting the café at lunchtime. Molly serve the mon to spare me. But him persist and eventually us talks."

Ward grimaced, hoping she didn't confess to that stuffed shirt scoring again. He had only so much forgiveness.

"The mon apologize time and again for misleading me about Velva Parham as well for not inform me him intend to marry that cow."

Ward forced himself to breathe while waiting and yearning to hear that she didn't capitulate.

"Lord how the mon alibi how he career demand such since he family lack influence. Him say him never realize during that time that him fall in love with me, and still adore me. You believe the mon have the damn gall to suggest secret meetings?"

"But you didn't cave," burst out of Ward. Then he sucked in and held his breath, hoping for confirmation.

"Believe that—even after the mon tell me him need me and shares no passion with that cow."

"Hope to hell you were stronger than previously."

"Very honestly, t'was hard because me have adore the mon—and because me horny. Lord, me never want to think bad of that mon. In me own way me love his conceited ass."

"So what happened?"

"Me tell he plain me have no desire for a back-street romance. Byrum become cross and remind me of all him have done for me—the places him took me that most poor-asses never visits, and the clothing him bought me."

Ward snickered, not surprised that the guy resorted to that tactic.

"You probably not believe that me become speechless. Yes, mon, this chick who rarely have trouble expressing me'self take a long moment before me find me tongue to cuss he ass proper."

Ward chuckled, and Darla chuckled with him. "Lord, me see red—red, mon—and tell that arrogant ass me going to dump all those fancy rags on he doorstep for he fat wife to wear."

Darla laughed, though her face reflected resentment rather than humor. "Lord, the mon angry, angry, and glare at me with fire in those eyes when he warn me to stay away from he home or him have me ruined. Then him stomp out."

"Wow! That's what I call ending a love affair."

"Still, me sad, because me miss the mon—and me stay a virgin 'til you bold self arrive."

"Oh, great. No wonder he's pissed. When I took this job, that had to have some meaning to you."

"I never thought it important, mon. Lord, me boiler melting and me need a fireman."

"So what you're saying is that I'm only the lucky guy getting a fast screw because you're horny."

"If that what you want to believe."

"He said you've been bedded by a lot of guys on the island."

"The mon a pig and a damn liar. Me marry Wilbur when me young, the first man on God's earth me intimate with. Since Wilbur pass away me succumb to only one man besides Byrum, then you bold self. Soon he score, that first rooster look elsewhere for a conquest."

"I want to care for you, but I have to know you're not available to any guy reaches for you. I want to feel special, not like a jerk."

"Me not a loose woman. Yes, me make two mistakes—one with a conceited ass who only care to feed he damn ego by have a conquest, and the other with a devious striver who put ambition before affection. Me making a mistake with you?"

Ward averted his eyes and stared at the wall.

She stood, wearing only panties. "You wants me naked or no? Jesus, Lord, say something."

He turned to her. "I don't know why or how, can't even explain it to myself, but I let myself get involved last night."

"As did myself." She went to him and took his face in her hands. "I yearn to kiss you."

He pulled her down to him. Their lips gently met. Passion increased to hunger that induced them to mash their mouths together and entangle their tongues. She pushed him down and lay atop him. He pulled off her panties. With her help he stripped off his skivvies. Then she straddled him.

Twisting atop him, she pulled him into her moist portal, enveloping his masculine probe in warm and loving folds. His hands enveloped her breasts, then grasped her buttocks as she gyrated on his swollen penus. Pressure billowing in his head displaced all of the doubts, suspicions, distrust, and uncertainties as he abandoned himself to ecstasy.

\#   \#

Thirty-Six

Ward wrinkled his nose at the emanations from the wooden crates piled high with finfish and shellfish of every size and shape, as he sauntered through the fish market in a brightly patterned shirt that'd make a Seminole proud. In one octopi flopped about in slime.

Fishmongers, mostly older women in long skirts and a variety of straw and cloth hats, with some draping once-colorful scarves over their heads, flailed at the flies that assailed their crude stands. Legions of locals bickered with the venders while examining the catch. A number of gnarled men bent under the burden of hauling dredges of iced fish to replenish the stands.

Ward stepped carefully through puddles from the hosing off of the remnants of the recently scaled, gutted and filleted fish. Seagulls scattered out of the paths of humans while quarreling over whatever they scavenged.

Reaching the open-air café on the perimeter of the noisy market, where he'd agreed to meet Poet for lunch, he dropped onto a decorative but wobbly wrought iron chair at a small table in the shade of an awning. It's proximity to the market kept it in the essence of that environment causing him to waver whether to take lunch there.

He threw a lazy wave to Pops hobbling toward him, mod in a collarless white shirt with dark blue piping. But the codger apparently wore the same wrinkled chino slacks as yesterday and the same sneakers. No mistaking those kicks, worn more on one side than the other, as well as having identifiable stains and dirt streaks.

Poet dropped onto a wobbly chair across the small table and puffed his exertion from the cross-town walk. "Bassa-bassa," he responded to Ward's inquiry of his well-being. When Ward stared askance at the reply, he translated: "Vincie for okay or no complaints."

"Sounds like you're going native."

Poet snickered as he signaled the waitress and ordered two beers and a menu.

Ward made a face, uncertain he wanted to take lunch while inhaling the pungency of that environment. The oldster had called him at the prosecutor's office to meet here rather than at Ward's suggestion of the Pilgrim's Pride Café. Ward hadn't pressed for an explanation. He'd had breakfast at the café with Darla to predispose of her bugging him about having lunch somewhere else. But he wasn't all that anxious to settle for this place . . . wished he'd insisted on the Pilgrim's Pride Café.

"Okay, Pops, what's the scoop?"

"An old pal snooping around in Curaçao informed me that Bajuk Ajakian and his cohorts were there at the time that jeweler got murdered. Info he dug up indicates that Interpol and the local police worked in concert to ensnare those who stole the uncut diamonds in an armed robbery in Rotterdam."

The waitress brought their beers; no surprise to Ward to receive Hairoun.

"What's the special for lunch?" Poet asked her.

"Whatever t'is you'all wants," she replied indifferently.

"You don't have a special today?" Poet asked.

"Flying fish." She said it impassively.

Poet bobbed his head around. "Okay, I could go for a fried fish sandwich."

Ward wrinkled his nose, not all that anxious to have lunch while inhaling the invasive smell of fish putrefying in the tropic sun. Plus, they had to continually wave off the pesky flies. But because he wanted to hear Poet's report he caved and dittoed the order. Hell, he didn't have to eat it if dining there became repugnant.

When she left, Ward mused: "Not surprised that the fuzz there didn't bust Ajakian and his mooks, since they apparently lacked evidence to tie them to the murder of that jeweler. But you'd think they had security cameras in that Rotterdam diamond center."

"The bandits were masked and immediately sprayed the cameras."

"Must have shaken up the fuzz in Curaçao," Ward said.

"Unable to find those rocks on them," Poet added, "they couldn't bust them."

"Hopefully," Ward said, "is that you have a line on Ajakian that connects him and Christopher to the murder of Torchy."

Poet wrinkled his face in confusion. "Isn't the diamond theft and smuggling a bigger story?"

"Only if it can be substantiated."

"Consensus is," Poet said, "that Ajakian felt boxed and didn't want to get caught with the diamonds . . . while unwilling to abandon them and relinquish that money."

"The reason he sought a conduit to get them off that island," Ward said. "So he recruited a boatman to smuggle them out of Curaçao, considering he had little hope of getting them cut there after snuffing that jeweler."

Poet nodded. "According to my source, eight foreign yachts visited the island at the time—one of them the Ole

Virginny. It doesn't take a genius to figure out that those diamonds got hauled out of there aboard Christopher's vessel."

Ward rolled his eyes back as his mind drifted back to the interview with Christopher's wife. He grinned while remembering her admitting having met Ajakian in Martinique, but hedged about an encounter in Curaçao. "Okay, but why then is Ajakian and his mooks so concerned that Christopher not end up in the joint?"

"Why else?" Poet shrugged. "Christopher hasn't as yet delivered the goods."

"Hard to believe, which brings us back to motive, or cause and effect. Why would a rich yachtsman smuggle uncut diamonds?"

"Could be he's not as rich as purported to be, making him receptive to obtaining a sack full of money. Then again, he could simply be greedy for more money."

The waitress plunked down their sandwiches on paper plates and left. Poet glanced at her retreating back, then hunched dismissal of her surly manner.

"Be helpful," Ward said, "if we knew what happened to those rocks."

Poet carefully grasped his overstuffed sandwich to prevent it falling apart. "C'mon, you have to believe they got hauled out of there aboard the Ole Virginny."

"With no evidence. Which still leaves us with the question: why did someone want Torchy dead? Was it unrelated to the diamond business?"

"Torchy was capable of anything," Poet said while chewing, "and might have pissed off Christopher. The guy was hated."

"So I keep hearing." The aroma of his sandwich induced Ward to pick it up as carefully as Poet had. "We need to learn where he stashed those rocks."

He bit into his sandwich, then groaned approval of the crispy fish with its spicy dressing. The area stench no longer bothered him as he chewed with relish. "Was Torchy's death unrelated to the diamond business?"

Poet shrugged, his jaws munching.

"So it's possible," Ward said, "that Torchy's murder was a random act, having nothing to do with whether Christopher smuggled those baubles for Ajakian?"

"Why not? The brute was some kind of incorrigible hoodlum. Women were deathly afraid of him. People nailed down their belongings when he was around. He'd steal the hair off your head."

"Yeah, yeah." Ward waved off the oldster's words with the overstuffed sandwich.

"Half a dozen stories circulating," Poet said while chewing with gusto, "where he raped guys' wives or girl friends. They wanted to kill him and the wives and girl friends swore they'd gut him."

"Why didn't they?" Ward asked, chewing non-stop.

Poet stuffed the last of his sandwich into his mouth, then wiped his hands and face with his paper napkin. After a long swig of beer, he said: "You had to see that husky stud with his hair done in those tight curls they call cornrows. Must have pumped iron to develop a body like the Caribbean Mister Atlas."

"Good sandwich," Ward said, finishing it off.

"Always wore sunglasses," Poet said, "even at night, like they were a badge of cool. Had a straggly mustache that needed a good dose of manure to mature it."

"Yeah, Pops, I get it: the most bad cat in town."

"Damned good-looking stud," Poet said, "but the embodiment of evil. Most folks, especially women, were frightened of him."

Ward gazed into space. "Why did Christopher kill him?"

"Maybe he laid hands on Vicki—Mrs. Christopher. That bastard had the gall to do something like that . . . didn't respect the altar of a church."

"But if he didn't make a play for her, Christopher had no apparent reason to kill him . . . so no free ride for justifiable murder. Any other motive can lead to conviction."

Poet drained the last drop of beer from his bottle, just as the waitress passed. He waved the bottle at her for a refill. "If Ajakian needed a hireling when he came to this island, he'd sure as hell end up with Torchy."

Ward grimaced. "Considering he has that Rastaman and the gutter-rat Frenchman, it's doubtful he'd need any more muscle in this burg."

When Poet didn't respond, Ward said: "Let's consider the big picture. If Christopher did it to protect his wife, he'd have pled justifiable homicide, rather than rot away in that dungeon. No jury on this island or anywhere else will convict Christopher, considering Torchy's reputation."

"Most condone him for the killing," Poet agreed. "Might give him a medal."

Ward stared into space. "There's more to it than a rich white Yankee versus a poor black local or something that happened in the heat of anger."

"No argument from me, detective."

"Why then," Ward asked, "are there guards around the yacht, considering it's docked in the safety of the Lagoon Hotel?"

"What I hear," Poet said, "is that Vicki never leaves the boat, even to visit her husband. She doesn't shop, doesn't eat out—nothing. Everything is sent in."

"But what is she frightened of?" Ward stared into space in his search for answers. "And why is Ajakian so damned concerned about Christopher getting convicted? What the hell is the connection?"

"We sure have a lot of questions to answer," Poet said. "I'll contact everyone I know and see what-all I can learn about Ajakian as well as about Christopher."

#   #

Thirty-Seven

Ward paused in the café doorway, enrapt by sight of Darla in that flowing skirt of dark blue and ivory with an Indonesian motif. Her white sleeveless knit shirt accentuated its sarong-like exoticism, and did justice to her knockout body. Remembering how she got those fancy togs set him to chortling.

After serving food at one table and taking an order from another, she disappeared behind the kitchen wall. He dropped into an unoccupied booth and breathed impatience until she reappeared, burdened with dishes of food. Finished serving them, she brushed past him on her way to another table.

"Hey," he called to her, "am I invisible?"

She cut her eyes at him. "Must be me the one doesn't be seen. What bring you inconsiderate self here past the hour for luncheon?"

"What the hell's rattling your cage now?"

"You find you'self a better place to take you meals?"

He started to explain, then took a deep breath, having learned yesterday to not fabricate stories. This chica had a stable of squeals, probably knew where he had lunch and with whom. "I met with Poet, that ex-newspaperman in a place near the fish market."

"Oh, you prefer the mon company to mine."

"No, dammit, it was business, discussing the case."

"You discusses a murder case with an old man who write poetry?"

"Cut me some slack, chica. He's got connections, knows a lot of journalists, and is getting me heads-ups to help make sense of a confusing case."

"What you reason for not take luncheon with the mon here? You ashamed if you white buddy learn you hugging up to some black woman?"

"Oh, come off it. I'd show you off on my arm anywhere on the island . . . in the best watering holes in Manhattan."

"So why you doesn't bring the mon to have luncheon with you here?"

"He picked the place. Ay Dios! Get real! You're my lady and I'd shout it from the roof of the café if you want me to."

"Me wants you to be considerate, not leave me to spend a whole day wondering if after you have you booty you lose interest in me . . . or perhaps you shamed to have you buddies know who you sleeps with,"

"What the hell are you talking about? We had breakfast together—remember?"

"And why we couldn't have luncheon together?"

"Madre de Dios! Why are you so cantankerous and so damned unreasonable?"

"What you say: it unreasonable to ask you to be considerate, especially after us bickers about this very thing last evening?"

"Shoot me, I'm absent-minded."

"Best you absent you inconsiderate self for a week and put you thing hang between you legs on ice. Don't even think about this booty the next seven days."

#   #

Thirty-Eight

Ward panted, splayed out on the bed, recovering from the mind-blowing passion of the past half hour. Thank God she'd gotten over being pissed at him. True, it had required talking a ton of trash and practicing some serious petting to get her into bed. But once aroused, she turned into a West Indian Vesuvius.

He stretched and yawned, indulging his lethargy while feasting on her fine parts as she padded off to the shower. Apparently she'd recovered from that exertion quicker than he. He shrugged to that and indulged his laziness by closing his eyes and goofing.

Hearing her return induced him to crack open his eyes, to see her don that blue sarong with its Indonesian design. That fine body triggered considerations of more libidinous exercise. Hell, he was no longer a rooster and might not have another round in him. Bull shit!

She glanced at him and her face crinkled with annoyance. "Why you doesn't move you'self, mon, to shower and dress. Me famished and needs to have some dinner."

"You're right. I'm laying here watching you dress and getting horny."

"Best you hie you'self into that shower, mon. You still has energy in you ancient bones after dinner us returns and tends to you needs."

#

"Something bother you?" Darla asked, aware of his pensiveness while he toweled off after stepping out of the shower.

"Can't get the case out of my head. Most everyone I speak to thinks it was ridiculous for Christopher to be indicted for murdering that launch-man."

"They right," Darla said.

"More than a few have pointed out the possibility of any number of people on the island nursing a grudge against Torchy, and eager to do him in."

"Believe that," Darla said.

"Fact is, those convinced that Christopher killed Torchy consider him justified."

"That the damn truth."

"You, however," Ward said, "are the only person I've talked to that accepts without question that he's the killer."

"You deny me having me own opinion?"

"It would be the first time. Why does Vicki Christopher hate Torchy?"

"The woman probably have good reason." Darla focused on the mirror while fixing her hair.

"There's something I'm missing. Maybe it's her reason for hating Torchy.

What's yours?"

"Mon, me going hate you, you doesn't hurry and dress, so us satisfy me hunger."

#   #

Thirty-Nine

Ward caved to Darla's choice of BASIL'S BAR & RESTAURANT at the Cobblestone Hotel. She lauded the place as a branch of the one on the island of Mustique in the Grenadines, where the rich and famous dine.

He'd read about that unique and privately owned island, the exclusive playground of a number of the ultra-rich and imagined those estates having mansions with swimming pools and tennis courts. Probably every one of them had a yacht a block long.

However, he'd heard the one here in Kingstown didn't charge prices like the one on Mustique, so donned his white cotton slacks with a nylon shirt dazzling with colorful geometric designs. Consequently, he welcomed the immersion into air-conditioning; grateful they didn't sit in a sidewalk café where he'd be acutely aware of the heat and humidity in that nonporous fabric.

A piano-player tickled out popular American tunes, somewhere in that candlelit ambiance. Ward noted that the celebratory crowd was predominantly white. The arrival of the waiter with a tray heaped with platters swept away all unrelated thoughts. He sighed approval after a mouthful of kingfish steak. "Damned good food. You come here often?"

"How me afford to come here often, mon? That why me like you bold self. You Yankee men spend like rich Vincies."

"You got no rich guys willing to splurge on you?"

"Nor a desire to have any and need to submit to those lechers just so them treats me to a fancy meal."

"So you're saying you've never been here before."

"Me said no such thing. Truth be told, me brought here by Byrum Josephs when us went places together."

"That figures."

"Yes, me realize now him bring me to this snooty place because news of it certain to get back to he wife of that time."

Ward snickered as he remembered how Josephs shed his ex. Gotta' give the guy credit for slick. Most men end up mortgaging their kidneys.

"At least me enjoy to come here once before," Darla said.

"Only once. Some sport."

"Him have a tiff with those Yankee yachtsmen and vacationers who want to have all they friends together near the piano over there for what they calls a sing-fest. Mon, those snooty folks tell the waiters to move the few Vincies, as if us goats or sheep to be put in a different meadow. And when Byrum resist, insulted that they ask such since us in the middle of we meal, some few of them become rude."

"You serious? They talked down to Byrum Josephs?"

"T'was before he appointed prosecutor and not yet have that standing . . . the reason those rich folks who thinks they owns the world dare to insult the mon."

"Really pissing Josephs off."

"Sure, mon! How you think us feel, among the few black people in that section and those uppity whites talking down they noses at we. Them throw a few dollars in we economy and us beggars must bow to they rich asses."

"Hey, you don't have to school me on the subject of prejudice. I'm Puerto Rican, remember? You can't grow up in New York without experiencing the disdain of Anglos."

"Then you understand why Byrum jump stink. No one want to be shunted aside by some arrogant Yankees and snooty English."

"Maybe that's it. Smoldering resentment is driving him to nail Chistopher."

Darla shook her head. "Byrum ambitious. Sure, him remember that incident and resent those people. But him anxious for the publicity come with prosecuting Mister Christopher, now it has worldwide coverage. Why you think him doesn't back off, even with all those reporters of different countries hounding he ass?"

Ward bobbed his head about while digesting that rationale. Then he grimaced, remembering that the slick prosecutor had nothing to lose since the New York detective figured to end up the goat if Christopher beat the rap.

"Why us discuss those things?" Darla asked. "This a romantic night. Come, dance with me. Hold me close and sway with me to this music."

Ward didn't need encouragement to press his body against hers. How many times does a love song reverberate in a man's heart? He buried his face in her hair and inhaled her aura.

"Call your daughter and tell her you're staying with me all night."

Darla laughed. "Me tire out you braggadocios ass in half of one hour."

#   #

Forty

Ward waved a greeting to Poet who hobbled toward the table. Morning sun formed a halo behind the codger's head, accentuating thinning gray hair brushed against a knobby skull. He wore another of his collarless knit shirts—this one in decorator heather. Like mod. But he wore the same old, same old, chinos and sneakers.

In dazzling contrast, Ward sported a colorful shirt with large tropical flowers and leaves. It took center stage amid THE LIME'S PUB's antique nautical ambiance, a conglomeration of paraphernalia from historic sailing ships plus the subdued effects of driftwood and photogravures of old-time steamboats and paddle wheelers. Its rustic charm was further enhanced by the uniqueness of one wall constructed of used and weathered lobster pots: square crates with wire attached to their wooden slats.

Ward had breakfast early at the Pilgrim's Pride Café, at which time he informed Darla of his intended meeting with the oldster—assuring her he'd have lunch at the Pilgrim's Pride Café. Damn real he caved to making whatever concessions to avoid discord. So he ordered only coffee at The Lime's Pub, while Poet had a cinnamon roll with his.

"You're an expensive date," Ward wisecracked.

"You'll consider my high maintenance worth the price when you hear the information I've obtained about

Christopher." He produced a sheet of paper. "Research from friends in Virginia. Ogden Christopher graduated Rice University at the low end of his class . . . typical of his being a classic underachiever."

"How in hell'd he get rich then?"

"Jelland Corporation of Charlottesville, Virginia, founded by his mother's family is a profitable enterprise that manufactures cigarette paper. His mother died recently leaving the firm to Ogden and his younger brother, Orville. The younger emerged as CEO and formed a consortium of share-holders. They voted that if Ogden didn't participate in the operation of the firm, he relinquished income from it."

"You saying they cut him off without a penny?"

"Couldn't do that. He gets periodic payments from his mother's trust plus dividends from the stocks he owns in the corporation. But he no longer receives a company stipend since he refuses to go home and become a working stiff."

"Putting a hurting on his financial ass," Ward murmured, "by reducing his income below his needs to support the lifestyle he's become accustomed to."

"But apparently hasn't induced him to cut back," Poet said, "at least as far as his wandering the Caribbean in the Ole Virginny," .

"So what we got is a wannabee rich-guy cut off from the where-with-all to finance his extravagance—a perfect candidate for smugglers."

"Topping that," Poet said, "he has a substantial obligation to his ex-wife and their two sons, one at Duke and the other in a private high school. Ajakian probably offered him too much to resist transporting those stolen diamonds."

"A relatively small package," Ward said, his eyes narrowed in speculation, "easy to conceal on his big-ass motorsailor. Okay, so we can circumstantially connect him to the diamond smuggling, but how do we tie him to Torchy's murder?"

"Why bother when we can apply our time and energy to the diamond smuggling?"

"I'm being paid to provide grist for the conviction of a murderer. Nobody's offered rewards for diamond thieves or smugglers."

"Don't you New York cops have the resilience to change your focus if something else is more promising?"

"Which story you think those syndicated newspapers in The States want most . . . an obscure European hold-up that's weeks old and yesterday's news, or the indictment of a rich, white American yachtsman for the murder of a black launch-tender?"

"Okay, we stick to solving the murder of Torchy, which will eventually touch on those diamonds and the Rotterdam hold-up."

Ward shrugged acceptance. "Let's work on learning how Torchy figures into it."

"Probably learned about that diamond business and tried to cut himself in for a share."

Ward sneered skepticism. "Torchy was a small-timer at best, with no chance of getting away with pushing around a heavy like Ajakian."

"But he had the balls to try."

"Naw. If anything, Ajakian hired Torchy, needing more muscle. I can appreciate that after waltzing with the bad-ass Rasta and the skinny frog-eater."

Ignoring Poet's gawking bewilderment, Ward turned his eyes upward in speculation. "If Torchy got out of hand, it's doubtful Ajakian expected Christopher to snuff him. The guy's an amateur at best and no match for someone bad as you claim Torchy was."

"He totally lacked human compassion."

"But if Ajakian had reason to have Torchy whacked he'd use one of his mooks, not a pampered yachtsman."

Poet rolled his eyes in concession. "Doubtful the body would have surfaced if Ajakian's thugs dumped him in the sea."

Ward stared at the wall constructed of weathered lobsterpots, as if trying to read something in the hieroglyphics of nicks, dents and scratches. "This thing is anything but cut and dried. There are so many suppositions. Did Christopher smuggle diamonds for Ajakian? And was Torchy also involved with Ajakian?"

When Poet didn't respond Ward scowled at the lack of answers in his head. "Why did Christopher kill the guy? Did he kill him in a moment of passion, having no connection with the diamond smuggling? Is it possible that someone killed Torchy for reasons we haven't considered?"

"You tell me. You're the detective—getting paid those big bucks."

#   #

Forty-One

"Ay chingalo, that was awesome." Ward sprawled out on his back, sucking air while recovering from exertion. He grinned adoringly at Darla's naked body, spread-eagled and beaded with sweat.

"Lord," she uttered, "you make me blow wild, damn bull."

"Don't turn me on so high if you don't want me to detonate."

"When you bold self departs this island me have a chance to rest from you mad passion. But, sad to say, me to miss you when you gone."

"Don't start anguishing before I leave. Besides, how do you know I will want to?"

"Because you come here by accident, with no intention to make you home here. Where you plan to go when that storm blow you off you course, and where you sure to go when you case finished?"

"Venezuela , to see how the super-spics live."

When she looked at him askance, he explained. "We survived day to day in that New York barrio. Some, like myself, aspired to move into the mainstream. Hurts to admit that I never realized enough of that dream, resulting from implicit limitations imposed by those gringos that dominate."

Darla shook her head, sympathetic to his memories.

"Yeah," he said, "it left a scar on my psyche for needing to struggle to overcome being regarded as an inferior by sonsofbitches whose poor-assed fathers or grandfathers migrated from somewhere in Europe. They made me feel like an alien every day of my life by repetitively implanting the designation of Puerto Rican as undesirable."

"But you enjoys inclusion when you visits Puerto Rico."

"Yeah, when there weren't any Yankee administrators and tourists around. We're acutely aware that our tiny island is a territory of the US of A and dominated by gringos."

He shook his head in dejection. "There's always underlying antagonism, stemming from increases of cancer because of the navy training exercises, including the bombings and shelling at Vieques. Plus there's resentment because of the take-over of good farmland for military installations. Nor do the locals appreciate it when real estate investors buy out low-income communities to build fancy condos for rich Yankees. It's just not the same as being in a country of Latinos independent of Uncle."

He snorted displeasure at the memories swirling in his head. "Actually, it wasn't too much different than being in New York."

"You saying you doesn't like New York?"

"Loved it! Loved the impressive buildings towering to the sky and enclosing crowded streets, as well as the clamoring activity of pedestrians and vehicles, the never ending parade of chicas, the posh stores displaying everything you wished you could buy, the camaraderie at the watering holes, and especially the hot-dogs and the pretzels from the street vendors."

Then he turned morose. "But I suffered the disillusionment of being made to feel like an outcast in

CALYPSO

my birthplace. I loved it and hated it—am left with great memories contaminated by smoldering resentment."

"Mon, you bitter. Me happy now me never join those who migrate to you country."

"Smart move. What's in your future?"

"Me working hard and sacrificing so me baby enjoy higher education and be more than me."

"You're not doing so bad, querida mia."

"You joking, mon. Me a pitiful small-island gal. Do you know me never been away from Saint Vincent, except to visit Bequia, and once to Saint Lucia."

"Ay chingalo, neither island is more than a long-ass stone-throw from this place. You've never been to the other Grenadines, to Barbados or Jamaica?"

"That is it. But me a proud woman and mother who survive tragedy. Me doesn't need no mon to depend on. And me doesn't want to be shamed again, like what happen when everyone pity me and whisper behind me back because Byrum Josephs use me to divorce Velva Parham, then cast me out with the trash when him marry with that cow."

"Hey, I hope I'm not leading you up the garden path."

"No, bold face. Me accept you for who you are, a sailorman passing through. Believe when me tell you me getting as much from this relationship as you bold self. Me like sex, yearn for affection, and love luxurious dinners. You paying through the nose to enjoy this fine ass."

"You don't hear me complaining."

"You think you ever pass back this way?"

"Is that what this is about?"

"Actually, no. And me not anxious to talk about things make me sad. Why you don't pour we a nice drink so us gets woozy."

#   #

191

Forty-Two

Ward climbed out of bed to pad across the floor to the little refrigerator. He filled two glasses with rum punch from a pitcher Darla made for him and kept there. After handing her a glass, he sat on the edge of the bed and stared into space while sipping his.

"What make you glum this time, mon?"

"Stymied at putting all the pieces of that goddam case in place."

"Mon, you has a week or more before Josephs must present evidence. Why you let that spoil we time together?"

"Sorry. I'm obsessed to solve this homicide and prove I'm a bad-ass detective. Problem is, I'm still on square one, in spite of having interviewed everyone with any involvement that I know of. There's got to be something I'm not seeing."

"Patience, non. What you doesn't see today you see tomorrow when you turn the page and read it from a different direction."

He grinned, amused by her attempt to console him. Then he rolled his eyes back as her words tumbled over the synapses of his analytical chamber.

"Madre de Dios! I've been staring at it all this time without realizing it. Why in hell is it that only one person on this island harbors no doubt that Christopher killed Torchy?

And why do you persist in the man's justification when <u>he</u> won't cop that plea?"

Darla averted her eyes, focusing on the ice cubes she sloshed around in her glass.

Ward searched her face. "Vicki Christopher has a good reason for defending her husband. But why do you?"

"Me has no part in that business, mon, and seeks none."

"Everybody else on this island thinks the prosecutor is pissing up a rope indicting Christopher. Most remind you that Torchy had a thousand enemies. But you simply accept that Christopher nailed Torchy. What the hell do you know that they don't?"

"How me know anything, mon? Me but a waitress."

"Stop the shit, Darla. You stated unequivocally that Christopher was justified in killing Torchy."

"Whatever that mean. Anyway, me entitled to have me own opinion."

"The way you defend Christopher sounds more like a statement of fact. What is it you know that I should?"

"You daft, mon."

"Daft, my ass. I thought we had something going for us—respect and trust."

"Us has passion." She lowered her eyes as she sipped her drink.

"It just might dissolve if we hide important things from each other—lose trust. If you persist in denying that you know anything, then you're lying to me."

She squeezed her glass, kept her eyes averted.

"Talk, dammit! A relationship can only survive in the light of honesty. I'm asking you to tell me why Christopher killed that launch-man."

She took another sip of the rum punch, before setting the glass on the scratched bedstand. "Best you not hear my story, mon, or us no longer have anything between us."

"If you don't tell me, then we have no basis for mutual respect."

"Torchy deserve to die. He lower than the belly of a snake, who strut about with those darkers hiding he eyes, cocky and grinning."

"I've heard the descriptions."

"The mon evil! Evil, mon! More evil than a scorpion."

"Yeah, yeah. Everybody in town knows he was a no-good hump. Why do you hate him with so much passion?"

She picked up the glass and turned it slowly in her palms. "The mon rape me."

"He what? Where? How?"

Darla took another sip, then resumed turning the glass in her hands, her glazed eyes following the rotating ice cubes. She leaned against the shaky metal headboard of the bed, her weight pushing it to clunk against the wall. But she didn't speak, only squeezed her eyes closed several times to hold back the tears.

#   #

Forty-Three

Ward stared at her—appalled while eager to hear every detail. But the pain etched in her face impelled him to back off and give her time to collect herself.

She sipped her drink, then stared at the ice cubes bobbling in it for long moments before speaking. "That snake stop by the café and tell he lie how him act as agent for a family in Bequia who fall on bad times and need to sell they collection of seashells."

"Seashells," Ward repeated, in a scoffing manner.

Darla cut her eyes to reprove him. "Collectors from all 'round the world scours the markets along both upper and lower Bay Street for shells found only in the waters of Saint Vincent and the Grenadines, such as certain cowries, hawkwing conchs, music volutes and different cones. Investigate for you'self if you not believe me, but expect to pay big prices for any you fancies."

Ward hunched concession. "Tell me what happened."

Darla remained bent forward, a morose expression on her face. "It no secret that me daughter have a collection since most on the island see Melissa often digging in the surf for them."

Ward shrugged, unimpressed by that announcement.

"Through the years me asks the fishermen to save shells for Melissa since her not able to pay the price them charges at the markets. It why it doesn't surprise me that Torchy learn of that interest. Lord, me sorry now it never raise suspicion when him approach with he surly grin. Come by his place, him invite, where him plan to set up a table to display them. Him say me sure to find something of interest—at prices far cheaper than me able to find elsewhere."

She snickered. "Lord, mon, me never trust Torchy, aware as everyone that he evil. One time me slap he paws off me body and curse he ass proper."

She sipped her drink. "Me doesn't deny me desire to see if he have shells that Melissa desire to have, but me doesn't trust he shifty ass. No, Lord, no way me go to he shack—on top of the beach near Calliagua, where the fishermen bring in their catch."

She shook her head in disdain at her gullibility. "That low snake call over he shoulder when him leave to come by after eight o'clock if interested. Him say expect to compete with others who coming. Mon, me never believe for the life of me why me doesn't realize the sly mongoose playing one he games."

She sighed. "Me too anxious to get a gift for Melissa. And me expect others to be about. So, that night, me went to he shanty. Lord, what him calls a house a damn lean-to, so weathered it surprise me an offshore breeze doesn't blow it away. The roof be crude, crude mon, of palm fronds, driftwood and other junk. And the doorway covered with a soiled tarpaulin, with newspaper tacked over what serve as a window."

Darla shook her head in reproof. "Me should never enter that grungy shack when him greet me with he evil-smile while hold aside that moldy canvas cloth. Lord, me shrink from brush against it, so step quickly into the shack, to be stunned by its squalor. And me full inside before it strike me that no others about."

She winced. "Damn lying snake have not only no people but nary a shell on the rickety table. But him now stand he muscular self in the doorway. That low snake have the gall to taunt me by tell me that me come because me desire he joint between me legs."

Darla clenched her teeth. "Lord, me curse the fool and call he rude—and let he know me sooner lay down with a cockroach than with he unwashed body. Him scoff as him grasp me arms and pull me against he. Me struggle to break free, but that brute wrench me around and pull me across the tiny room. Believe, me exert me'self to prevent be drag to the mattress on the floor. Lord, me recoil at have me body touch those rumpled and soiled bedcovers. But him force me down onto it and drop on top of me."

She averted her eyes and shook her head, as if to expel memory. "Me scream loud as me lungs allow, desperate to attract attention of someone walking on the beach—even at that late hour. Lord, me feel me head rock. And me blink and blink to clear fog from me eyes—before me realize him strike me. Me head sting even in memory."

Ward hung on every word, horrified but enthralled.

"Damn bully grin in he evil way as him show he fist and tell me him to punch me to pulp if me make another sound . . . taunt me by tell me how me go home for me daughter to see me bruised face. Pictures flash in me mind of other women with they faces beaten raw by him. Lord in heaven, me doesn't want to suffer they shame."

She sipped her drink. "But me can do nothing, so clamps me eyes closed and try not to know what he do next. But it make me sick, so me try to twist free. But him slap me hard—so hard, mon, it make me head ring."

Darla wiped the tears leaking down her distraught face. "Never in me life me so humiliated. But me keep me eyes closed and suffer his thrusting that ugly thing in me."

Ward struggled to keep from turning away from her.

"God in heaven, him make me so shame, me doesn't know to this day how me endure."

#   #

## Forty-Four

"Finally him let me free to stumble home. Lord, me cry all night—though careful to hide that anguish from me daughter. No, Lord, me never sleep a wink, hard as me try, fearful that he claim me as his woman."

Darla again wiped tears from her face. "The low snake have done that to others, and shame they so them doesn't want to show they faces. Them know every person see they bruised faces and whisper how them have rough sex with that brute. Lord, me be strip of pride and me life ruin."

She sighed then sipped her drink. "Me has no other way to earn me living, so must continue waitressing. God, me apply a ton of make-up to conceal those bruises. And me pray him doesn't show up to bray how him have me last night. How me to explain why me went there? How me to explain it to me daughter?"

Darla paused for a few deep breaths. "Thank the good Lord the morning pass without incident. Some stare hard at me bruises, but not one person mention one word that Torchy brag about town that he have me in he bed. Yes, some few sure to speculate how me get those bruises. The island have no lack of woman-beaters. Me able to live with that, so long as none learn me receive them from Torchy."

"So he didn't go to the café to taunt you?"

"Bless God, no. After work me go home and drop on me bed. Lord, me not know how long me weep . . . and how much me pray Melissa never learn of it and lose respect for she mama."

Ward compressed his lips as he sought words with which to console her.

"Lord me worry how me survive day after day worrying when that brute say something to ruin me life. Besides, me fear that the low bastard even walk in me house and declare me as he woman . . . might be he rape sweet Melissa. Lord in heaven, me need to prevent that."

Darla blew her nose and wiped her tears. "Me get up the nerve to go back to that shack—taking the Webley service revolver of me dead husband. Yes, me did. And me sneak in when me find no one there. With no idea what to do, me hide in a closet of crude boards with the door covered by another piece of that moldy canvass.

"Lord, that place fill with junk—and it stink from mildew and unwashed clothes he hang on nails or dump in piles. But me clench me teeth and wait to kill he black ass."

Darla took a few deep breaths. "Lord, how me bones aches from crouch in that tiny space stuff with smelly clothing, scattered footwear and junky boxes. Lord know how long before me decide to give up and go home. Me start to rise when me hear people arrive.

"Me peek out and gasp to see not only Torchy but that Armenian gangster and he two thugs. Believe, mon, me careful not to make a sound and bring attention to me'self —more frightened than ever."

She took a deep breath, then sipped her drink. "Lord, me fret that foolish decision for go there, but it leave me little choice but stay quiet until him guests leave. And pray God the mon have no reason to go to he closet. Lord, what me to do if he and they stays late, trapping me in that smelly place?"

She shook her head in condemnation of what she'd done. "Mon, it blow me mind when Torchy have the gall to call that hovel a house and tell Mister Ajakian how he please to have the mon use it for a meeting. That Armenian move about with care to keep from brushing he fine clothing against anything in that squalid shack."

Ward clenched his teeth to contain his curiosity of why they met.

"A few minutes later me stun again when Mister Christopher and he blonde wife walk into that hovel. Lord, what those imperious American yachting folks doing there with their heads downcast like servants instead of upraise in the manner of gentry? Mon, they address that Armenian like he the lord of the realm."

Ward perked, consumed now.

"Believe it shock me to hear Ajakian demand those folks give him diamonds. Mister Christopher, with his head still hung, explain that he hide them in a hole in the reef of Canouan when told that the coast patrol searching vessels. Him claim him fear that they confiscate he yacht if them finds contraband on board."

Ward nodded, brightened by that enlightenment.

"Ajakian order the mon to retrieve them. Mister Christopher say how him try the day after the coast patrol search and clear he vessel. But him fail to find where he hide them when he go back. Him tell how he compass coordinates not correct. Ajakian barked liar at the man, but Mister Christopher insist he dive a number of times but fail to find them. Still, he know they there."

She took another sip. "That Armenian tell he thugs the American need to be convince to give up those stones. That one-eyed Frenchman put he knife to the throat of Mister

Christopher, and force he to lean against the wall with he head bent back and he eyes popping with terror.

"Then the woman scream when that bad-faced Rasta rips the front of she dress and ruffle she breasts. Gallyvan cover she mouth with one hand and squeeze she tits with the other—more to put fear in she heart than excite either she or he'self. Mister Christopher beg them to stop, even though the knife at he throat constrict he voice.

"Jesus Lord, me fear me throw up. Me have all me can do not to cry out. It cross me mind to bust in on them and shoot that Rastaman—but me lack confidence of survive a gunfight with those thugs."

Ward shook his head, astounded—and refrained from questioning her.

"Mon, me never before fire a gun. The thing so heavy me barely able to hold it. Besides, me had all me to do to keep me knees from buckle and make me fall against something that tumble and make noise to give away hiding there."

She drew a deep breath. "Frighten and without courage to intervene, me watch and listen as Torchy beg Ajakian to let him thump Vicki Christopher's pretty ass. Mister Christopher plead with them not to hurt he wife. Him promise that him return to the reef and dive until him find the gems."

Ward nodded to that, enthralled that the details were falling in place.

"That Armenian tell he thugs the Christophers need more convincing, so Gallyvan bend Mrs. Christopher over the back of a chair and screw her back end, though both still clothed. Lord, how the woman screech. Lord me has all me can do to stay still. Me swallow so me doesn't vomit. And me fear if me move me cause some of that junk to fall on the floor . . . bring those thugs to attack me."

She took a deep breath. "Mister Christopher yelp how he to find those diamonds, so that Armenian tell Gallyvan to release the woman. That bad-skinned Rasta scowl as him amble over to Mister Christopher and grab the mon's genitals. Then him brag how he learn in prison to enjoy mens. Lord, he have that white mon squeal when him squeeze he buns and tell he how he always desire to thump a white mon."

Ward shook his head, appalled.

"That Armenian warn Mister Christopher that they doesn't get off the next time. Both be rape, then be skin alive. They have two days to produce his rocks. Mister Christopher say how him to dive the first thing in the morning, soon after him get air tanks from the chandler shop at the Lagoon Hotel Pier."

She again breathed deeply. "Ajakian warn him not to attempt to flee, that him have agents in every corner of the world. They then to suffer the worst hell, and have they yacht burn. While the Christophers hurry away, tears in they eyes, Torchy call to them that he to visit their yacht later to thump Mrs. Christopher.

"Those ruffians laughs and ask Torchy if he have liquor. When he say no, the French gutter-rat suggest they goes to a place on the hill where they get booze and be sure to find them some fine whores. So them go off together."

Darla exhaled volubly. "Lord, me force me'self to breathe while me wait until those hoodlums no longer near-by. Only God knows how long before me have courage to slip out of that shack. And, Lord, me spent from fright, and need to stumble along the beach until out of sight of that evil place. Then me lean against a palm tree and puke out me guts. No, me never before tell anyone a single word of what happen that night."

"Unbelievable," Ward murmured as he went to her and gathered her in his arms to console and reassure her.

#   #

## Forty-Five

Darla sucked in breath, exhausted from sobbing. She wiped her eyes. "It why me believe with heart and soul Mister Christopher not deserve to be punish for kill that scorpion."

"I understand how you feel, but crimes have to be punished if we're to preserve civilization and the rule of law."

"The mon save me from disgrace. In some ways him save me life."

"How do you know that? Did you see him do in Torchy?"

"No, mon, of course not! How me to see what done? Him out on a damn boat."

"What makes you so sure that he, and not his wife, did the deed?"

She sipped her drink, with her eyes averted. Ward searched her face as he murmured: "Maybe that deckhand did it."

"No! Caleb never kill nobody."

"How in hell you know that?"

"Caleb a true Christian, and never harm a human being."

"Pardon me for being a skeptic, resulting from twenty-eight years of police work. How can you know who killed Torchy?"

"Lord, mon, you hear me tell how Torchy threaten to rape the mon wife."

Ward remembered the dockworkers speculate why the Christophers returned to their yacht then came back ashore to spend the night at the hotel. Now he understood their fear of remaining on the yacht anchored out in the stream, fearful of an assault by Torchy. He glanced to Darla. "So your assumption is that Christopher did him in."

"What you do if it you and you woman?"

"It wasn't though, and I'm not about to speculate on the basis of hypothesis."

"Whatever that mean. All I say is that after what they do to he, then he wife, him have every right to kill that snake."

"Then why isn't he pleading justifiable homicide? Besides, based on your account of what happened in that shack the guy would be more likely to kill the Rasta or Ajakian."

"The mon set me free and need reward, not punish." Darla picked up her glass and wandered to the little window. While sipping her rum punch she gazed at a centipede scampering across the upper part of a low wall.

"Come on, Darla, you came this far. You have to tell me how and why you're so sure Christopher killed Torchy."

"Lord, me promise never to reveal that."

"To who? And is that person more important to you than me?"

"No, mon, me not say that. Besides, how that secret affect you."

"It tells me that you care enough to trust me and share with me. If you don't tell me then I'll know there's no hope for this relationship."

He winced, remorseful for pressuring her like that—laying the same bull on her he did when grilling a skel. Dammit, he felt driven to know. But he delayed questioning her further as he watched her wander back to the bed and sit. Dios, she looked so forlorn.

After a short silence he said: "Only two people besides Ogden Christopher can disclose what happened on that launch. Vicki Christopher didn't impress me as someone who'd take you into her confidence. That leaves the deckhand, Caleb."

When Darla didn't respond, he studied her, hoping to read something in her facial expression or body language. But she transmitted nothing to hang an assumption on. "Okay, I'll grill Caleb to get the entire story."

"No! That poor mon not want to say things against folks important to him."

"He doesn't have a choice."

"Why, mon, when you you'self say Christopher justified to shoot that snake. No, mon, Caleb never say one word."

"He'll be subpoenaed."

"Why you doing this?"

"Dammit, I took this job to clear a homicide, and you two hold important keys to putting it to bed."

"How you can violate things I tell you in confidence, mon? It not fair to use all I say to convict Mister Christopher."

"We don't know that he'll be convicted—do time anyway. Probability is, it'll support extenuating circumstances—for murder anyway. Diamond smuggling is a separate issue."

"You must never utter one word of that which I tell you here today."

"Don't have a choice. I'm a cop—have been one most of my adult life. It's my commitment to law enforcement."

"Why you must be so holy? You believes, as does me'self, that Mister Christopher doesn't deserve to be punish for kill that snake. What you do if it you wife?"

"Probably the same damn thing. The difference is I'd plead justifiable homicide, not try to stonewall the police and the courts, and rise above justice. But his concern is concealing the diamond smuggling, which likely will result in the confiscation of his yacht, besides imprisonment. He gambles on beating the murder rap. He will too if I don't have evidence to present."

"Mon, me sorry me tell you those things." She slammed her glass down on the nightstand, splashing liquid on it. Jumping up from the bed she snatched her skirt off the chair and stepped into it.

"Hey, where the hell you going? We've got a lot to clarify."

"Get someone else to pump for you information. You take me in you bed, then use me." She thrust her feet into her shoes. "Now you betrays me."

"I'm doing my job. I'm pursuing justice."

"And you pursuing someone else for you booty." She slipped into her blouse, scooped up her straw-like handbag, stuffing her underthings into it. "Best you learn to have loyalty to you friends over police work." She stormed out, slamming the door behind her.

"Where the hell you going?" But she'd already left. Ay chingalo, why did she have to rush out like a raging nut? Why couldn't she see his side of it and understand that he'd been conditioned over the years to serve the law? She had no right to expect him to suddenly turn his back on everything he'd been steeped in—the ethics that guided him for twenty-eight years.

Chingalo, he'd have to smooth things out at the café tomorrow. But, goddamit, he didn't relish suffering her moody-assed cantankerous attitude until she relented.

Meanwhile he needed to rehash everything he'd been told, put it in perspective, corroborate all of that testimony. Dios mio, he finally had it all: motive, means, and opportunity—even if he lacked substantiation. But, just maybe, he'd get that from Caleb if he got lucky enough to get the guy alone.

#   #

Forty-Six

Ogden Christopher rubbed the sleep from his eyes while two guards escorted him into the stark interview room. He looked emaciated in his oversized, faded and rumpled prison tunic as he tottered along in leg chains, befuddled by being taken there that early in the morning.

Obeying the gesture of the guards, he sat in the wooden chair across the small table from the seated constable. He blinked, confused as he watched the guards leave and clank the door closed behind them. Then he turned to stare quizzically at the uniformed man across the table.

"You remember me? I Constable Booker, who take you into custody in Union Island and bring you ass back here."

Christopher nodded. Worry lines ridged his face. "Are you here to press additional charges?"

"Why you think that, mon? You deserves additional charges?"

Christopher twirled his hands. "Then what?"

"I here as an emissary for Bajuk Ajakian."

"But you're the police!"

"Mister Ajakian say to tell you he lose patience, mon. He want that which you pledge to deliver to him. And he doesn't going to wait 'till you free of this place."

"You're the law. How can you represent Ajakian?"

"Keep you voice down, and stop you nonsense. I mean this meeting to be painless. Long as you cooperate, you doesn't have to worry you be harmed."

"Harmed? But you're the people who're supposed to protect me."

Booker slammed his palm on the table. Christopher jerked away from the resounding smack, shrinking as far back as the chair allowed. His thin face contorted with fright and bewilderment.

"Mister Ajakian send me so you know being in this dungeon do not place you beyond his reach, doesn't save you ass from the ravages of brutes."

"Oh, God! Oh, God!"

"God ain't help you sorry ass, mon. You needs to tell me where that package be found if you cares to survive another dawn."

"I don't know. I don't know."

"How you don't know? What in that package, anyway?"

"I don't understand. Are you intended to know?"

"Probably dope. It what you fools transports. But you doesn't need to tell me. Onliest thing important is to learn where that package be, for Mister Ajakian to fetch."

"Maybe I should have my lawyer here."

"You a fool? You want to die tonight?" He slammed his palm on the table again.

Christopher again jerked back, to shrink into his shoulders. His long face with its prominent nose and ears sagged with hopelessness.

"To save you ass you needs to tell that mon what him desires to know."

"How can you represent those people? You're the law."

Booker slammed the table top again. "Stop you naïve shit, mon. I here for a purpose. Believe you ass suffers if you doesn't send instruction for Mister Ajakian to retrieve that package. I shoot you dumb ass me own self, you mention a lawyer again."

Christopher blinked repeatedly, hopelessness etched in his long face. "I've already told him I hid it in the reef off Canouan."

"Say what?"

"I pushed it into a hole just inside a crevice. Thought I'd recognize that huge scar again with the anemones growing around it. Went back but couldn't find that spot. There are so many fissures and so many plants and strangely shaped coral. It confused me."

"How you can not find the place again if you mark it?"

"I didn't mark it, for fear a mark might attract curious reef divers. That crevice struck me as a natural landmark. But it was late in the afternoon, almost dark, with everything covered in shadows, distorting my view of it." He waved his hands to accentuate his confusion.

"You tell me you hide something of value and know not where you put same?"

"There are so many crevices. Maybe I saw it from a different angle when I dived to retrieve it. I somehow lost track of how deep I searched for a hiding place."

"But you makes notes, no?"

"Probably confused the navigational coordinates. A fraction of a degree could put me off one hundred feet or more. One part looks like all the others."

"Seem to me yachtsmen supposed to be navigators and know how to return to any place on earth."

"I'm a capable navigator—no matter what—"

"Then how you not able to find what you hide? When you dive again, it the same time of day?"

Christopher rolled his eyes upward in memory. "No, it was earlier. Actually, that's what I was doing when the coast patrol took me into custody."

"Lord, lord, lord. So that the reason they find you scuba diving, surprised that you not in full flight."

"I was trying to retrieve the damn things and get Ajakian off my back."

"I has no reason to disbelieve you, mon. But Mister Ajakian doesn't want to accept you lame excuses."

"What options does he have—until I get out?"

"He tell me to bring to this place one big-dicked black stud to make a tunnel in you white ass unless you tells him where to find he package."

"No, please!" Christopher shrunk back and clasped his arms around his chest. "Twice I tried to find the damned thing."

"Best you think about you health and that of you wife and find a way to lead that mon to that place you secret his goods."

"My wife is protected."

"You think two sleepy guards protects anybody? We needs only to arrest them on some trumped-up charge and you wife naked—naked, mon. That bad-ass Gallyvan strut across you gangplank and shove he dick in you wife's ass."

"No! Please! Don't let them hurt her."

"Give me something that Mister Ajakian accept. That the onliest way to save you white ass and that of you pretty wife."

"Caleb!" And when Booker's brow creased, Christopher repeated: "Caleb. My crewman. He was with me when I hid it. I was chicken about diving alone, even though the top of the reef isn't very deep."

"That old man dive with you?"

"It was getting dark and I was reluctant to go down there by myself, never knowing what I might encounter in those depths—hammerheads and bull sharks, maybe a mako. So I took Caleb along both times."

"That old man?"

"He's an experienced diver . . . better than me. He agreed when we went back that we didn't have the right part of the reef. That damned thing runs for miles, and we couldn't find the exact location in that reef. I tried!"

"You sure Caleb know where to search for that thing?"

"Absolutely. Caleb will find it. He'll do anything for me."

"Okay, I tell that to Mister Ajakian. For you sake I hope that old man find the place and save you from become a woman."

"Please!"

#   #

Forty-Seven

Ward stretched and groaned, groggy from tossing and turning all night. Goddammit, he yearned to become the hero, not the butt of criticism, which is what he faced if Josephs failed to win a conviction. And he wanted the balance of that ten grand to pay down Ramón's tuition at law school . . . relieve a hell of a burden.

While briskly walking to the courthouse, he mulled over every thing Darla said last night; re-examining it after sitting at his desk while shuffling papers. Nothing she'd told him could be substantiated, consequently served as credible evidence. And no way he dared to consult with Josephs and put Darla at risk.

He doubted that pompous prick had any compunctions about charging her with obstruction and sending her to prison, especially considering his grudge because of her threat to dump those clothes on his wife's doorstep. That thought fueled a momentary chuckle.

But the gravity of the situation erased that and compelled him to pore over his paper work, reviewing everything in an effort to connect things and be able to present his findings without involving her. Dammit to hell, he needed corroboration.

The old deckhand qualified as the only credible witness, with Darla only able to offer suppositions. But Ward doubted he'd persuade the guy to flip on the people who probably bought his silence with the promise of financial security in his waning years.

Wagging his head, he searched his brain for an inducement to convince Caleb to tell what he knew, considering the oldster risked termination of his employment. Doubtful the geezer would find other yachts to hire him when they had a choice of younger and more agile men. No, Caleb was imprisoned by his age and financial dependence on his benefactors. Ward sniggered at the improbability of this tight-ass government offering some kind of pension as an incentive. Hell, they allotted only ten grand for a professional investigator in a capital crime.

And what were his chances of convincing Interpol to give Christopher immunity on the diamond business for testifying against Ajakian? He'd get better odds at a racetrack. Doubtful Interpol would forgive the guy that smuggled those rocks out of Curaçao, and left them with albumen dripping off their frustrated jowls.

Yeah, Christopher didn't plead justifiable homicide because out of the slammer he was vulnerable to Ajakian and his thugs. He also had to worry about implication in diamond smuggling—resulting in confiscation of his yacht.

Josephs wouldn't hesitate to send a man to prison for the rest of his life, whether or not the guy deserved that harsh sentence. Political hunger drove that prick, to gamble for all or nothing. Winning a conviction made Josephs a hero, champion of the Vincies, and opened the door for him to become the next prime minister. Losing cost him nothing, having the New York detective as a scapegoat.

Ward snapped out of his mental rambling when Booker arrived and clunked the door closed behind him. Dropping into the squeaky chair at his desk, the grouch replied unintelligibly when Bivens asked where he'd been all morning.

Unconcerned for that, Ward concentrated on his files, reviewing everything again. But he found nada to present in court. Shaking off the torpor induced by reexamining everything over and over, he decided to go to lunch.

#

Aware of the lack of reporters when he exited the building he assumed they chased more topical events until the trial. Ogden Christopher and that murder rated as stale news until then.

Threading among milling tourists and locals, he waved off peddlers. His belly growled at the prospect of suffering the moodiness of Darla. He'd be lucky if she snubbed him for only ten or fifteen minutes . . . Probably get served by the heavy gal. Actually their relationship figured to worsen when he grilled that old deckhand. So making up with her today was an exercise in futility.

When the café came into sight he paused and stared at it. His ears pulsated with the cacophony of motors growling and horns blowing. Quarrelsome birds flitted about, contesting for roosting places and morsels of food.

With his gut churning, he decided against subjecting himself to her surliness. So he turned and plodded toward the docks to find an eatery without touristy prices. Finding an empty table at a sidewalk café on Grenadines Wharf—an area patronized by dock workers and deckhands—he sat and ordered. But he found the food tasteless and the beer not cold enough for his liking.

Still, he drained the bottle, but left half the food. Okay, he'd go to the boatyard since they promised to have his baby ready today. Conyo, he yearned to have it tugging at his hands, with the breeze disheveling his hair. Yes, he wanted to feel free, if only for a short time. But he needed first to pay his check.

\#   \#

Forty-Eight

Ward poked his head in the doorway in search of the waitress. He did a double take when he spotted the familiar face at a table in the corner. It damned sure looked like Caleb, the oldster who crewed on Christopher's motorsailer. He moved closer to be certain, since the oldster bent over the table nursing a stubby glass of dark liquor.

Yeah, the old codger had that religious medal on a round piece of leather dangling around his neck. So, stifling a triumphant grin, he approached, optimistic that the leathery deckhand could provide information needed to lay out his case. Hell, the old guy had also been with his employer in Curaçao and at that dive sight off Canouan—might have aided and abetted, as well as witnessed lighting up Torchy. Maybe that's why he'd remained tight-lipped . . . being complicit.

When he dropped into the chair across from the man, the oldster peered up with squinted eyes questioning the intrusion. Ward read inebriation in those blood-shot orbs.

"Do me knows you?" the oldster asked.

"Sure, you're Caleb who crews on the Ole' Virginny. Taking time off, right? I'm taking time off also."

Caleb scowled as he peered at the interloper.

"Why don't I buy you a drink? We can chat a little." Ward waved over the chubby waitress. "Another drink for this gentleman and a beer for myself."

Caleb continued to gawk his confusion. But when the chubby waitress set the Hairoun in front of Ward and the stubby glass of dark rum in front of him the oldster perked up. He finished the little left in his glass and pushed it aside, then lifted the refill and gestured appreciation to Ward. Like most men he considered a free drink a boon.

"You celebrating something special?" Ward asked.

"Lord God, no, mon, me repenting." His slurred speech indicated he was almost in the tank. "Me seeks communion and forgiveness."

"Why? What's the problem?"

"A private matter, mon. Do me know you?"

"Share it with me and I'll drink with you." Ward raised his bottle.

Caleb held up his stubby glass, clinked it against Ward's bottle, then sipped the rum. "Me needs to drown sorrow and be absolve."

"Better bring this man another," Ward called to the waitress. "He's got a big sacrament."

Caleb gazed in disbelief at his benefactor. Then he stared at his squat glass for a moment before slurping down half its content.

"Drink to your heart's content," Ward said. "Plenty more where that came from." Noticing the chubby waitress had gone to the bar, he called to her: "Might as well bring the bottle."

Caleb's eyes widened with surprise, then delight when she placed it on the table in front of him. He grinned and drained his glass.

"How 'bout sharing your problems with me," Ward said.

Caleb hung his head and swayed it side-to-side.

"No way I can help," Ward said, "unless you tell me about it."

"How you to save me, mon, when me condemn to hell?"

"Just might be able to if you explain it."

"Me render falsehoods that violates me Christian faith."

"Tell me about it."

"Why, mon? What purpose that serve?"

"How will you know if you don't share it with me?"

Caleb stared at him with rheumy eyes—bloodshot and glazed by remorse. After a moment he said: "Not more than two weeks past me swear to the prosecutor to tell the truth. But me lie before God."

"Tell me why you lied," Ward said, "and I'll try to get you absolution."

"How? You not a priest, mon." He scrutinized Ward's raucous shirt and baseball cap. Then he winced as recognition dawned. "You that damn copper irritate Miz Christopher on the boat."

"True, but I have influence. Explain your problem to me and let me put in a good word for you."

Caleb picked up his glass, stared at it for a moment, then slurped some. He stared dumbly at his benefactor. "That prosecutor ask if me with Mister Christopher when that bully be kill."

"Were you?" Ward held his breath as he watched Caleb bow his head and wag it, but remain silent. "Talk to me. Tell me about when you and Mister Christopher went on that launch with that bully."

"It what the prosecutor ask. And, Lord in heaven, me lie before God."

"Tell me the truth to erase that lie."

Caleb took another swallow of rum then wagged his head again. "Mon, me violate me Christian vows by tell that prosecutor me sees nothing."

"What did you see?"

Caleb bowed his head and mumbled: "Me be sentence to damnation and to live in hell for all eternity." Then he sobbed uncontrollably.

Ward shifted to the seat alongside him and ran his arm around his shoulders. "Nod your head if you know who killed Torchy."

But Caleb wept uncontrollably, his body convulsing. Ward clenched his teeth to invoke patience while searching the man's face for an indication to direct his inquiry—some way to open the guy up. Dios en cielo, he was desperate for that information.

"Tell you what: don't take me into your confidence by telling me something you don't want to. Just nod if you know who killed Torchy."

When Caleb continued to sob and didn't respond, Ward said: "Don't mention any names. That'll be your secret. Just nod if you know who did it, which will be the first step to forgiveness."

Ward forced himself to breathe while the seconds ticked by, with hope withering since the oldster didn't respond. Hell, he wasn't sure if the codger heard him, that sad old man so consumed by his mental turmoil. And maybe too much rum denied Ward breaking the guy—after spending all that money getting him sloshed.

"You need to set yourself free," Ward said. "Were you there when it happened?"

Caleb kept his arms wrapped around his body. Long seconds passed before he bobbed his head up and down, then said in a barely audible voice: "Lord forgive me for lie about see it happen that awful morning."

Ward held his breath, fearful of saying anything to shut Caleb down. It grated in his gut when the oldster only sobbed, instead of revealing more. So he leaned closer and whispered in the oldster's ear: "You need to cleanse your soul of that awful secret."

Caleb appeared oblivious to the advice as he lifted his head and trained his eyes on the empty glass.

Ward filled it. "I'm going to give you advice, Caleb—man to man. No Christian can live with that guilt. Unless you unburdened your soul you might go insane and will not perform as required on your job, resulting in disappointing your employers."

"No, mon, me never disappoint those wonderful folks who treat me good all these years, and promise to take care of me in me old age."

"Being Christians too, they'd want you to cleanse your conscience."

"But them tell me to say nothing about that awful morning."

"What they said is not to testify about it to the prosecutor. But you can confide in me. Why were you there that morning?"

"Me spend the night with a nice woman in the hills above the town."

"Lucky you. What happened in the morning?"

"Me return to the pier for take a launch to the yacht and surprise to run into Mister and Miz Christopher." Caleb broke down to blubbering.

Ward squeezed his shoulders. "What happened then?"

Caleb glanced up with vacant eyes. "Nothing. Them only buying tanks and such for diving from the wharf chandler."

"Why? What did they intend to use it for?"

Caleb sobbed again. "Why God let me be born to witness that awful day?"

"God picked you because he knew you for an honorable man who will expose the truth to the world." Ward clamped his teeth together to keep from saying anything else. He'd learned a long time ago that silence sometimes is more productive than questioning.

Caleb picked up his squat glass and gazed at its contents. After a second he slurped some rum, then stared at what remained.

Ward breathed deeply to contain his impatience—knew he'd brought the troubled little man to the brink of confession and only needed to nudge him over the edge.

Caleb leaned toward him and whispered: "Me confides in you by confess me sins, but you must never repeat what me tell you. 'Fore God, you must never repeat it."

Ward's breath caught from the excitement of anticipation, hoping the oldster accepted his nod since his Catholic upbringing inhibited his verbalizing that promise. If he vowed to keep the secret then revealed it he defiled that sacrament.

Caleb leaned closer, his head almost in Ward's chest. "Me violate me Christian oath when me lie and tell that prosecutor me see nothing on that launch that day."

"Tell me what happened."

"It mystify me, mon," Caleb said in a pain-laced whisper, "to see Torchy take dive tanks and such from one launch to put in another, with nothing wrong with the first boat. Only later did me learn that Mister Christopher hire the other one to carry he and he wife, along with that equipment to the yacht."

Dismay contorted Caleb's face as he wagged his head. "Torchy rude, show Mister Christopher no respect and have the damn cheek to refuse me'self riding in that launch with those folks. Me doesn't understand to this day why Mister Christopher never stand up to that bully and chase he ass off."

Ward nodded to urge the oldster to continue.

"When Mister Christopher do stand up to the ruffian and say him not going board the launch without he crewmon, Torchy back down. Miz Christopher clutch she husband arm and sob. All the years me know that woman her strong. Lord, and now her blubbers."

Ward harnessed impatience—denied himself interrupting, though he'd heard all that from the dockworkers.

"Me sorry for them folks, though me know not how to help—too old to fight that bully. So me try to end it by say me not need to board the mon launch. But Mister Christopher angry—angry, mon, and say him want me along. So me stay quiet."

Caleb chuckled as he rolled his eyes back. "Mister Christopher tell that bully to keep the diving equipment. Torchy show shock and screw up he face, then say it okay to bring they crewman. Me never know why Torchy have more interest in Mister and Miz Christopher ride in he launch than leave with those tanks and such, to make himself some few coppers."

He slurped more rum, almost emptying his glass, so Ward filled it. Caleb bobbed his head in appreciation. "When all we aboard us head into the bay. But soon us into the harbor Torchy say him take we to Canouan to dive for that package in the reef."

Ward drew in breath in anticipation of hearing what led to Torchy's demise . . . mere words away.

"Mon, me wonder how that bully know of that matter. Mister Christopher angry —angry, mon—and tell the bully him fear him run off with the diamonds and leave he and him wife to face an angry Mister Ajakian. Torchy laugh while head for the cut from Blue Lagoon."

Ward nodded to coax Caleb to continue talking.

"Me wonder how Torchy know that Mister Christopher hide that object look like a salami in a hole in the reef. Lord, me never know it have diamonds. Why in God's name a person push a bag of diamonds into a hole in the reef?"

Caleb turned questioning eyes to Ward, who waved him to continue narrating.

Caleb shrugged and slurped some rum. "When us go back the day after to take that package from those rocks us doesn't find them. God be me witness, us dives for hours but doesn't find that crevice. Because me believe Mister Christopher record the place, me doesn't bother. So us not find that place."

Ward breathed deeply to retain patience.

"Mon, that reef have all manner of funny plants and rocks and such for endless kilometers. It swarm with fish of every type and color, some too beautiful to describe. Sometimes strange twig-like things look to lay dead on the coral but of a sudden flutter and swim away. Lord, me frighten of that place with all its strange creatures."

"Yeah, yeah. What happened next?"

"When us surface to change air tanks the Coast Patrol arrest Mister Christopher. It fall upon me to take the Ole Virginny back to Kingstown. Poor Miz Christopher sob all the way."

"Let's talk about the launch with Torchy," Ward said.

Caleb shrugged and stared at the far wall. Quiet for a few seconds, he nodded to memory. "Torchy ignore Mister Christopher and steer for the open sea. Him laugh in he evil way as him say him head for the dive site. Then him threaten

Mister Christopher that if him not come up with the package in two hours, Torchy thump Miz Christopher."

Ward drew a deep breath, aware he was close.

"Every two hours, Torchy threaten in he wicked way, that Mister Christopher doesn't produce the diamonds him again thump Miz Christopher. The brute pound he bare chest and brag how him go fifteen times in one day and wear out the woman.

"Poor Miz Christopher, her sobs out of control. Lord, me doesn't know how me doesn't jump that brute. But what an old man can do against that ruffian? And me serves no purpose to those folks dead."

Ward gasped when Caleb dropped his head onto his arms on the table and sobbed. Dios, the oldster couldn't stop now. Too many times he'd been frustrated by a mook clamming up after starting to talk. Damned if he understood what possessed someone to abruptly stop the flow of confession.

But he accepted he needed to be considerate of the codger's fragile condition. So he patted his shoulders. "You're almost absolved."

Caleb peeked up, his eyes widened with confusion, then flashed recognition.

"You need to tell the rest." Ward hoped the oldster hadn't swilled too much rum.

Caleb nodded as he turned to rest the side of his head on his arm. "Me not know then that Mister Christopher have return to the yacht the night before and fetch he shark pistol—not that me ever learn why. And me believe it rude to ask."

Ward wished he'd skip those peripheral parts, but decided against interrupting, fearful of the oldster taking umbrage and clamming up.

"Mister Christopher angry—angry, mon, and shout at Torchy when him head for the cut to leave the harbor. Him point he pistol at Torchy. That bully blanch, mon—lose all he color. Mister Christopher demand us be take to the yacht."

Caleb sighed, then sipped some rum. "Next thing me know Torchy spin the wheel to swerve the launch hard over. Mister Christopher lose he footing and pitch forward—as do me'self and Miz Christopher. Mister Christopher scrambles to regain balance, but when him look up him see Torchy point a pistol at him."

Ward's eyes bulged.

"Mon, things happen so fast—so fast, mon. All we wonder where Torchy get he gun. But we come close to crash into a boat at anchor, and Torchy have to turn the wheel to keep from hit it. While him do that, Mister Christopher raise he pistol and shoot.

"Torchy tumble off he bench and stare at Mister Christopher. Him push he'self up and raise he own pistol. Mister Christopher shoot again and again. Torchy fall back against the gunnel and lay still."

Caleb breathed heavily from residual horror that etched deep lines in his ebon face. He swung his head back and forth. "Lord, me never before see a man be kill."

"Yeah, yeah. Then what happened?"

"Me lurch over to the helm and grab the wheel to veer away from crash into boats at anchor. Lord, the eyes of Mister Christopher tell how he sad for have to kill that brute. So me stay at the helm while Mister Christopher hug and console he wife.

"When us reach the yacht, us put Miz Christopher aboard, along with the diving gear. Then Mister Christopher and me'self take a rubber dinghy with a small outboard motor in tow and drive the launch out to sea some few kilometers.

"Me help tie chains around Torchy with ropes, then dumps he mean ass over the side. After us get into the dinghy, Mister Christopher shoot holes in the bottom of the launch. When it sink the mon toss that small pistol after it."

Caleb flagged his head in remorse. "Us then returns to the yacht and Mister Christopher make me swear to never tell all that happen. So you swear to never tell all that I say. The Lord be me witness, me never testify against those fine folks."

Ward drained the bottle into Caleb's glass, but sat there as he ran all that had been said over and over in his head. Yes, he had a witness to the murder, but lacked corroboration—essential for a conviction. Even if he did it'd be justifiable homicide—getting Christopher off the hook.

Anyway, he doubted he'd convince Caleb to tell his story to a jury . . . certainly not if he was sober. Besides, he doubted the codger had the stamina to stand up against the cross-examination of the defense attorney, who'd make a laughing-stock of him.

Okay, Ward accepted that at least he had it laid out. While pondering how best to utilize the information he watched the old man's head drop to the table. A moment later Caleb snored drunkenly.

Ward paid the bill and left, to head for the boatyard with all he'd heard tumbling in his head.

#   #

229

Forty-Nine

"Ooh-ooh!" Ward sighed, elated by the wheel's metal spokes caressing his palms. Dios en cielo, how he'd missed plowing through the chop. Yeah, and he dug the pulsing of the motor vibrating in his feet as he putt-putted away from the boatyard and across the bay. Believe that he yearned to bend on sails and put her through the paces. But too much demanded his attention to indulge that frivolity.

The bane of a cop is his commitment to solving crimes and clearing cases . . . taking bad guys off the street. Ward made his mental concession to that mind-set years ago, and since enjoyed the pride of contributing to the safeguarding of society. Or, at least, to the snooping out and arresting of those who offended honest citizens.

Cops all too often put catching the bad guys ahead of attentiveness to their families, resulting in high percentage of divorces. Incredibly, in the face of broken marriages of the veterans, newbies anticipated their loved ones indulgence of the cop's obsession.

He grimaced, aware of that being one of his errors in his first marriage . . . but only one. Shaking his head to erase memory of Rosalía, he concentrated on the list of things-to-do that tumbled about in his mind. First he needed to stop at the Lagoon Hotel Pier to stock up before mooring his sloop in the bay, where it would be a hell of a lot cheaper than docking. Plus, he could live on the boat and save hotel costs. With Darla pissed at him he didn't need the convenience of a shore pad.

Patching up their relationship required concessions he wasn't eager to make. A man can have his guts gouged only so many times. And Ward had reached his limit. Besides, he needed to concentrate on the case. Darla sure as hell wasn't about to contribute. Matter of fact, every procedure from here on would more than likely increase antagonism between them. Ay Dios, she'd really scathe his ass when she learned he'd grilled Caleb.

No way he wouldn't use what he'd learned from that pathetic old man. Yes, he'd subpoena him if he had to, as well as Darla for corroboration. Depend on that erupting another flare-up—maybe a damn volcano. So, for the time being, it made sense to relegate their relationship to limbo. All indications pointed to it heading there anyway. Sure it wrenched his heart, but some things have to be accepted as inevitable.

Approaching the pier, he spotted Poet lounging on a bench near the railing. The oldster set down his bottle of beer and strolled over to catch the line Ward tossed him, then drop it over a cleat.

As Ward stepped ashore, he noticed that Pops wore a navy blue knit shirt—with a collar. How do you like that? Must've run out of collarless shirts . . . or laundry soap.

"Interesting," Poet said, "that you named your boat Calypso?"

"Seemed appropriate since I acquired it in the Caribbean."

"Greek mythology has her on the mystical island of Ogygia—somewhere in the Mediterranean."

"Really? Didn't know that."

"Yep, Calypso was a siren, or seductress, who failed to induce Odysseus to stay with her."

"Sounds familiarly like my life."

When Poet stared quizzically at him, Ward shook his head. No, he decided against sharing the improbability of extending the romance with Darla. "What brings you here, Pops?"

"You told me yesterday you'd probably pick up your boat today and bring it here to stock up. Figured I'd meet you and relate the news. Buy me a beer to keep my throat lubricated while I give you the latest poop."

"Thought you were nursing one when I pulled in."

"That one's 'bout finished."

Ward shrugged concession and sat on the bench Poet had occupied. The oldster signaled to the waiter to bring two beers. "Learned from my Paris source that one of the two Turks killed in the diamond center robbery in Rotterdam had been a close friend of Ajakian as well as a neighbor in Monaco."

"Circumstantial," Ward said, vexed by being fed banality that wasted time. "It doesn't tie anyone to anything. Probably why Interpol hasn't bothered to take Ajakian into custody, lacking substance to charge him with something that'll stand up in court."

"But it opens avenues of investigation," Poet said stubbornly.

Ward snickered. "Your buddy in Paris has to finger Ajakian and that Turk doing the robbery in Rotterdam."

"No such luck," Poet said as he glanced up to the waiter who set their bottles of Hairoun in front of them.

"So far," Warm grumbled, "you haven't earned that brew."

Poet scowled. "Ran into a Vincie crony with a forty-foot cabin cruiser. When Edgy doesn't have a charter he takes his friends fishing."

"Okay, so you and a bunch of beer-heads tank up and maybe catch a few lunkers."

Poet shrugged that off. "Heard whispers on occasion that Edgy runs contraband—not that I know what. Never asked, so he never told."

"That bit of drivel doesn't justify the price of your beer either."

"How about Edgy bragging about landing a top-paying charter with Bajuk Ajakian, to scuba dive in one of the islands of the Grenadines."

Ward's jaw dropped.

Poet postured smugly and took a long swig: "They're presently taking on stores in preparation of sailing in the morning for—"

"Canouan," Ward said.

"How'd you know that?"

"It's why I get those big bucks."

"Anyway, surprised the hell out of me to learn that the dapper Armenian is a scuba diver."

Ward wrenched his cap sideways. "Sonofabitch if they're not going to search for those rocks Christopher stashed." When Poet gaped at him, Ward said: "Just as you assumed, Christopher smuggled them out of Curaçao for Ajakian, then stashed them in those reefs."

"How in hell do you know that?"

"I'm the sleuth getting those megabucks, remember?"

After chuckling, Ward added: "Considering Christopher had trouble finding the cache, despite being the one hid them there, how the hell does Ajakian expect to succeed? Did he also book scuba divers?"

"They encouraged Christopher's deckhand, Caleb, to go along."

"Conyo, of course!" Ward pulled his cap down to shade his eyes while he stared at the horizon. "Just left him three or so hours ago. They must've sobered up the old coot, then used a lot of duress . . . or kept him in that stupor to control him."

"I'd think they'd enlist him simply by offering money," Poet said, confused.

"Not that dedicated old man. He's stubbornly opposed to doing anything to hurt the Christophers. Anyway, we need to sail to Canouan to keep them under surveillance."

"You for real? Expect your dinky sailboat to keep up with Edgy's cabin cruiser? He has twin diesels in that baby."

"We won't have to if we're in place when they show up. We know their destination, so it's only a matter of being there when they arrive in the morning."

Poet gazed at the small sailboat bobbing at the dock, then at the choppy sea and shook his head. "I'd just as soon wait here for you to return and report day-old news."

"You want that scoop, Pops, you sail with me to where it's happening. Keep in mind that all facets of this case will be on your buddy's charterboat. Ajakian and those diamonds are tied into Torchy's murder."

Poet frowned, gazed hard at the sailboat, then shook his head, expressing reluctance to cross open seas on it.

"We'll scope out the action, amigo," Ward said, "and when we see them retrieve those diamonds we'll call the Coast Guard or the local Coast Patrol to take them into custody. Caught red-handed with those stones, one or the other of those toughs will roll to save his ass."

"How can you be sure?"

"Skels turn into rats when cornered. They'll sell out their best buddies to get a lighter sentence. Hell, they'll squeal on their mothers for a walk."

"And you guys are receptive to letting them off easy?"

"Trading up. It's how we take down the bosses. And it's how the crowded court dockets get cleared. I'm hoping Caleb can be convinced to testify about Torchy's murder, having been an eye witness."

"How in hell you know that?"

"More important is: the minute Ajakian retrieves those diamonds, he kills that old man, snuffing that important witness."

"Kill that harmless old guy? I don't believe it."

"Get real, Pops. Ajakian is a stone killer. Once he has possession of those diamonds, he erases all traces tying him to Christopher. You want to save that little guy from being murdered, you accompany me and be ready to step in. Besides, you want an exclusive, you have to earn it by being embedded—a witness to accounts."

Poet again scanned the white caps. He shook his head at the little boat, then at the wide ocean beyond the headlands, finally at the sun leaning toward the western horizon. "Don't believe I'm caving to this."

"Pack a few things to tide you over for a few days while I'm getting my stuff at the Mango Inn and taking on stores."

#   #

Fifty

Ward volubly exhaled exasperation as he paced the limited space allowed by the armored cord of the public phone bracketed to the wall of the lobby connecting the hotel verandahs. He kept the handset pressed against his ear while forcing himself to suppress vexation for having to hold on while being shunted from person to person.

All he'd requested from Interpol was to be connected to the agent in charge of the theft of uncut diamonds in Rotterdam. But he ended up having to repeat the request and answer the same questions for one foreign-sounding person after the next.

It took effort to remain civil while admitting for the umpteenth time that he didn't have specifics, such as date and location, but knew it was the robbery of a jewelry center that occurred during the past month in Rotterdam. They bounced him around the divisions, claiming that because of the lack of precise information they searched to connect him to the person assigned to that case.

Finally he heard a gruff voice with a guttural accent. "Inspector Dietzen here. Does the caller have information concerning the uncut diamonds stolen at gunpoint from a diamond center in Rotterdam?" He sounded bored as well as skeptical. Ward knew that attitude all too well, resulting from following up on too many dead-end leads.

Most were imparted by well-meaning people, unaware their information was irrelevant. Pursuing a case generally became exhausting. Listening to a lot of unrelated babble during the course of the investigation wore on them. Detectives lose enthusiasm after a number of hummers and become pessimistic of callers thereafter.

"I'm Ward Perez, a retired New York City detective."

"And your information, sir?" Inspector Dietzen didn't sound impressed.

"Believe I can recover those diamonds, not simply locate them."

"Then you know where they are."

"Before I answer that, let me ask: has DeBeers offered a reward?"

"The equivalent of fifty thousand of US dollars for information leading to their recovery."

Ward had all he could do not to yahoo. "How much do you think they'll pay for retrieving them, significantly more service than tendering information?"

"Contact DeBeers for that answer. However, for the moment, please inform me how you came to have such information."

"I'm a stickler for face-to-face negotiations. Any chance you can have a DeBeers' representative come to Kingstown in Saint Vincent, an island in the southern Caribbean, rather than discuss sensitive things over the telephone."

"Am presently in Curaçao and quite aware of the location of Saint Vincent."

Ward's eyes widened with wonder at the technology that permitted telephone calls made to Europe to be transferred back to another island in the Caribbean . . . then remembered being shunted from the United States to India when inquiring about computer technical advice.

"If convinced of dependable information leading to recovery of the diamonds," Dietzen said, "I and a DeBeers' representative working with me here, shall travel to Saint Vincent within a day or so."

"Okay, then let's set the record straight. I don't presently possess them, but I'm confident I will within the next few days. Yes, I'm pretty sure I'll learn where they're cached. Sure, I can be contacted through the office of the Prosecutor of Saint Vincent and the Grenadines. Yes, I'm in his employ."

"Aha." Mention of that office apparently stimulated interest. "Expect me in Saint Vincent within two or three days."

#

Ward returned to the dock to complete the loading of stores. He'd already gotten his affects from the hotel and stowed them. He grinned when he spotted Poet trundling onto the wharf, toting a canvas carryall. The oldster glanced warily at the western horizon, where the sun edged below a cloudbank.

"Ask me," Poet grouched, "we'd be better off departing early in the morning than sailing at night. So what if Edgy arrives before us, considering they'll likely spend hours searching the reef for the diamonds."

Ward shook his head. "Not willing to take that chance. With Caleb along they might locate the cache quickly and be gone before we can have them intercepted. Those thugs will certainly kill Caleb once they retrieve those rocks. No way they'll leave witnesses."

"Okay, but I'm not all that anxious to bobble out there in the night."

"Relax, I've studied those charts, and crossing Bequia Channel is a jump of about five miles—two flaps of a seagull's wings."

"Damned big seagull, considering your distance estimate is from the protrusion of land at the end of Blue Lagoon to Bequia Head, the northernmost part of the island."

"What's wrong with that?"

"It's just the start, with two or three miles to the jump-off point, then a run of another eight or ten miles down the length of Bequia before setting off on the next leg of about another dozen miles to Mustique, with an additional dozen or so to Canouan. So much for your seagull."

"Make it a frigate bird then. I'm planning to sail eighteen miles in the sheltered Caribbean from Bequia to Canouan Island, instead of island hopping the ten or twelve mile runs to Mustique and then to Canouan. Effortless, baby." He pulled his Yankee cap tight on his head before slipping the mooring lines.

#   #

Fifty-One

Ward steered between the shoals sheltering Blue Lagoon, to skirt Young Island, with its array of boats moored in protected areas. Stone cottages on the wooded islet peeked through a profusion of manicured foliage, with flowers in every shape and color. Myriad birds fluttered around that upscale paradise, skimming across the white sand— unusual in Saint Vincent, where most beaches are covered with gray and black lava granules.

Ward trimmed the sails to track south by southwest, with a fresh easterly driving them on a broad reach. Invigorated by being back to sea, he squinted against the dazzling reflections from the thin band of sun teetering on the horizon. To steer clear of Bequia Head, the northern point of the island designated as their first jump-off point, he tracked a bit west of due south.

He beamed, elated by bouncing across the chop after a brief hiatus from sailing, as well from the creaking of the rigging from the boat straining under the force of wind. He even welcomed the combers that broke against the starboard bow and sent spray halfway up the length of the hull, accepting the washes of mist with equanimity; rather than duck from it as Poet did.

He nodded to his accomplishment when Bequia Head came into view, silhouetted against the darkening sky. It had taken a little more than an hour, thanks to the fresh breeze. Ward skirted the island and its dangerous shoals, as well as avoided competing with the press of boat traffic on the west coast, especially in the vicinity of the popular harbor of Admiralty Bay.

Poet stared morosely at the sun descending beyond the edge of the world, causing the land to fade from view. Ward, meanwhile, kept an eye out for running lights of other vessels while rounding the southern end of the island, a rocky promontory notated on the charts as West Cay.

The moon and stars provided limited visibility because of the profusion of clouds, but sufficient in Ward's opinion to opt for a direct route to Canouan. "Hope to hell you have a good compass," Poet remarked, the lines etched in his face indicating his concern of getting lost in the expanse of sea.

He gawked when shown a small, hand-held gadget. "Please! You don't really intend to cross eighteen to twenty miles of open sea in the black of night, with the most rudimentary of navigational equipment."

Ward directed the oldster's attention to the nightsky where stars peeked between clouds. "Best compass in the world. All we have to do is sail straight at Sagittarius, that collection of bright stars off the port bow, while keeping the Northern Cross behind us." He pointed out Polaris. "We'll be sailing due south with the current out of the west pushing us a few points east, the correction needed to hail our destination."

When Poet grimaced, Ward said: "Expect it to be a fast crossing with that following wind."

Poet didn't respond, just kept gazing at the receding land until the navigation light off West Cay dimmed, indicating they left land in their wake.

Ward gripped the tiller as wind zizzed in their ears for more than two hours, whipping up spray and windrift. He pointed ahead to the lights of Petit Canouan, an islet a few miles north of their destination. Within another hour he brought Poet's attention to the illuminated beacon off the north coast of Canouan Island.

"Thank God," the oldster croaked.

"Amen," Ward added, exhaling angst. He'd postured with bravado throughout the crossing to mollify Poet's fears while traversing the dangerous ocean. He now relaxed, having reached the anchorage of Charlestown Bay, a wide gulf on the Caribbean.

He scanned the headlands sheltering that tranquil roadstead, illuminated by the lights of shoreside buildings as well as scores of impressive motor and sailing yachts. A bulky, steel ferry occupied one of the three piers jutting into the bay, while a solitary launch lapped at the dinghy dock of the Tamarind Beach Hotel. Shadowy palms bowed and waved in the distance, in concert to the bobbing of the half dozen motor and sail yachts anchored in the bay.

After tying up to an unoccupied buoy and furling the sails, Ward hailed the shore launch, which conveyed them to the Tamarind Beach Hotel. An impressive complex, it had an informal restaurant-bar on the patio under a thatched roof. They decided to dine there since it didn't require changing clothes—unlike the indoor dining areas that acceded to West Indian formality. Both ordered conch-burgers and sweet potato fries. Ward ordered a bottle of the house burgundy to wash it down.

Poet giggled as he clinked his glass against Ward's, gleeful for having survived. He talked incessantly, releasing the anxiety pent-up during that crossing. And he drank non-stop. "Hey, this bottle's empty," he complained. "Better order another."

"Let's not get tanked, Pops. We're going to need our wits about us when those mooks arrive off the reef."

"A goodnight bottle so's we'll sleep well."

\#   \#

Fifty-Two

Ward flailed at the intrusive sunlight while groaning acceptance of the dawning of a new day. Sitting up, he winced from pain in his head and muscles throughout his body. Those damnable birds amplified the agony of his hangover with their chorus of matins; a few harmonizing, but most discordant.

He and Poet slept on the cockpit lockers flanking each side of the boat because it had been too hot below in the cabin. Consequently he now rubbed his neck while flexing his back and shoulders to relieve the stiffness from that hard bedstead. He gritted his teeth against the punishing reminder that he'd imbibed too much wine. Groaning from the throbbing in his head, he gazed at countless watercraft ranging from crude island vessels to multi-million dollar yachts.

Sunlight haloed the wooded hills of Canouan, silhouetting trees and rocky tors in stark relief. He remembered reading that Canouan meant Turtle Island in the Carib Indian language. Those ancients obviously associated it by its crescent-shape and rocky, shell-like hunchback.

Ignoring the pain and throbbing, he rose to stumble to the fresh-water nozzle on deck to splash water on his face. Having slept in his skivvies, he donned teal-colored shorts and a yellow tee shirt emblazoned with a garish advertisement for a sporting event that occurred two years ago in Spanish Harlem.

While making coffee, he watched Poet struggle to his feet and dunk his head in a bucket of water. Then the codger took a mouthful of water, gargled and hawked up phlegm. Ward tried not to be nauseated by those exhalations, but it took effort to resign himself to the guy's need to expel the coagulated mucus accumulated in his sinus passages.

When Poet finally concluded his noisome evacuations into the surrounding baywater, he sat on the gunnel in his boxer shorts and gazed morosely out to sea. Ward drank a mug of coffee and treated himself to two of the sweet rolls they brought back with them last night. Poet nibbled on one, made a face and put it aside. He drank the coffee and looked awful.

Ward let go the mooring line, then raised the sails by himself, but left cleaning up the coffee mugs and the percolator to Poet. He steered them out of Charleston Bay, then sailed west, with the fair breeze leaning the sloop to port. Opting for caution, he gave a wide berth to Glossy Hill, the western promontory of the island. Then, leaving that threatening area astern, he turned south, picking up a following wind to belly his sails.

He couldn't suppress grinning while watching Poet, blue around the gills, struggle to don a cloudy white tee shirt that struck Ward as a departure for him. Of course he wore his chino trousers and weathered sneakers. Obviously settling in the tropics hadn't induced Pops to adopt shorts.

Despite awareness of a passage that coursed through South Glossy Bay, dividing Canouan and Dove Cay, an offshore islet, Ward again opted for safety by ignoring the shortcut and steered wide of Dove Cay, tracking south by southwest.

Once he'd rounded that promontory, which constituted the southern extremity of Canouan, he turned north, requiring he sail into the wind. That necessitated he tack first this way then that, staying close on the wind, to claw his way up the eastern side of the island.

For the best part of an hour he searched the desolate shoreline, rife with reefs and shallows, for an entrance to Friendship Bay. Spotting a cut between two low peaks and the treacherous reef that sheltered the bay from the restless Atlantic, he scanned its surface, a chorus of small ripples.

Dark patches marked reefs, which he estimated the tops to be no more than six fathoms beneath the surface. Unsure which reef they'd search for the diamonds, the smaller one, with a length of about one nautical mile, lying south of Friendship Point, or the longer one to the north that ran almost two nautical miles, he threaded the narrow passage between them to the calm waters.

Recovered from his hangover, Poet joined Ward in surveying the area and concurred it benefited them to anchor in the lee of the smaller reef, close enough to enjoy full view of both. They doubted Ajakian or any of his people knew of their sloop, so hoped to be regarded as picnickers enjoying the solitude of the isolated beach. Both realized the peril if discovered . . . never doubting the Armenian wouldn't leave any witnesses.

They took turns keeping a lookout for Edgy's boat. Ward took the first watch, then snoozed when relieved, but responded when Poet alerted him to the large cabin cruiser approaching the southern end of the larger reef. So Ward rummaged in one of the lockers and extracted the second-hand binoculars he'd purchased in Saint Croix of the Virgin Islands, his first landfall after departing Puerto Rico. That short run underscored his need for them.

With that magnification he read the name on the transom of the distant vessel as REGALIA, which Poet confirmed as Edgy's boat. Scanning the decks, he identified Bajuk Ajakian strutting about in a marine blue and white outfit topped by a white mariner's cap.

He sniggered at the vain pudgeball while watching him direct Gallyvan and little Caleb in preparing to dive. The one-eyed frog-sticker tended the air tanks, aided by a black man which Ward presumed to be a Vincie and one of the crewmen.

Even from that distance, he made out Caleb gesturing with flailing arms toward the reef, apparently uncertain of the exact area to search. The others appeared equally irresolute. Ward chuckled, remembering some of the witless wonders he'd dealt with in his police days. Damned few bad-guys had real smarts.

He and Poet resigned themselves to the long vigil, taking turns emerging from shade to roast in the sun while surveilling the cabin cruiser through the binoculars. And they thanked God for the offshore breeze that provided a modicum of comfort while watching Gallyvan and Caleb surface time and again during the long day, to slump on the deck while Bonbieu and the crewman changed their air tanks. As the day waned, the divers inched up the two-mile long reef. Somber faces on the Regalia reflected the lack of success.

Ward shared their disappointment, needing them to locate those diamonds to provide him with evidence.

#   #

Fifty-Three

Bajuk Ajakian hunkered in the shade of the cabin while yearning for the divers to relieve his anxiety. Too much had gone wrong since the day they barged into that diamond center with guns in hands. Two additional guards they hadn't expected foiled their grand plan by assailing them with shotgun fire.

Mustafa Erkaban and the other Turk were killed. That's how he ended up with Bonbieu, a confederate of Ismet Okyar and driver of the get-away minivan. The three survivors fled with only a portion of the intended take.

Bajuk Ajakian balled his fists to contain emotions as he stared at the dark shadow beneath the placid water that spread away in a wide crescent, haunted by endless frustration since then. He'd stifled angst for much of the day resulting from negative reports each time the divers surfaced to change tanks. Be damned if he didn't dread another failure connected with those bloody baubles.

What kind of idiot cached something of considerable value without carefully recording that location to simplify retrieval . . . if in truth he hid them in the reef? Caleb swore they had, which alleviated some suspicion.

Unable to dispel that torment, he gazed around at scrubby hills on one side and the endless ocean on the other. Only the stationary sailboat with its single mast, wallowing in the small bay beyond the reefs, stood out in conflict with the harsh landscape. He assumed its occupants anchored there to picnic.

What sort of dullards spent the entire day on the beach? With a boat like that, one would think they'd race before the wind, challenging nature. Agh, he had more important concerns.

He jerked to attentiveness when the divers surfaced again. But their long faces mirrored their frustration. That continued failure wore on him.

#

Ward and Poet watched the divers climb aboard and collapse on the deck. Growing darkness induced those on the Regalia to end the search and raise anchor to head south. Ward assumed they'd spend the night in Charlestown Bay on the leeward side of the island.

Deeming it wise to avoid further proximity with them, Ward took his sloop up the north coast, tacking into the freshening breeze, sailing more east than north to steer clear of the ragged shore. He fought the headwinds for two hours before rounding the north end of the island, then pass offshore of shallow Maho Bay and finally reach Corbay, an anchorage protected by promontories.

Palm trees bowed and waved to them from the beach. Gulls and terns screeched resentment of the intrusion. Brown pelicans squatting on pilings stared quizzically at the newcomers.

After anchoring the sloop, they paid two boys in a rowboat to take them ashore, where they happened upon a thatched roof suspended on crude poles that served the locals as a restaurant. And they found the food better than expected, cooked on an open fire by Mama Mahalia.

A cigarette dangling from the corner of her mouth, the chubby woman prepared and served them a meal of lambi: fresh snapper and the flesh of the seashell called conch. They washed it down with beer; rum the only other liquor available. Ward concurred with Poet's decision to avoid waking up in the morning hung over, not eager to hear the oldster's exhalations again.

#   #

Fifty-Four

Ward got them underway early, to run south in the Atlantic, propelled by a brisk following wind which bellied both sails like lopsided wings—the huge mainsail to the starboard side of the boat and the smaller Genoa jibsail to port. It left little for Ward to do but man the helm and hold them on course. And it allowed him to enjoy the gulls and cormorants that raced him, gliding at times to wait for the sailboat to catch up.

The sun's glow enveloped the monotony of scrub-covered low hills in elongated patterns, some in shades of green and others in shades of brown, with the two shades combining at times. Frigate birds with forked tails soared high in the near-cloudless sky.

Arriving off the reefs, he spotted the Regalia anchored a half mile offshore of the southern quarter of the larger reef. So Ward sailed seaward of the yacht and anchored a mile or so north of it.

He and Poet got out fishing poles, hoping to allay suspicions. They chanced that no one aboard the cabin cruiser recognized them as the sailboat in Friendship Bay the previous day. Both wore wide-brimmed straw hats they'd purchased from a peddler in Corbay last night to hide their faces in the event someone aboard the Regalia scrutinized them with high-powered binoculars.

Ward scanned the horizon, wishing for other boats to join them and make them less obvious. But among the only vessels that passed the entire day were a cruising trawler, a rusty island freighter, a big sailboat that bustled past with its canvas snapping in the fresh breeze, and a sports fisherman that anchored south of them for a short time. No, it didn't relieve Ward of worrying that those on the Regalia become suspicious of being staked out.

#   #

Fifty-Five

<u>Why?</u> a voice resonated in Bajuk Ajakian's brain. Why are they cursed to fail at locating that bloody package? Did that witless oaf conceal that bag of diamonds so thoroughly that it defied rediscovery . . . or did he run some sort of game? If so, he'd bloody well suffer the worst hell imaginable.

He applied effort to refrain from squealing his anguish while spending the day watching Gallyvan and Caleb surface from each dive to change air tanks and dive again. They inched up the reef, almost to the center, with the lack of success increasing his angst. Were they, in truth, expert divers capable of locating that cache, or did they exaggerate their capabilities?

Every time he questioned Caleb that leathery old salt assured they hid the damnable baubles in some sort of fissure in the rock—less than halfway up the reef. Be damned if they'd already arrived at midpoint. To which half did the bloke allude? And now to amplify disappointment, the advent of nightfall signaled time to suspend the search again. How many days must they be distressed by lack of success?

He glanced out at the sailboat that wallowed there all day, suspicious of it. Interpol hadn't bothered to arrest them hitherto since it lacked evidence to tie them to the robbery. That innocent looking vessel might be positioned to radiotelephone larger and faster boats upon awareness of retrieval of the diamonds.

How close, he wondered, were the patrol boats? Were there airplanes, perhaps helicopters nearby? Would this exercise turn out to be a trap . . . if it didn't prove futile altogether?

Quite right, it could be a different sailboat than he'd seen yesterday. He had no ability to differentiate one from another, since the craft never interested him enough to familiarize himself with particular makes or models. Besides, it defied credibility that Interpol didn't employ a faster, sleeker vessel.

Why, he wondered, didn't they observe him with binoculars from the wooded hills, where he had no ability to discern them? But then, he doubted they had awareness of his presence, having been careful to conceal his whereabouts from Interpol. No matter how many times he dismissed it as ridiculous he failed to suppress suspicion that the blighters surveilled him from that dratted sailboat.

Unable to continue ignoring the bloody thing, he called to Edgy to send some people to check out that pesky vessel. Make certain, he added, it isn't the authorities keeping track of them.

Edgy, a robust man, chuckled at the prospect of law enforcement utilizing a craft like that and doubted that they were anything except what they appeared. But since his well-paying charter insisted, Edgy sent two deckhands in a rubber dinghy propelled by an outboard motor to investigate.

#

"Oh, oh," Ward said, bringing Poet's attention to the skiff, "they're checking us out."

Both men watched the dinghy approach. "Only two," Poet said. "That's not too threatening."

"Depends," Ward said, "if they're only snooping us out or intend to harass us."

"What do you suggest we do?"

"Keep fishing," Ward said as he tightened his grip on his pole, mentally and physically preparing himself for whatever transpired. He forced himself to breathe easy and not show trepidation as the boat approached. When it drew close he warned Poet: "Two Vincies cradling shotguns."

"You're a cop. Don't you have a gun."

"Never expected to need one, investigating a suspect already incarcerated."

Ward ignored Poet's expression of surprise, reacting to a pull on his pole. He yanked it back hard, to sink the hook in whatever nibbled at it. His pole bent, inducing him to reel in line. Within minutes he had the fish alongside. Deciding against bothering with a gaff, something the Vincies might construe as a weapon and induce them to react by peppering them with buckshot, he heaved it aboard.

The two Vincies cheered when a large grouper broke water. Aware of their excitement, Ward held it up for them to see. They cheered again.

"Us sees you'all here to fish," one of the Vincies yelled to them.

"And we now have dinner," Ward called back.

"Then have you more luck," the other grinning Vincie yelled to them as he turned the dinghy about and headed back to the cruiser.

\#   \#

Fifty-Six

Ajakian scowled his dissatisfaction at the report of two white men fishing. Shaking his head at Edgy, he silently admonished the man for sending two illiterate Vincies on a mission such as that. Growing darkness halted the diving for the day, adding to his discontent.

Dejected, he stared at the water roiling past as they headed back to Charlestown Bay. His gut growled with the realization that nothing about this venture had gone as planned. Those bloody baubles persisted in remaining undiscovered. But what alternative had he, except to continue searching? Obtaining them had required considerable investment, which he determined to recover. Fact is, their absence threatened to deny him a comfortable future.

True, not more than two or three millions of US dollars might be gleaned from the bloody things. However, he had not the least intention of sharing it. Offing the French gutter-rat shouldn't necessitate effort. Doing the African very well might. Besides, he rather liked the burly bugger. But when the time came he'd damn well put aside sentiment and do what he must. First, however, they need locate that damnable cache.

Every prior endeavor required guile as opposed to violence, and had been reasonably successful. This one, his only participation with weapons and violence, denied him the fruits of his daring.

The compulsion to live in the more flamboyant style of Mustafa had induced him to join his friend in that perilous venture. Worst part was the necessity to invest part of his nest egg in financing the abortive robbery. Having spent far more than intended left no option but to conclude this business successfully so he'd emerge with the where-with-all to live financially security.

He'd have been wiser not to have been seduced by the prospects of wealth when they discussed the enterprise over cocktails on the verandah of a restaurant in Monaco. It didn't register that Mustafa Erkaban intended to charge into a diamond center in the bustling business section of a prominent city and steal the bloody baubles at gunpoint. Bajuk expected that they'd utilize guile; perhaps bribe a courier to surrender them and claim he'd been held up.

But while casing the facility he and Mustafa gleaned the information that there were five times as many uncut diamonds as anticipated. The prospect of obtaining a share of fifteen or possibly eighteen millions of dollars by one bold stroke dissolved Bajuk's reticence to brazenly rush the bloody place with guns blazing to snatch the bloody things.

No denying he became eager to execute once he'd enlisted Gallyvan, believing the black man a super-being who, by his very existence, assured success.

#   #

Fifty-Seven

Ward pranced the deck, worried that they pushed it, stalking the prey for the third day. Hell, even a landlubber figured to recognize it as the same sailboat. But without alternative, he'd sailed back to the ocean, to anchor south of the Regalia this time, and as far seaward as their binoculars permitted. They hoped to be less familiar at that distance and in that direction, especially since they donned nautical caps, fearing the straw hats would be a dead giveaway.

He grinned at the oldster's yellow polo shirt, another departure from his modish collarless jobs, but the same old chinos and sneakers. It pricked his curiosity why Pops persistently wore long pants rather than shorts.

"Always envied the reporters," Poet said, "who got to go out on stakeouts with the police. Never realized the strain of vigilance, nor the boredom."

"We get what we came for," Ward said, "it'll be worth the time and effort."

"Long as I don't get caught in a shoot-out."

"Violence is part of a cop's commitment to being a peace-officer. We take down bad-guys, and sometimes we get taken down."

"Damned commendable, by God. Doubt that most people appreciate the selfless commitment a cop makes when he pins on that badge."

"That dedication grows stronger with time," Ward said, "especially when we realize we're all there is between the community and packs of barbaric bad guys."

"Can't argue with that."

"I'm thinking we oughtta' get poles into the water," Ward said as he scanned the yacht. "Makes sense to give some semblance of being out here to fish, so they don't start wondering about us again."

"Didn't I catch enough yesterday," Poet retorted, "only to have those lovely lunkers traded to Mama Mahalia in exchange for her cooking a couple snappers for us."

"Plus all the sides and the beer. Beats the hell out of paying for a meal. You're lucky I caught so many fish."

"You? I caught the four biggest. All you caught were innocent juveniles."

"Just get your line in the water, Pops, before I hook <u>you</u> up for bait."

#   #

Fifty-Eight

Bajuk Ajakian strode back and forth along the railing, jaunty in his marine blue shorts and white polo shirt decorated with a yacht club insignia. He'd dressed flashily, hoping for it to elate him, wanting to feel upbeat rather than morose. Nothing is gained by fretting about failure.

He glared at that damned sailboat. It had to be the same one. Surely Interpol had ability to devise better surveillance. Did they think him too much the bloody boob to be unmindful that they waited for him to retrieve the package before alerting others to close in on him?

However, he considered it premature to strategize elusive action. Far more important was to locate the bloody baubles to relieve anxiety that had gripped him for weeks since arriving in the island of Curaçao.

That sack of uncut diamonds had quite a heady bit of intrinsic value, yet remained virtually worthless until properly doctored. To accomplish that required finding a diamond cutter with no aversion to working with stolen stones.

Mustafa dealt with a diamond cutter in South Africa, but hadn't shared that information, and lay dead in that diamond center. Forced to flee Rotterdam they lacked knowledge of an expert to cut the diamonds and make them unrecognizable as well as valuable. Actually, they dared not approach anyone in Europe.

Bajuk remembered having read that Jewish diamond cutters fled Europe during the Hitler era and relocated in Curaçao. So he and his surviving cohorts headed there . . . to an island remote from the police dragnets of Europe.

While gazing out the window of that tiny room of an inexpensive hotel in the Otrabanda district of Willemstad, the main city of Curaçao, he fretted he lacked sufficient lucre to continue financing the enterprise. Not only did he need to provide the necessities for himself, but for the other two as well, since they bordered on beggary.

Damned if he intended to indulge them with accommodations in the expensive tourist hotels of some of the other districts. For that reason he subjected himself to checking into that cut-rate gaff. Staring at rows of attached three-storied Dutch colonial buildings trimmed like gingerbread houses and painted in a variety of pastel colors, he wondered how to know who to approach.

Telephoning a chap in Paris he remembered having illicit connections, he learned of a jeweler in Willemstad named Levy. They found his shop in a line of attached storefronts with brick arches on a narrow street in the district of Punda.

A morose and bearded oldster in yarmulke with wire-rimmed spectacles perched on his long nose, the jeweler sniffed incessantly while inspecting the stones. His thin face remained devoid of expression as he assured he'd be able to convert them into unidentifiable gems with considerable value.

When Ajakian asked him how long to expect it to take, Levy flagged his elongated head like a bloody pendulum before replying in his laconic manner that he required at least four or five days to study them in order to resolve where and how to cut. He'd droned on about how the shaping of diamonds was an art requiring he understand the facets of each gem. At that time he'd be able to discuss with Bajuk his fee, then shrugged his lack of objection when Ajakian asked if he'd accept a percentage of the stones as payment.

Ajakian and his cohorts wiled away the time exploring the pleasant island and indulging themselves in touristy pastimes. The promise of enrichment buoyed their spirits. But that bubble shattered upon receiving a telephone call from Levy after two days, requesting a meeting at his shop the following noon.

Distrustful by nature, Ajakian arrived with his underlings at the jeweler's shop an hour before the arranged time. Gaining entrance through the rear door presented little challenge for Gallyvan, who expertly picked the electronic lock. They entered stealthily to find Levy talking on the telephone.

So they hugged the wall and seethed upon realizing he conversed with the police, setting them up with the place bugged. Ajakian assumed the bloody coppers waited nearby, and the moment he and his cohorts took possession of the baubles, they'd move in and arrest them with that damning evidence.

When Levy terminated the phone call, Ajakian gestured to Bonbieu, who dispatched the betrayer with a thrust of his stiletto. Without uttering a word to be heard by electronic eavesdropping equipment, they grabbed their bag of diamonds and fled. Ajakian flagged a scolding finger at the other two to prevent them taking anything else, concerned that any sound alert the police, as well the probability those baubles would be identified as from the stock of Levy.

Anticipating the authorities closing in on them as soon as they discovered their squeal had been murdered, Bajuk concealed the diamonds in a wooded section of the suburb of Montaña Abao, to erase that connection with the Rotterdam robbery, as well to the killing of Levy.

Returning to their dismal hotel rooms, they awaited the anticipated police raid and the search of their accommodations, their personal affects, and their persons. Since no diamonds were found in their possession, the police lacked reason to detain them. Ajakian accepted they'd be under surveillance thereafter.

Unwilling to simply discard millions of dollars, after all they'd been through, as well because of his deteriorating financial situation, Ajakian racked his brain for a way to get the stones out of Curaçao. It defied credibility to approach any other jeweler on the island. Surely, the police had cowed all of them by unrelenting attention. Those that might have been amenable would now be averse to dealing with desperadoes who brutally murdered Levy.

#   #

Fifty-Nine

Ajakian scowled, daunted by the realization that he had little chance of departing Curaçao while in possession of those bloody stones. He and his cohorts knew they'd be thoroughly searched at airports or cruise-line docks, leaving only illegal means of egress.

So he scoured the waterfront for a conduit. People from both countries passed back and forth with minimal scrutiny on the ferry to Venezuela. Ah, but surely the authorities checked departing passengers more thoroughly since the murder. They'd quite likely have photographs and recognize any of the three suspects, consequently apprehend them in possession of the diamonds; damning evidence to result in life imprisonment.

During his quest for an escape duct, Ajakian observed the Venezolanos who brought farm produce, meat and seafood in motorized schooners to the Schottegat, the wide waterway and harbor of the city of Willemstad. Curaçaoans crowded the quay called the Floating Market every day to shop from those Venezuelan boats.

It strained credibility to expect the authorities to allow him to slip away in one of those vessels in possession of the evidence. So he considered encouraging one of the crews of roughneck seafarers to transport either the Jamaican or the

Frenchman to Venezuela so that man might smuggle the bloody baubles off the island.

He surmised that if he made himself apparent in public, attracting the major surveillance, it might relieve his less-identifiable henchmen. Yes, he'd disguise one or the other so that man could slip past the authorities.

But Bajuk doubted those gutter-rats were any less averse to share than he—therefore found himself unwilling to relinquish control of the diamonds to either of them. Snickering, he wondered if they suspected that he never intended them to enjoy a share.

Seeking viable alternatives, he contacted his Paris connection again, who gave him the name of a jeweler in Havana, Cuba. But Havana presented a distance too far to bridge.

He rented a car to scour the island in hopes of finding the needed conduit. Happening upon Carracasbai, a small port some eight to ten kilometers from Willemstad, he scanned the boats in the bay.

Three yachts bobbed out there amid the many stubby native fishing boats, but he couldn't very well proposition some rich yachtsman to smuggle them out. Those pillars of morality, some of which earned their fortunes by devious involvements, were certain to posture piously and report him to the police.

And the stubby fishing craft didn't imbue confidence to weather that journey. His eyes widened when he read the nameplate on one of the tall-masted luxury vessels: <u>Ole Virginny</u>.

Quite right, he'd been a guest on that motorsailer while vacationing in Martinique not too many months past with the man and his wife. The name Christopher came to mind, as did a conversation he had with the husband, Ogden. He brightened; encouraged that he'd convince that chap to transport him and the stones out of Curaçao.

Then he wrestled with the temptation of slipping away, abandoning his cohorts. He hadn't shared with them information of the Cuban connection, nor of Christopher and his yacht. He'd bloody well rid himself of them simply by slipping into anonymity—certain of inventing a new identity in Havana.

#   #

Sixty

Ajakian jerked out of his introspection, aroused by the sound of the divers' heads bursting through the surface. He clenched his jaws upon reading failure on their faces. Shaking his head against his persistent misfortune, he pounded the side of his fist against the plastic coaming to expel his frustration. Bonbieu patted his shoulder, to impart sympathy, aware of the distraught lines etched in the man's pudgy face.

Ajakian flagged his head. "Only an imbecile caches valuables without carefully diagramming their location for later retrieval. I curse the day I entrusted those diamonds to that blunderer."

"We had no so many options, mon patrón. The police in Curaçao, they search us many times. If they find us in possession of those rocks, we end up to rot in the prison."

"Quite right. It became imperative to transport them away from Curaçao. But I should never have entrusted them to that idiot. Can't bloody believe I didn't detect his lack of ingenuity when I first encountered him in Martinique."

"Aha, so that is how you know the Americain. Gallyvan and myself, we wonder about that."

"During a vacation to Martinique with my wife and Mustafa Erkaban, who brought a French dancer of the chorus, we enjoyed a drink before dinner at the bar of the

Lagon Bleu, rather a delightful place overlooking the yacht club of Marin. Having struck up a conversation with the Christophers, an American couple, led to all of us dining together. During the evening we accepted an invitation to cruise the coast of Martinique on their motorsailer the following day."

"But how you know to trust that rich yachtsman to smuggle the diamonds out of Curaçao?"

"Late in the afternoon of the following day, when we'd finished cruising, and were indulging ourselves with drinks in a quaint little bar near the marina in Anse Mitan, Christopher became quite drunk. Morose actually, as he confided in me that financial reverses might force him to sell his beloved yacht. At the time his dilemma had no value. Actually I considered it a nuisance to be burdened by such during a celebratory bash. Rather suspected the boob was feeling me out for a loan."

"You knew not the importance of that information."

"Not until that day in Caracasbai, when I gazed at the moored yachts and glimpsed the nameplate: Ole Virginny."

"Aha! You discovered the means to remove those baubles from Curaçao."

"Still, he frustrated me, refusing whatever I offered, reluctant to have fugitives aboard, fearful of interdiction resulting in the confiscation of his vessel, as newspapers had reported happening to several smugglers."

"But somehow," Bonbieu said, "you convince him."

"The greedy bloke was seduced by the opportunity to avail himself of several hundred thousand of dollars, but not at the risk of losing his motorsailer, considering that its value far exceeded the amount offered."

"You promised so much of money?"

"Imperative to enlist his help. It took a bit of doing to concluded an agreement with him to take only the diamonds, easily concealable, for two hundred fifty thousand US dollars—to be paid upon delivery."

Ajakian half-smiled as he remembered deciding then to take his blokes along, in the event he needed muscle to regain possession of the baubles after arriving at their destination.

"The rotter adamantly declared his destination as Kingstown in Saint Vincent," Ajakian said, "not Havana, claiming that all who knew him expected him there for the races later in the month."

"What matter to us," Bonbieu asked, "since he remove them from Curaçao, to save us from arrest? Also do we now have those gems to convert to a future of luxury. But do you have so much of money to pay such an amount?"

"I concerned myself only with inveigling him to remove the baubles from Curaçao. Later in Kingstown I intended to encourage him, with a gun to his head, to transport us to Havana."

"Ha ha, with no chance to receive payment."

"Still, I feared he might run off with the stones. One can't trust desperate people. For that reason, I impressed upon him that the diamonds in their present state had little value, gaining appreciable worth only after being cut by a talented jeweler. However, should he entertain deceit, it would result in the death of his beautiful wife."

"Surely that made him attentive to you."

"Bloody coward all but balked out of the deal, but I assured him he need not fear so long as he did not abscond with the basically worthless pieces of carbon. Christopher swore he wanted only to earn the fee, since he had no contacts who bought uncut diamonds, or any other contraband. The sooner he rid himself of those rocks and received payment, the happier he'd be."

"For that reason, you chanced to transport them by his yacht."

"Little did I realize the anguish I'd suffer in retrieving them."

Bonbieu grinned as he forced himself to continue to be patient until the diamonds were retrieved and the Armenian converted them to money, then slit his throat and take the money for himself. Still, there remained the African to deal with. But he need not worry about how to kill that one until the time came.

Yes, they had greater strength, but not the ability to outwit white men.

#   #

Sixty-One

Ajakian paced the deck, unmindful of the late afternoon heat, mumbling how that bloody sailboat out there wore on him. True, it anchored in a different location but he swore it appeared as the same bloody vessel. The two Vincies sent to investigate yesterday reported two Caucasians fishing, neglecting to have learned their nationalities.

By Jove, one of them could be that detective. Struck by the realization, he yelled to Edgy: "Send the boat again. But this time have Bonbieu accompany the two Vincies. He'll bloody recognize the bloke of one of them is that Puerto Rican."

#

Ward and Poet yawned more often as the day wore, struggling to remain alert while scrutinizing the cabin cruiser. Hour after hour crept monotonously by, with their boat rocking in concert to the motion of the sea, lulling them into boredom.

Late in the day, with the sun descending among billowing clouds on the western horizon, Ward jerked to alertness when he became aware of the dinghy headed his way. "There's that boat again," he called to Poet.

"They might be more aggressive this time," Poet said.

Ward used the binoculars to scope it. "Bad news. They're sending that little frog-sticker along this time."

"What are we going to do?" Poet asked. "He'll recognize you sure as hell."

"And they have shotguns again. Haul in the fishing gear. We need to hoist anchor and get the hell out of here."

"You expect to outrun Edgy's cruiser?"

"Just that dinghy for now. We'll race into Friendship Bay, then beach the boat and run for it."

"Can you do that—without damaging your boat?"

"Believe that I'm not happy to take that chance. But survival is the most important thing at this point."

"And where do we run to—on an open beach?"

"To beyond those dunes so we can duck from their shotgun fire."

"Hey, I'm eighty years old. How far and how fast you think I can run?"

"Fast as you need to, Pops. We don't have alternatives, having no weapons to defend ourselves."

"Edgy's a good buddy—won't let anyone hurt me."

"He's a smuggler who deals in dope and guns. Like other miscreants, his primary concern is avoiding arrest. Doubt he'd hesitate to eliminate either of us as witnesses."

Poet winced, then shrugged concession as he joined Ward in reeling in fishing line, Then both tensed, startled by the shrill horn of the Regalia.

It baffled them to see the dinghy respond to the repeated blasts by swinging about and heading back to the cabin cruiser. They scanned the yacht and watched with open mouths when muscle-bound Gallyvan clambered aboard with more alacrity than he'd shown of late.

Sensing the Jamaican's excitement they gripped the railing while watching the dinghy pull alongside and the Frenchman leap aboard. He helped Gallyvan rig a marker with an anchor and drop it over the side, in a precise location, a bit more than halfway up the reef. Ajakian joined them in scribbling intersecting lines on a cardboard. Everyone on the Regalia displayed animation.

"More'n likely found the cache," Poet said breathlessly.

Ward's face wrinkled with perplexion. "Then why in hell do they need to mark the place with a buoy and then diagram the location? If they recovered the thing, why the hell aren't they taking it aboard and hauling ass?"

"What the hell's going on with Caleb?" Poet asked.

They gawked at watching Caleb, who struggled to climb aboard, had succeeded in hoisting himself onto the gunnel. The Frenchman and the Jamaican slammed him repeatedly on the head with stubby shark bats. Caleb fell into the water to float lifelessly, face-down. They could see the blood slick widen around his body. Then the cruiser spouted water from its stern as it headed north with the seas boiling in its wake.

"Why?" Poet gasped. "For God's sake, why?"

"Because he has no more value to them." Ward wiped his face with his hand in an attempt to dispel the horror he'd witnessed. "Dead, he can't reveal anything."

"The lousy sonsofabitches!" Poet balled both fists.

"Your good buddy, Edgy."

"Murdering bastard!"

"Taking low-lifes like those off the street is what drives cops," Ward said, the earnestness of his statement etched in his face. He kicked over the engine and cut through the chop toward Caleb as fast as it was capable of propelling the vessel, rocking through the chop against the force of sea.

"I understand cop-motivation now," Poet said, gripping the helm molding, impatient to reach Caleb.

"Most of us have trouble defining it to non-cops," Ward said through clenched teeth. "But it's what motivates us to continue pursuing law-breakers through the years."

Poet nodded, while scanning the area they'd last seen Caleb.

Ward grimaced, because by the time they reached the area where Caleb's body had floated the roiling chop had erased the blood slick, leaving no trace.

They got out gaffs and dragged for half an hour, without success. Ward considered diving for the oldster, but hesitated because Caleb's blood surely attracted predators. Besides, the man had been underwater too long to survive. Darkness forced them to quit.

Ward struck the water in anger with his gaff. "Heartless bastards!"

"Tell me how to help get them. I'll do whatever it takes."

"First we need to figure out where they're going."

"They headed north."

"Right. If they were returning to Charlestown Bay they'd track south like they did the last two nights." Ward yanked out his charts and studied them.

"Maybe they're going somewhere," Poet offered, "to hire more divers."

"Why'd they kill Caleb then? Think, Pops! They snuffed the only diver with some idea of where to find those rocks. Obviously the search is ended. What's the next step? Where the hell did they head? We've got to find them, especially if they've retrieved those diamonds."

"But we didn't see them hoist anything aboard."

Ward nodded as his eyes narrowed while peering into the darkness. "Why in hell would they leave a marker if they've retrieved them? It's pretty obvious that they left the marker with intentions of retrieving them under circumstances that won't get them caught in possession of the damning things. We need to go after those rat bastards."

Poet stared questioningly at the darkness all but blotting out the seas, getting steadily rougher as the storm built. "Ask me, they headed for Kingstown. Otherwise they'd have elected to go to Union Island—south, not north."

"Agreed, so let's head there—rather than spend endless hours searching other islands—especially with bad weather building."

#   #

Sixty-Two

Ward bent on sails and steered north. Poet hunkered in with him behind the low housing for the long and windy run, committed to failure if they didn't encounter the Regalia in Kingstown. Their little sloop pitched and yawed while rolling from side to side, pounded by the combers and buffeted by the wind.

Showing only a storm jib and a reefed mainsail, they beat to windward, hour after hour, struggling to make headway against a fury building to almost half a gale. Angry seas crashed across their bow, tossing the boat from wavetop to wavetop while blinding the two men with spray and soaking them.

They squinted into the wind, their faces taut, haunted by the realization that the Regalia might head to any number of places in the Grenadines. To the northwest lay the privately owned island of Mustique, with huge rocks projecting through the ocean surface at both the north and south ends, endangering any craft unaware of them on a dark and stormy night. And due north, a line of shoals threatened the unwary in the vicinity of Bequia, an island favorite of yachtsmen.

Ward denied himself being daunted by those perils and forced himself hour after hour not to succumb to exhaustion. He released a long sigh when he spotted the beacon lights at the approach to the harbor of Kingstown. "Gracias a Dios!" escaped him as barely more than a whimper. Having spent every ounce of his energy, he doubted he had enough left to do more than get his sloop to the pier of the Lagoon Hotel. Screw mooring out and dealing with shore launches this late at night. He didn't give a damn about cost.

But it depressed him not to spot the Regalia anchored anywhere in the bay or docked at any of the piers. Of course, they could have gone to docking places and anchorages unseen from that part of the bay. They were endless, not only in that region but up and down both coasts.

Poet informed that Edgy moved his boat around to confuse the authorities and avoid surveillance. Ward blinked, suffering a sinking feeling that he'd made a wrong decision. It might have been wiser to wait off the reef of Canouan for them to return?

Perhaps before those mooks arrived back there in the morning he could dive. To where? The buoy marked a broad area of reference. He'd need their graph to know exactly where to search.

#   #

Sixty-Three

Ward and Poet staggered onto the open-deck verandah, both drenched and disheveled. They knew they wouldn't be welcomed in the inner lounge in their condition. No way, hombre, not in a posh West Indian club, where decorum is practiced more rigidly than in England. Still, they had to pretend indifference to the disparaging expression of the waiter and the few snooty patrons remaining there at that hour.

They slumped in wicker chairs, fatigued and panting while waiting for the haughty waiter to obtain then serve the vodka on the rocks they'd ordered; no beer tonight, both needing revitalization.

When the waiter finally returned with their drinks on a tray both grasped them from his hand, denying him properly placing them on coasters. After consuming half the liquor in their glasses with the first swallows, they loudly sighed appreciation of the restorative affects. The waiter, steeped in British West Indian custom, pranced away, with his head quivering with condemnation.

"You planning to contact Darla?" Poet asked.

Ward winced, having not given it thought. Nope, he wasn't about to explain why to Poet. So he replied: "Kinda' late for that." But he knew he yearned to hear her voice. He'd been haunted the last three days by unrelenting memory.

Okay, he needed to call her, and hoped time and separation dissipated the bad feelings.

So he took another swallow and exhaled concession before struggling out of the wicker chair to stumble to the telephone bracketed on the lobby wall. After dialing he breathed deeply to prepare for the encounter—and tensed when he heard the click of it being answered. "Hi, this is Ward."

Silence. "Hello. Hello, Darla?"

"Why you wake me at this hour of the night, mon? You get you bold self drunk or something? It sound so, with you words slurred."

"Not drunk, just tired as hell, after sailing back from Canouan. Yes, in that blow. Man, what a grueling trip."

"But you safe, and me happy to hear that. Why you call at this late hour?"

"Needed to talk to you—to hear your—"

"What you have to say cannot wait 'til morning?"

"It's been three days since—"

"Why then me doesn't hear one peep from you in all this time? You sails off without so much as a by-you-leave, with no regard for whether me agonize from be deserted."

"Hey, it was you stomped out of my hotel room. I never walked out on—"

"And what you excuse that you doesn't bother to contact me all this time? It obvious, mon, you not feeling too badly that we break up, ending the affair with no pain on you part."

"Come on! Get real!"

"Real? Mon, it obvious this brownskin gal not on you mind when you set upon you voyage."

"That's ridiculous, Darla."

"About as ridiculous that you wake me tonight. You a selfish mon who give no thought to others and simply sail

CALYPSO

off for three days, then think you can ring me on the phone to have booty ready for the sailor's homecoming."

"Why are you so goddam cantankerous?"

"Why you inconsiderate? Where you been these past three days?"

"On a stake-out. We shadowed that Armenian and his hoods down to the reefs off Canouan, where they dove for the diamonds. Yes, those diamonds. Guess Ajakian got tired of waiting for Christopher to get sprung and retrieve them so searched for the damned things himself."

"It surprise me not to hear it come to that," Darla said. "But, that aside, best you tell me about it in the morning, not wake me in the middle of the night."

"I'm on the verandah at the Lagoon. Come on down to talk this out over a couple of drinks rather than growl at each other over the phone."

"Best we doesn't see each other anymore. It only lead to one or both of we hurt the other. This thing doesn't going to work."

"Are you crazy. We have to see each other—to talk—even if we end up splitting. We owe each other that much, to conclude it face to face."

"So you say. But me say t'is better us have no more contact."

"We're going to have contact until we settle this thing. You hear me? You're not here within twenty minutes, I'm going there, to bang on your door until you answer it."

"Lord God, don't come raising no row, frighten me daughter, and wake me neighbors, stirring new rumors. Me suffer enough with that Byrum Josephs business, then Torchy."

"Then come here and talk to me. Believe that if you don't, I'm going there."

"Mon, you lose you fool mind? You can't wait for morning?"

"No way. You're either here in twenty minutes or I'm going there."

"Jesus Lord! Don't ruin what left of me life."

"Then get your ass down here."

"Very well, me dress and go there to talk with you. But that be it. Remember that you bold self have retain no right to fondle this body. You hear what me tell you?"

Mumbling acceptance Ward hung up, then tromped back to the table, shaking his head to dispel irritation. He'd avoided her surliness for three days. Why in hell did he demand she join him tonight—when he was too tired to sleep? He sniggered at letting her rile him and rued having persisted she come.

Dropping into his chair, he drained the vodka. When Poet asked whether Darla agreed to join them, he nodded. Then he flagged the waiter and ordered another round of drinks. Both slumped in their wicker chairs, too spent to converse.

#   #

Sixty-four

Ward and Poet struggled to their feet when Darla entered. She greeted Poet with a curt nod, but only cut her eyes at Ward. Poet mumbled a nicety. Ward waved her to a chair, then flagged the condescending waiter for drinks all around.

Darla sucked her teeth as she sat. "Best you explain why you call me from me bed at this hour—hopefully not to again spout you holy justice."

"You have to understand that my life has been spent bringing in the bad guys and protecting society from the predators. It's who I became over the years because of training and indoctrination. It's not something I can simply turn off."

"But why you must use me?"

"I don't want to use you, just the information you imparted. But I won't without your consent. You're important to me, Darla."

"So you saying you doesn't breathe a word of anything me share with you?" She glanced to Poet.

"Not even to him. And I won't unless you agree to let me use it to bring justice to Ogden Christopher, and to little Caleb, who they killed today."

"Caleb—killed! What you say?"

"We witnessed it with binoculars, Poet said, "too far away to intervene."

Darla drew in breath, but refrained from saying anything while the waiter served their drinks. He glanced disdainfully at the two roughly dressed white men he considered ill-mannered, and all but smirked at the black woman of the working class they entertained . . . at the Lagoon Hotel.

Darla waited until he left then demanded: "Tell me about Caleb."

"The Jamaican," Ward said, "and the gutter-rat Frenchman bashed his head in with fish bats."

"Lord God in heaven!" Darla's face twisted with wrath.

"I intend to bring them to justice," Ward said. "I'd like you to help."

"Of course me help, mon. But how those things me know not hurt Mister

Christopher? That mon set me free. Me do nothing to hurt he."

"Trust me on this, Darla, to use the information to advantage."

"Me going to be a fool again and trust you jiving ass. But tell me how it happen those low bastards murder a nice old man like Caleb."

Ward and Poet took turns relating to her the events of the past few days,

concluding with their vain pursuit of the Regalia.

"Lord, me doesn't believe this!" Darla exclaimed.

"Whatta' you mean," burst out of Ward, "you don't believe?"

Darla waved a hand at him. "T'is what me overhear at the café me doesn't believe. Lord, it happen that even though me doesn't see Edgy or his boat me learn the mon on his return to Kingstown."

Both men tensed.

"Lord God in heaven," Darla said, "it happen not more than some few minutes before me shift end. The gal who run with Edgy stop by the café and brag how she mon radio-telephone how him returning from the Grenadines and want to take dinner with she. Lord, how that gal crow how her to give he a night to remember, since him to take on stores for a long trip tomorrow."

"Did she mention his destination?" Ward asked.

"Me never ask such. Me shift end and me anxious to get home to fix dinner for me daughter."

"Chingalo!" Ward grimaced at his ill luck to have only limited information about something so crucial.

"Mon, me never think all that she brag have value."

Ward pursed his lips as he stared at the black night beyond the railing. "Yep, that had to be the reason they killed the old guy. They found the cache but didn't retrieve the diamonds because those rocks tie them to the robbery in Rotterdam, as well as to the murder of the jeweler in Curaçao."

"Sounds right," Poet agreed.

"The Regalia hadn't been stocked for a long trip," Ward rationalized, "so returned to Kingstown rather than take on stores in small ports. An accomplished smuggler, Edgy knew he'd raise fewer eyebrows in the larger metropolis of Kingstown than in the small provincial ports."

"Besides," Poet contributed, "it permits Ajakian and his cohorts to pick up personal belongings."

Ward pointed a finger of commendation at the oldster. "That conceited pudgeball isn't about to leave all his bad rags behind. They intend to retrieve the diamonds in the morning and flee to God knows where, leaving Christopher to stew in that prison."

"There are more than a few docks and moorings in the area," Poet said, "where Edgy might have taken his boat. I'll call a friend with a car to provide us with wheels so we can search for it."

Ward shook his head. "Unimportant now that we know the boat returned to Kingstown and have deduced what they plan."

Poet stared blankly at the detective, unable to appreciate how that limited knowledge sufficed. But Ward didn't explain it. He pushed himself out of the chair and crossed the lobby to the public telephone.

Considering the hour, he couldn't expect anyone to be at the courthouse, so called information. "Yes, I need the home phone for Prosecutor Byrum Josephs."

"Sorry, sir, we not permitted to give out such."

"I'm Ward Perez, an investigator for the prosecutor. This is vital."

"If you on he staff, sir, why you not have that information?"

"Didn't realize how important it would be to have it. It's very important I talk with him."

"Sorry, sir, we not permitted to give out certain numbers."

"Okay, then let me give you mine so you can inform the prosecutor that Investigator Ward Perez awaits his call. It's urgent that the prosecutor calls me as quickly as possible." He read the number off the public phone. "Be sure to call Prosecutor Josephs immediately. This is a national emergency."

#   #

## Sixty-Five

Ward hung up, and leaned against the wall, breathing deeply to imbue patience. Minutes passed but the phone didn't ring. His luck, the guy wasn't home. Or the hump didn't take the call seriously.

Maybe the operator didn't have the moxie to call Sir Pompous at that hour, in spite of his having categorized it as imperative. Grimacing, he returned to his table, racking his brain along the way for an alternative strategy. Darla and Poet stared at him, expectantly. Both scowled annoyance when he didn't relieve their curiosity.

Ward dropped into the wicker chair and lifted his drink. But he barely got

the glass to his lips when the telephone jangled. For a second he wrestled with whether to take a swig first or rush to the telephone. The telephone won.

"Ward Perez here. Yes, sir, still working the case. Didn't think I needed to check in without having something useful to report. Yes, sir, I have now. Been shadowing Ajakian and his thugs on a trip they took down to the Grenadines. Yes, sir, it is relevant. Actually, I believe I've solved your murder."

"What do you mean, solved it? We both know who the murderer is."

"Yes, sir, you're absolutely right, but I can now prove it wasn't justifiable."

"That is certainly gratifying."

"I need you to keep certain people in town tomorrow, sir. Yes, that Armenian, Ajakian, and his two henchmen."

"I don't understand."

"They chartered the Regalia, a cabin cruiser that's owned and operated by a known smuggler called Edgy, with intent to sail to Canouan tomorrow. I need them denied exit from port."

"We need substantive reason to detain people here, just as you do in New York."

"You busted and incarcerated Christopher without a solid case."

"If that is all you have to say, I'm ringing off and returning to bed."

"No! No, listen to me. You've got to keep those guys in port tomorrow. There are any number of witnesses who saw Ajakian take Christopher's crewman, Caleb, aboard the Regalia when it sailed three days ago. Well the Regalia returned to port without Caleb—because they murdered him off the reefs of Canouan."

"Are you certain? My God, why? How?"

"Bashed his head in with shark bats."

"You witnessed his murder? But why didn't you prevent it?"

"Too far away—watching it all with binoculars. Too bad because he was a witness to the killing of Torchy."

"A rather reluctant one who denied possessing that knowledge."

"True, sir. And unfortunately he's not around now, but his murderers are. You let them depart in the morning and they flee for good."

"Good riddance to a bad lot."

"They leave and they take all the pressure off Christopher, since there's a relationship. He'll be liberated of indictment on other charges, and will file self-defense and justifiable homicide on the Torchy charge. There isn't a juror on this island will convict him for defending his wife. You'll be left to explain your impetuous decision of indicting him . . . and especially of incarcerating him in that dungeon."

Silence, which Ward broke with: "It could end up politically embarrassing."

"What exactly would you have me do?"

"Take them into custody. I'm sure they returned to their hotel rooms for the night. And I doubt they'll resist being busted, thinking they're Teflon."

"Whatever do I do with them after having them taken into custody?"

"Arrange for them to be at an informal meeting at the courthouse the morning of the day after tomorrow. I'll have the package all tied up nice and neat by then, after which you can make the formal indictments."

"I'm rather uncomfortable with that arrangement."

"Oh, by the way, sir, there's an Inspector Dietzen from Interpol, along with a DeBeers representative due to visit the island."

"Stopped by this afternoon and inquired for you."

"Have them there too. And Christopher as well. Day after tomorrow we'll put this whole thing to bed."

"Whyever should we transport Christopher from the prison?"

"Just do it, sir. Please! We need his testimony to tie up all of the loose ends."

"What testimony? To date he's been particularly uncooperative."

"Just have them all there, sir, and I'll wrap up your case in bright red ribbons and make you look like a hero. You can invite Texas Jack Hower to the press conference."

"I'm rather reluctant, detective, to accommodate your request."

"Just do it, sir. Trust me."

"You disappoint me I promise you'll regret it."

Ward stifled a chuckle as he signed off and hung up. <u>Trust me</u> had its particular significance in The Apple, and it wasn't to convince one. He bobbed his head in thought as he returned to the table. Chingalo, he hoped he'd convinced Josephs to hold those two mooks in town. The guy didn't and Ward worried it'd put his ass in jeopardy.

He dropped into his wicker chair and gestured the waiter to bring another round of drinks. When it arrived, Ward raised his glass. "Here's to a giant-sized crapshoot."

"What that supposed to mean?" Darla asked.

"It means Poet and I succeed tomorrow or your old boyfriend will put kinks in this tired spic ass."

"Succeed at what?" Poet asked, gazing boozily at Ward.

"We're going back to Canouan and dive for those diamonds—needing them to present as evidence that'll put those mooks away for the rest of their miserable lives."

Poet gawked. Shaking the alcoholic fog from his head, he asked: "What makes you think Ajakian and his thugs will allow you to do that?"

"They'll be in custody. All arranged."

Poet stared dumbly at Ward. "Made that scary trip once—then back in a gale."

"It's not a matter of choice, Pops. The diamonds are the evidence that connects all of the perps to the crimes."

\#   \#

Sixty-Six

Ay chingalo! Past six!

Ward bounded out of the hotel bed, awakening Darla. "What happening? Mon, where me be? What in hell happening?"

"I should have been up an hour ago. Me and Poet should be on our way."

"Oh, Lord!" Darla sat up and rubbed her eyes. "Me fall asleep in you bed. Why you didn't wake me? What me to tell me daughter?"

"That you slept over at the Lagoon. That'll impress her."

"Stop you nonsense, mon. This not a joke. Me needs to explain to me daughter why me stays out all night—like some loose woman."

Ward didn't respond to that, busily splashing water on his face and under his armpits, then toweling off. After pulling on faded denim shorts he donned a tee shirt emblazoned with a multi-colored square daubed by a surrealist—the clothing he'd worn yesterday. Shoving his bare feet into his sneakers and grabbing his baseball cap and sunglasses, he bolted out the door before Darla struggled off the bed.

"Where you go and leave me here by me lonesome? Mon, you doesn't know you rude for not see me home?"

Her voice rang in his ears as he hurried onto the pier behind the hotel. Searching around he fretted that Poet had gotten too bombed last night to make it back to the boat this morning. Sure, he could sail to Canouan by himself, but he'd like to have someone on the boat while he dived for the diamonds.

Dumbest thing a diver can do is not have a person on the surface to help or call for help if needed. Problem was, he didn't know how to contact the oldster if the guy failed to show. He'd never gotten Pop's address and didn't know if he had a phone, much less its number. How dumb is that? Oh gracias! He expelled relief to spot Poet sprawled on a bench near the boat, looking like he spent the night there. Okay, Ward accepted the need to rouse him from a boozy fugue.

Upon closer inspection, Ward realized that the oldster had gone home to change and shave. He wore a gray and white striped collarless shirt as mod as it got. It made a guy wonder where he got all those in-your-face cotton pullovers. Probably a mail-order-catalogue junky. Damned if he hadn't also donned freshly laundered chinos. Same old, same old sneakers.

Ward shook the guy awake, after which Poet struggled out of the chair. His stumbling indicated he hadn't fully recovered from that infusion of booze. But it irritated Ward to have the codger sputtering at him about being late. Ignoring that, Ward harried the sleepy guy who tended the chandlery to obtain half a dozen dive tanks.

After getting that equipment aboard, along with some easy-to-prepare food and containers of hot coffee, they let go the mooring lines to get underway. Ward stood the helm, motoring his sloop down the narrow channel out of Blue Lagoon, kissed by the morning sun as they passed between the channel markers guiding them safely between reefs and shallows.

Once in the open roadstead, he and Poet bent on canvas and tacked past Young Island, where tropic flora waved departure to the vessel, as did a variety of sea birds with their railing symphony.

A steady trade wind drove them south by southeast with sails bellied and straining under a broad reach. The mast groaned and the rigging creaked as they cleaved through the medium chop. Puffball clouds scudding across the blue skies promised fair weather.

Ward sighted mountainous Bequia Head a mile to starboard after little more than an hour. He took the windward course to make time, steering east of the island, out of the sheltered seaways of the Caribbean and into the heavier chop of the Atlantic.

Despite favorable conditions and easy sailing, Ward anguished whether the pig-headed prosecutor detained Ajakian and his thugs. If the Regalia showed up, there'd be no way for he and Pops to deter them from acquiring the diamonds, or to deter Ajakian and his mutts from fleeing to parts unknown. Worse consideration was that he and the oldster might end up statistics—missing at sea. They couldn't expect any help, since the police rarely patrolled the windward side of Canouan, a desolate area most people, as well as boats, avoided.

So much depended on the stuffed-shirt prosecutor doing his part. And the one person in this world Ward didn't want to have to depend on, was Byrum fucking Josephs. Ay Chingalo, he had to wonder if this wasn't a really dumb undertaking.

"How will you know where to search?" Poet asked.

"Dah. They left a buoy."

"That only marks the area of the reef where the diamonds are hidden. Dah. How will you know exactly where the gems are cached?"

Ward stared dumbly at him, lost for a reply.

"Surely, Mister Smart-ass Cop, you don't expect the damned things to be hanging on a coral pronghorn waiting for you to pluck them off."

Ward stared out at sea, irritated that Pops had nailed a fault. Dammit, he hadn't permitted himself to think about anything other than success. He sure wished he'd gotten a peek at the schematic Gallyvan and Bonbieu had sketched.

"Assuming you don't get lucky, don't find the diamonds, what are you going to tell the prosecutor?"

Ward didn't acknowledge Poet's question. He breathed deeply as he watched the seas roll past. Sometimes you just didn't want to think about alternatives.

Concentrating on sailing, Ward let the current correct their course to a more southerly direction as he skirted the west coast of Mustique, thus avoiding the dangerous shoals north and east of the island, especially the rocky little Baliceaux Island and all of the cayos around it. His primitive charts identified the Pillories, a group of mountain peaks that protruded through the surface of the sea.

Soon after, he adjusted his course again, to give Montezuma Shoal a wide berth. The chart notated that a ninety-foot dredge had sunk off its east side and lay in forty feet of water. Anything that far down didn't pose a threat. Hell, he only drew five feet, and that because he'd extended the keel to attain better stability, especially in stormy seas.

The further along he got, the more the prospects of failure haunted him—driving home the realization that finding the diamonds wasn't a given. And he didn't have a speck of evidence to justify indicting Ajakian and his two cold-blooded killers without those diamonds to tie them to the crimes?

Would a jury convict them for the murder of Caleb simply on the testimony of he and Poet, considering they observed it from a distance that required binoculars to see the incident. And they alternated using those, ruling out both observing the action at the same time, which stretched corroboration to a thin line.

What were his odds of convincing Christopher to testify against Ajakian? If not, Ward knew goddam well he'd need to flip both of those mooks against their pudgeball boss, needing one to corroborate the testimony of the other. How likely was that, considering the grudge they had against him for beating on their asses?

After skirting Mustique and the chain of rocky islands south of the fabled island retreat of the rich and snobby, he had a stretch of about a dozen knots, during which he needed to clear a series of frightening reefs called Savan Island and Savan Rocks, with all four of the rocky brutes protruding through the surface, probably the peaks of mountains rather than islets anchored by coral reefs. He didn't know for certain, and only cared that he avoided them.

Sighting Petit Canouan, more a rocky volcanic peak than an island, rising some four hundred feet above the surface of the choppy sea, he steered due south. Within a half hour he could see the hills of Canouan. Gracias a Dios. He began to engender a fondness for The Turtle.

After finding the marker left by the Regalia, he anchored a distance off the reef, concerned with not damaging the fragile coral structure. Both searched around and breathed their relief at not seeing any other watercraft, especially no Regalia.

#   #

Sixty-Seven

"So far, so good," Ward said while changing into bathing trunks. "No sign of Ajakian and his thugs." After donning his diving gear, along with two air tanks, he loaded a spear gun.

"That thing isn't legal in these waters," Poet said.

"Fishing with it is illegal, which I'm not planning to do. But if I encounter any sharks or barracudas, common off these reefs, I want to be prepared. No way I'm going down there without an equalizer."

After cleaving the surface, he dove to the top of the reef, to be instantly engulfed by swirling schools of brilliant yellows and blues and pinks and reds and greens, in a myriad of shapes. The legions of exotic fish topped any of the other dives he'd made, even that reef twenty miles off the coast of Cabo Rojo, Puerto Rico or that extraordinary reef paralleling the coast off Guánica.

Diving deeper, he encountered sinewy plants that wavered with the motion of the water, as well as spongy-looking growths in bright and luminous colors, all interspersed by schools of fish and jet-propelled squids. Turtles of every size, tiny to mammoth, glided through the water. He found the big ones with those horny beaks scary. And giant manta rays with trailing wand-like tails made him uneasy, though he'd been told they were gentle—not dangerous. Still. . . .

Pursuing his sole purpose, he concentrated on finding the place Caleb had recognized and hoped it would be identifiably marked. Gambling that the oldster hadn't been mistaken, he accepted that he searched the correct section of the reef. Even then he dreaded covering an area the size of a football field.

Okay, he accepted the logic that they'd pinpointed the exact spot but left them hidden to avoid being apprehended while in possession of that damning evidence, with no intent of taking possession of them until they had the ability to flee the area. It defied reason that they'd have jumped the gun and offed Caleb if they hadn't located that cache.

Schemers like Ajakian generally were paranoid, distrusting every one. Having discovered that hiding place, he was reluctant to take possession of the diamonds until after returning to Kingstown to take on stores and obtain personal gear. Then they'd retrieve the rocks with a fully stocked boat so they could flee and avoid indictment.

Ward shuddered when it occurred to him that those killers might surprise him down there, to shoot a spear up his ass. Chingalo, especially that Rasta, who sure as hell bristled for payback. Dammit, he thought he'd left all the scary shit behind when he retired. Hadn't he anguished enough on some of those assignments in Brooklyn and Spanish Harlem? Chingalo, it still took doing to put himself in a bad place.

Swallowing to suppress his bugaboos, he focused on finding the goddam diamonds so he could get the hell out of there. Gallyvan didn't strike him as a whiz kid, but probably had enough smarts not to kill the guide before arrival at the destination.

Still, there weren't any obvious indications of a stash, so he scoured the craggy reef, inch by inch. The coral formed lumpy rocks in places and tree-like branches in others.

Colorful anemone flowers bloomed in garish patches. Fish large and small swirled around him in a never-ending kaleidoscope. But nowhere did he find any place to hide a small package. And after an hour and a half he surfaced to replace his air tanks.

\#   \#

Sixty-Eight

Ward ground his jaws, with frustration increasing after the fourth dive. Six hours of diligent searching revealed nothing. He knew he had two hours of daylight at most before the sun dropped west of the craggy hills of Canouan, immersing the area in shadows. Then he'd be denied sufficient visibility to continue the underwater search. What the hell would he tell Josephs if he failed to produce that evidence?

The few times he'd found holes or crevices in the coral big enough to stash a bag of diamonds, a spotted moray eel emerged from it. They scared the hell out of him, charging out after him with their fangs bared. He'd heard stories of how divers had been chomped on by those ravenous mothers, some as big around as his arm. They'd needed to cut the heads off the brutes. Then it still required prying open those vise-like jaws.

Skimming along the undulating reef with its ragged formation, he happened upon a crevice partially concealed by vegetation. It sure struck him as the kind of place you'd hide something, since the cut in the coral made a natural mark to find it again. But a goddam moray eel appeared out of nowhere.

Lacking the cojones to mess with the devil thing, he withdrew a few feet, giving it all the space it wanted. After glaring at him with those beady eyes, it turned and slithered into the crevice, and into a hole behind the widespread petals of a flowering anemone. So much for that location.

Eager to avoid contact with the scary leopard of the sea, he searched a distance away from it, hoping to find another natural or man-made marker, while keeping tabs on that devilish thing from the corner of his eye. The brute went only halfway into the hole, then jousted with something in there, and withdrew after a few thrusts.

Ward gaped at that pugnacious beast retreating. What coral-dweller chased off a moray eel? Another moray eel maybe? But the big mother would exert its dominance by chasing after the interloper, fluttering its fins and baring its teeth to advertise its being a bad-ass to the watery world. No other eel appeared.

Nothing so much as stuck its head or a claw out. Then what the hell could it be? He'd never heard of anything small enough to hide in that hole that's bad enough to take on a moray.

He flicked his flippers to propel himself to hover a safe distance from the hole. But he couldn't see past the anemone blossoms to determine whatever hung out in the crevice. Okay, he probed it with his spear gun. Wary of whatever might charge out after him, he kept his finger on the trigger. But nothing came out. And the spear went in only so far, thumping something without the consistency of coral, perplexing him and provoking interest. What could it be?

He probed with the spear, to feel density in places and not in others. He tried to snag it, but failed to no matter how he angled his thrust. Dammit, he had to know. So he inhaled courage and reluctantly inserted his hand, probing until he reached in up to his elbow. Holy shit, it felt like canvas or cloth or something.

He grabbed as much of the velvety substance as his fingers could grasp and pulled hard. The sombitchen thing barely budged. What the hell could it be? God, in his infinite wisdom grew a lot of extraordinary things on this earth, especially on these reefs. Ward needed it to be that certain package.

If Christopher stashed the bag of diamonds in that hole, more than likely he'd have wedged it in tightly to prevent reef snorkelers from helping themselves to it. Okay, he'd try again. But it continued to resist, despite his grasping it with the tips of his fingers and applying every ounce of strength. Por fin! He finally budged it.

Encouraged, he continued to grasp and pull, enjoying minimum success. Finally, he worked enough of it free to be able to grip it and give it a concerted yank. The salami shaped package popped out, knocking him off balance.

He bobbled it, and in his effort to contain it, he almost lost the speargun. It took all of his concentration in that weightless environment to hold onto both the package and the weapon. Below him the reef fell away forever. He sure didn't want that package plunging down there. And he damn sure didn't want to swim among those morays without the speargun.

Probing the package with his fingers, his eyes widened. He tried to howl his joy, but the mask around his nose and mouth muffled sound. Then his breath froze in his throat. From the corner of his eye he saw the flash of white. He turned to see the shark flashing past, then whipping around and streaking back the other way. Swarms of small fish dashed away in havoc.

Holding his breath, he backed off with as little movement as possible, so as not to roil the water and attract its attention. The circling ten- or twelve-foot-long monster looked vicious—scared the hell out of him.

Ay chingalo! The package slipped from his fingers. He snatched for it—but fear of too much movement attracting that man-eater inhibited his effort. The damned thing bounced off the coral to free-fall between schools of small, colorful fish, farther and farther away. No-oo!

Despite his apprehension of the shark, he dived, unhappy about having that monster above him, blocking his escape. Hopefully, that beast stayed there, didn't follow him down into the depths. The water turned murkier the deeper he dove. How far down did he need to probe?

Then he saw it—hanging from a pronghorn of coral. It might have been funny if that fucking shark wasn't circling above him. He kept an eye on the beast as he dropped to where the package hung precariously. Hovering, he grasped the damn thing before pulling it away from the clinging coral . . . while clutching the speargun.

Glancing up at the circling shark, he dreaded the ascent, and would have preferred to wait for the brute to swim away, attracted by other prey. But his tanks had only a few minutes more of air. So he flicked his flippers to propel himself upward, his spear gun at the ready. He hugged the reef in an effort to camouflage himself, having heard that sharks have poor eyesight. His luck, this mother had twenty-twenty.

Passing the scary demon, with eight or ten feet between them, he reached the top of the reef, which encouraged him to thrust upward. Damn real he kept a wary eye on the circling monster. Popping through the surface, he searched for his boat.

Wouldn't you know he sighted it two to three hundred feet away? Thank God he could see pretty far down in the clear water. No sign of that damned shark at the moment. If it came hunting him he hoped to shoot its ass before it ripped a piece out of him. No way he liked having his feet dangling down there, to get snapped off before he put a spear in that ugly mother.

Gripping the spear gun in one hand and the bulky package in the other, he breast stroked his way toward the sloop, pumping with his flippers but careful not to roil the water too much. His flippers generated more motive power than his encumbered breaststroke, but awareness that motion in the water attracted sharks inhibited excessive movement. Still, he yearned to speed up, with that fucking predator circling below him.

Realization of the other danger impelled him to search around. Gracias a

Dios—no other craft in sight. Apparently Josephs had detained the bad guys. Scanning his sailboat, it irked and puzzled him not to see the oldster. Okay, Pops probably snoozed, bored by the long day and affected by all that booze he'd consumed last night. At least he hoped that was it.

It felt like it took half a lifetime to inch closer to his sloop. He called to Poet but failed to arouse the oldster. With the wind in his face he knew his voice didn't carry all that far. And huffing and puffing from exertion didn't leave him much calling power. The whole time he suffered the eerie feeling that the shark lurked below him, sniffing his toes. So he kept the spear gun ready.

Where the hell was Poet? Did something happen to the oldster? He labored for breath while determinately stroking, and finally reached the rounded hull. Grasping the gunnel, he yelled: "Shark! Give me a hand!"

The oldster appeared and helped him scurry across the coaming, to get his legs and feet out of the water and into the boat. Exhaling his reprieve, Ward threw the tubular sack at Poet's feet.

The oldster stared dumbly at it. "Tell me it is. By God! Tell me it is!"

Ward sat up, extracted the knife from his weight-belt and cut an opening in the velvet package. They howled their joy.

A voice in the recesses of his mind taunted him that his next challenge was to tie Ajakian and his two mooks to those stones or his efforts will have been in vain.

#   #

Sixty-Nine

Ward paced in front of the Courthouse and Parliament Building, his eyes darting up and down the peopled streets as he searched for Darla and Poet. The snooty glances of local bureaucrats wearing shirts and ties irked him. Some even wore suit jackets . . . in that climate. He sneered back at them, flipped his head at a few. Who the hell were they to look askance at him?

He'd worn his white linen guayabera shirt with its squared tails outside of laundered chinos. In keeping with his penchant for the demonstrative, he'd had it tailored in Puerto Rico with an abundance of lacy swirls in complimentary shades of white. Hell, it was boss on that island.

Nevertheless, he'd rarely worn it, saving it for special occasions. A day in court qualified, especially one in which he'd lay out his case and prove himself as one super-ass detective.

Caribbean Hispanics considered it acceptable business dress. Actually, it even qualified for less-than-formal evening wear. Hell, it made sense in the tropics. Screw them and their snooty English affectations. Hombre, he'd be the object of admiration in Puerto Rico, Cuba, or the Dominican Republic.

Clutching a small duffel bag, he paced back and forth, irritated that Darla and Poet hadn't as yet arrived, needing

303

them to testify. He checked his watch , concerned with His Lordship getting antsy. Josephs didn't impress him as one who'd condone lateness—tardiness as he'd probably allude to it. Parakeets screeching in a nearby tree amplified his concern and irritability.

Gracias a Dios, he spotted Poet coming up the street in his quickstep hobble. Damned if the oldster wasn't togged out like a businessman in a gray seersucker suit, white shirt and regimental-striped tie. Chingalo, does he think he's going to preside at the meeting?

While trying to decide what smart-assed comment to make, since the oldster wore those scruffy sneakers, he followed Poet's gaze, to see Darla approach from the opposite direction. Madre de Dios, he felt like he stared at the Queen of the May, in a two-piece cotton knit dress, dark blue with lighter blue polka dots, its jewel-neck enhanced by a gold necklace that matched the gold-tone buttons on the front of the blouse. Gold rings dangled from her earlobes, swinging with the rhythm of her knock-out walk. Chingalo, she sure got her some bad togs from that fling with his lordship.

Ha, he chuckled when it occurred to him that Josephs was about to review these bad rags he'd bestowed upon his paramour. Then he shook off that distraction and waved them to follow as he led the way, weaving through the usual multitude in the corridor. The courtroom door swung open just as he reached it, almost hitting him in the face.

Byrum Josephs emerged in a huff, the personification of importance in his dark striped suit and red power tie, his brow creased with concern. "Perez! T'is past time. I feared you'd fail to appear and make me a laughing-stock."

Haughtier faded as he glanced past Ward and identified those accompanying the detective. His brows furrowed with questioning as he pushed the door closed behind him, then leaned against it to prevent anyone entering or exiting. He glanced back to Ward to scowl criticism of his guayabera shirt.

"I'm less than five minutes late." Ward checked his watch while pretending unawareness of Josephs' disapproval of his attire. Fuck him, it worked in Puerto Rico.

"Tardy is tardy," Josephs said while adjusting his horn-rimmed glasses to better stare at the other two. "Why are these two here?"

"They're going to testify. This is Poet, er, Harry Gundersen, a retired reporter for the Cleveland Plain Dealer." Then he gestured toward Darla.

"He know me name." Darla sucked her teeth and shuffled from foot to foot.

Josephs grimaced while glancing around at the people swirling in all directions to attend to one official business or another. He sighed relief when no one paid attention to Darla, to possibly trigger gossip.

Gesturing to Poet,he said: "This, I believe is the chap with the reputation for writing trite poetry. Will he now rhyme something substantive to bolster in some way the indictment of Christopher?"

Without waiting for a reply, he turned hard eyes on Darla. "Are you here to embarrass me? Surely you're aware your presence will fuel innuendos."

"Whatever that mean. You investigator ask me to be a witness."

"They're both witnesses," Ward said. "Their testimony will nail—"

"Testify to what? Are you referring to actually witnessing anything or simply mouthing hearsay?"

"Poet was with me when they clubbed poor old Caleb to death."

"Observed from a distance of two kilometers more or less while sharing a single pair of binoculars—which questions credibility."

Ward shrugged acceptance of the probability of a defense attorney disparaging it.

"I will not permit you to make a spectacle of this hearing, despite it being informal. Neither of these people need be here." Josephs pulled open the door and strode into the courtroom, clunking the door closed behind him.

Ward stared at it—dumbfounded. He flailed his hands while probing for words to express his frustration and allay the wounded feelings of Darla and Poet.

Darla sucked her teeth. "No way this gal go in there with that pompous ass. You going to have to present you case without testimony from me." She glanced around self-consciously, apparently concerned that some of the people sweeping past might have overheard Josephs deride her in public and spread hateful gossip around Kingstown.

"Hey, come on, Darla, you witnessed that whole thing with the Christophers and Torchy and Ajakian and his bunch at the shack on the beach."

"Best you find another way to present you case. Me never testify for that pompous ass." She turned and strode toward the exit.

"Nor I," Poet said as he hobbled after Darla.

"Hey, you can't cop out on me now."

"I didn't," Poet called over his shoulder. "Your high and mighty employer did. I'll be at the café with Darla."

Ward gaped as they exited the building and let the door swing closed behind them. He stared down at the small bag in his hand, dreading that everything had fallen apart. A moment ago he'd been on the threshold of celebrity. The Puerto Rican whiz kid had the case in hand—on the verge of clearing it. Now he had slim hope going for him. Sure he had the diamonds, but needed to connect them to Ajakian and his thugs.

He shook his head to dispel the cloud of negativity while inhaling determination. No way he'd lose this chance to prove himself and send a TV-message to his old buddies in blue—a news report he'd fantasized rankling those deputy commissioners.

#   #

Seventy

Ward pulled open the door and ventured into the small chamber with its raised podium facing a dozen rows of wooden bench-seats; miniature in comparison to New York courtrooms. Glancing past the glowering prosecutor, he spotted Ogden Christopher, forlorn in oversized prison garb, flanked by Constables Booker and Bivens. First time he'd seen either wearing sidearms; probably because they'd been assigned to guard the prisoner.

On the far side of the small chamber Bajuk Ajakian huddled with the Frenchman and the muscle-bound Jamaican. The dapper Armenian wore a beige suit of worsted wool with expensive foulard tie. Gallyvan, with his wiry beard, looked like some kind of West Indian guru in his loose-fitting gray outfit and colorful skullcap, with his dreadlocks dangling from it. Skinny little Bonbieu reminded him of a refugee from a homeless camp in his wrinkled clothing. He wrung his soiled mariner's cap between skinny hands while incessantly blinking his good eye; the glazed one locked in a sightless stare.

Two others didn't ring any bells of familiarity. Ward approached them. "Hi, I'm Ward Perez, the prosecutor's investigator."

"Henrik Dietzen of Interpol. This is Henrietta Spiezer of DeBeers."

Ward shook hands with the tall Inspector then the stocky woman. "Excuse me for a minute." He crossed to Byrum Josephs, who resembled a smoldering volcano, prancing impatiently up and down the center aisle.

"We need to talk privately."

Josephs glowered at him, his facial expression alternating between obstinacy and perplexity.

"It'll take one minute."

Josephs scowled but let Ward usher him out to the swarming hallway. Ward pushed the door closed behind them while the prosecutor searched around with furrowed brow, then registered both relief and disappointment not to see Darla.

Ward disregarded the man's questioning eyes as he spoke in a whisper so as not to be overheard by passers-by, aware of his employer's social sensitivity. "Considering your case against Christopher lacks the essential ingredient of a witness, and the only one I came up with they murdered, are you ready to deal for a different conviction?"

"What in bloody hell are you saying, Perez?" Josephs jerked his head back as he glanced around. Since no one appeared to have overheard his outburst, he turned back to Ward, but spoke in a subdued tone. "Have you misrepresented yourself when claiming to have this bloody business wrapped up?"

"Not exactly. What I—"

Why were those two brought here . . . to embarrass me?"

"No, sir, as witnesses."

"Is that the best you offer, an expatriate American who plays the fool here and—"

"Don't say it, sir. You'll really piss me off. Chill while you take into consideration that the only two witnesses to

Torchy's killing were the old deckhand and Christopher's wife."

"Bloody waste—in both instances."

"True, she doesn't have to and almost certainly won't testify against her husband, while, of course, she will speak volubly in his behalf—probably weeping and distraught when explaining how her husband defended her from being brutally and sexually assaulted by Torchy."

Josephs blinked, his pomposity deflated.

"Bottom line," Ward said, "is we don't have witness one to challenge Christopher's claim of killing in self-defense."

"Then why this outrageous charade?" Josephs clenched his teeth to stem his excited comment as he glanced around, concerned with whatever he said being repeated by detractors. "Why have you let me make a fool of myself by assembling these people? Whatever are you up—"

"Without a witness it's not likely you're going to win a conviction. You lose and the world press will make a mockery of you."

"Then you forfeit the ten thousand dollars. I'll petition the return of all monies dispensed to you. And I'll see you're charged with fraudulent intent for having me detain those three and then gathering the others here today."

"I'm sure you don't want me to manufacture a case."

"Damn you! Are you saying you have nothing to present after all you've put me through? Have you brought me here to be humiliated? Is this by design of Darla? Have you two conspired to—"

"I'm saying I've devised a situation that will save face in the world press. But it isn't going to convict Christopher. Actually you're going to need to offer him immunity to serve as a witness."

"What in bloody hell are you up to—damn you?"

"Look, sir, this whole thing has been about diamond smuggling."

"I don't give a fig about anything of that sort. I specifically engaged you—"

"You should, sir. It's the best chance you have for a conviction. The reason for this whole mess stems from Christopher smuggling uncut diamonds that Ajakian and his two thugs stole in a high-profile hold-up in Holland."

"Having no bloody connection with the murder charge against Christopher."

"It has everything to do with Christopher, and the reason the Interpol inspector and the DeBeers agent are here."

"Damn them and their purpose for coming!"

"They're going to be useful to you, sir, in getting convictions."

"In what bloody way? What possible information could they possess with respect to the murder of Torchy?"

"Torchy had an association with Ajakian. The reason for his murder had to do with those diamonds. That's why I needed the freedom to search the reef off Canouan. And I got lucky and found them." He waggled the duffel bag.

"That's why you wanted Ajakian and his people detained . . . so they couldn't interfere with you extracting some diamonds?"

"However, sir, we don't have a case against anybody for stealing and or smuggling them."

"What in blazes are you telling me now, Perez? A moment ago you said you recovered that evidence from the reef. Is this business balls up?"

"We have the diamonds to return to Interpol and DeBeers, but we don't have a perp because we have no way of proving how those stones got there in the first place."

"Oh blessed God!" Josephs held his head—then glanced around, self-conscious for having raised his voice and expressed dismay amid that multitude of passers-by who might take note of his behavior.

"Look, sir, if we can convince Christopher to testify that Ajakian hired him to smuggle them out of Curaçao, and that he cached them in the reef, we can convict Ajakian. But you know and I know Christopher isn't about to do that unless we offer him immunity so he doesn't put his own ass in jeopardy."

"How in bloody hell does that impact on the murder of Torchy?"

"It permits Christopher to plead justifiable homicide since he no longer needs to fear indictment for diamond smuggling."

"Absolutely not! Under no circumstances will I—"

"Consider the facts, sir. We have little chance of convicting him for the murder anyway. Aren't we better off dealing nothing for something."

"This is ridiculous, Perez." Again Josephs jerked around to glance self-consciously at those that passed close enough to have heard his angry outburst.

"For years, sir, Ajakian has evaded conviction in many parts of the world. Every country in Europe would like to send him to prison. You convict him and you'll have accomplished what many European prosecutors wish they could have. You'll be a shining star to world-wide law enforcement."

Josephs' face lost some of the tenseness, though his brow remained furrowed with skepticism. After a moment of consideration he rejected the proposal with a shake of his head. "Christopher's testimony alone will not be sufficient to convict. Ajakian need only deny the charges and make us a laughingstock."

"Not if we have corroboration, sir. Once we announce the charge against Ajakian, that Jamaican will jump at the chance to get off the hook. He's the kind of punk you can flip. We'll entice him with immunity too."

"Why do we not simply throw open the doors of the prison, set everyone free?"

"You fail to convict Christopher, sir, and Texas Jack along with every other media motor-mouth is going to chew you up like a rag."

"Blast you, Perez!"

"Consider, sir, that if you have a rock solid case against an international crook like Ajakian, they're going to focus on that story. Fact is, most of the reporters have milked the Christopher story for all they can get out of it and left the island to pursue more topical news."

Josephs tilted his head as he considered that assertion. Breathing deeply, he said: "Very well, we'll permit Christopher to plead to justifiable homicide so long as he allocates to the crime. Then, of course, he'll need to testify against Ajakian."

"With immunity."

"Without immunity. By jove, he stands trial—"

"Get real, sir. We have no case against Ajakian without Christopher. Why in hell would Christopher incriminate himself? Not likely, sir. We need to offer him an incentive."

"For what bloody reason, pray tell?"

"Because if we let Ajakian leave the island and disappear, Christopher will no longer fear indictment on diamond-smuggling charges. He'll claim justifiable homicide and very probably be exonerated by a jury of people who hated and feared Torchy."

Josephs glared at the detective. But as the seconds ticked by his demeanor softened. "Very well, we'll allow him to plead himself out of the murder charge then—"

"He knows damn well he doesn't need to trade off the murder charge. He beats you hands down on that. He knows it. I know it. You know it, sir. So let's give the guy immunity, the only chance we have of convincing him to testify."

"Damn you, Perez, you had better have a rock solid case against this Ajakian."

"I've got a case if I convince Christopher to testify against him. The only way I can do that is by offering immunity from indictment for diamond smuggling. Then I'll insist he confess to killing Torchy in self defense."

"Do you truly expect he'll agree to that?"

"Justifying your arrest of him, sir, and making you one big-ass hero in Kingstown. And, of course, that justifies my receiving the balance of the ten thousand."

"What kind of games are you playing, Perez? What exactly—"

"Give me a few minutes to confer with Christopher before we start the proceedings." Without waiting for Josephs to object, Ward pulled open the door and ushered the prosecutor back into the courtroom. All eyes turned to them, glaring impatience.

Ward exhaled, drained since he'd achieved only a small step in a large undertaking, with the biggest challenges still ahead. He'd learned by experience not to anticipate how a mook will react. Sure as hell don't depend on his or her testimony.

#   #

## Seventy-One

Ward suppressed anxiety as he strode across the small courtroom to approach Christopher. He gestured the gaunt man to move aside with him, but the two constables refused to relinquish possession of him. Ward turned entreating eyes to the prosecutor, who grudgingly nodded approval.

Exhaling relief, Ward took Christopher a few feet away to pitch him beyond ear-shot of others. After listening for a few moments Christopher smirked and shook his head, unconvinced that the proposal was in his best interest.

Ward blinked back prospects of defeat as he pitched harder, but Christopher continually shook his head. "I'll take my chances at a trial. Probably should have my attorney at this hearing."

Chingalo, Ward didn't want things confused by a lot of legal entanglements. "You go to court, you get convicted."

When he saw the skepticism curling Christopher's lips, Ward pulled the convict further away and spoke in a whisper too low to be overheard by the others. "We've appealed to Caleb's Christian ethic and convinced him to testify."

"I don't believe that!"

Ward expelled relief that Christopher responded differently than if he'd been apprised of the murder of Caleb. So he pressed the issue. "The man is a devout Christian, possessed by conscience and compelled to expunge his guilt."

"I refuse to believe he'd say anything that harms me."

Ward expressed alarm by the loudness of the objection, fearful of others surmising what was said and informing Christopher of Caleb's demise. He drew Christopher a few feet further away and spoke to him in hushed voice.

"Let me relate the sequence of events on that launch with Torchy: how you obtained your thirty-two the night before, after that episode with Ajakian and his thugs at the shack of Torchy, then how Torchy insisted on going directly to Canouan to dive for the diamonds. He threatened to sexually molest your wife if you failed to locate the cache in that reef, so you brandished your gun. But he swerved the boat hard over, knocking you off balance, then came up with his own pistol. However you pumped one bullet into him, then pumped two more when he threatened to shoot back."

Christopher gawked, his widened eyes probing Ward's face.

Ward patted his back. "We're willing to let you plead to justifiable homicide, with the understanding that the prosecutor will absolve you of willful murder and drop the case against you. But you have to testify against Ajakian."

Christopher smirked and shook his head.

"On top of that," Ward said, anxiously, "we offer you immunity from prosecution for diamond smuggling. You get out of jail and will no longer fear confiscation of your yacht. Ajakian and his two hoods will be incarcerated, relieving you of that worry. You need to accept that this is the only way you can accomplish all those things."

Christopher blinked repeatedly as he stared at the wall, then appeared to relent. "Why can't I simply testify against Ajakian and you drop the other charge?"

"Too much press. The prosecutor needs to save face. Hey, it's not like we're asking you to submit to some kind of hardship. You're not going to do time or nothing. Once the trial of Ajakian is over you get to sail away with your lovely wife."

Christopher stared hard at Ward—strife-lines in his face. Ward held his breath, fearful of the man responding negatively. "Besides," he said, desperate to convince, "this arrangement is going to save you those healthy legal fees if you go to court."

Seeing Christopher's brow arch in deliberation, he pressed on. "And you avenge being terrorized by those thugs. Remember that Jamaican molesting your wife, then grabbing a handful of your genitals, threatening to rape you?"

Christopher gasped, then scowled and turned away. Ward patted his back again. Christopher flexed his jaw before turning back and nodding affirmation.

Ward exhaled, then called to Josephs: "We're ready to begin." Crossing to the defendant's table, he dumped the contents out of the canvas bag. Ajakian and his cohorts gaped at the glassy objects rolling around.

"That bloody sailboat!" burst out of Ajakian.

Ward turned away from the pudgeball to ask the DeBeers representative to identify the diamonds. She studied them with one of those little ocular devices.

Leaving her engaged, Ward took Inspector Dietzen aside for a whispered conference. "While I've retrieved the diamonds, we have no way of proving that Ajakian stole them and cached them there unless the yachtsman who smuggled them out of Curaçao testifies to that. But that requires offering him immunity from prosecution."

Dietzen drew back—dumbfounded. Recovering, he sneered, but Ward spoke before he verbalized objection. "We have zero chance of convicting anyone without testimony that Ajakian arranged to have those diamonds smuggled out of Curaçao."

Inspector Dietzen snorted unwillingness to accept that lack of alternatives.

"Let's not jerk each other around," Ward said. "Either you want to be able to pin that Rotterdam hold-up on Ajakian, or you don't. Your choice."

Dietzen shrugged concession. "That one yachtsman only."

Ward nodded happily as he turned his attention to the DeBeers representative, who'd completed her perusal. It relieved him to hear her announce: "Yes, these are the uncut diamonds stolen at gunpoint from the center in Rotterdam."

Ward swung around to Gallyvan, who resembled a guru with straw-like dreadlocks spilling out of a colorful tam. "I'm betting there's an open warrant against you in Jamaica. Testify that your boss stole those diamonds from that center in Rotterdam or you'll be sent back for prosecution, and one long-ass term in prison."

When the Jamaican's eyes widened Ward knew he'd guessed right. It'd be embarrassing if the guy countered that he had no outstanding warrants.

But Gallyvan's next words made Ward feel like he took one in the solar plexus. "Me doesn't testify nothing against Mister Ajakian. True, mon, me naught but a gutter-rat. But me one loyal rat."

"You rather do hard time in Jamaica?" Ward asked, hoping that threat impacted on the burly Rasta. He purposely hadn't mentioned punishment for implication in the Rotterdam robbery, lacking confidence in Inspector Dietzen extending immunity to skels who participated in that escapade.

"They must first convict me ass. T'was a street fight, most a year ago, and those that witnessed it likely fade away by now. Me take me chances."

Byrum Josephs coughed—all but choked. Ajakian beamed smugly. Ward swallowed and glared at the Jamaican. "Don't say you didn't have your chance, maybe to even get off the hook with that Rotterdam robbery."

Gallyvan's eyes widened. Then he he sneered and turned away.

Ward sucked in resolve and turned to Bonbieu. "Your turn for a deal. But you got just one minute to accept. Yes or no?"

Ward winced when Tuerto sneered. He knew he had to convince the frog-sticker or lose the game. "To start with, we gave Mister Christopher immunity to testify that he smuggled those diamonds out of Curaçao for Ajakian. All you have to do is substantiate that testimony."

Bonbieu stared dumbly at him, didn't respond.

Ward felt himself sinking into the quicksand of defeat. "You're wanted in France as well as Holland. You help or your miserable ass goes back there to stand trial and do time. The Interpol detective is standing right there, ready to take your slimy ass back."

Bonbieu scrutinized Inspector Dietzen, then the woman, with his good eye before returning his attention to the American. "I receive immunity also, and no be take back to Europe. I have permission to leave this place without fear of arrest by Interpol?"

"We can arrange something," Ward said.

"Hold on!" Inspector Dietzen growled.

Ward swung around to him. "You got your diamonds back and you're going to have Bajuk Ajakian, the mastermind, to indict. The diamond center robbery in Rotterdam will be cleared. Every cop in Europe will envy you. You give to get. You don't give, you don't get. You know the drill."

The inspector bobbed his head about in indecision. Ward sucked for breath as he watched the Interpol inspector agonize which way to go. "Get real, inspector. This isn't the first time you offered a deal to a small-fish to net a big one."

"But in this instance," Dietzen retorted, "exist mitigating circumstances."

"Hey, you don't make this deal, Ajakian walks. You make it, you get credit for collaring an international criminal that nobody else succeeded in busting, plus you clean up the Rotterdam mess, and the killing of the jeweler in Curaçao."

Dietzen closed his eyes momentarily, then slitted them open to stare at the American detective.

"It's up to you," Ward barked. ". . . Your chance to be a hero."

Dietzen shrugged. "Let us see how this business plays out."

Ward turned back to the Frenchman. "Last chance. You in or out?"

Bonbieu grinned crookedly as he took a few steps to separate himself from Ajakian and Gallyvan. "I have loyalty only to myself, unlike the savage, so will testify only with immunity and to leave this place without that Interpol."

Ward turned to Inspector Dietzen, hoping the guy didn't object and disrupt things. Man, he couldn't afford a balk at this juncture. The inspector screwed up his face but refrained from remarking. Ward exhaled as he turned back to Bonbieu. "Looking good, baby. You just got yourself the break of a lifetime."

"Hey, you'all never offer me immunity," Gallyvan yelped.

"You had your chance," Ward grumbled. "We got a witness now."

"Why, mon? You'all needs carburation for get a conviction. You going need this child's testimony."

Ward thought about the guy's argument: how it was a street fight and there probably wouldn't be any witnesses left, so doubtful of a conviction in Jamaica. One perp more or less in the Rotterdam thing shouldn't matter too much. He hunched as he admitted: "You got a point. We always need carburation." He turned to Byrum Josephs and Inspector Dietzen. "Your call, gentlemen. Grant this guy immunity and the chance to split the island and you've got the case wrapped up tight."

Dietzen grimaced. Josephs sneered disapproval of the Jamaican's attire and dreadlocks. Ward held his breath for the long moment it took Josephs to nod concession, then announce in his pompous way: "All three will testify. Therefore I indict Ajakian."

"You will only detain Ajakian in preparation for extradition to the Netherlands," Inspector Dietzen growled, "where he shall face numerous criminal charges."

"Right here in Kingstown," Josephs said, "in my jurisdiction."

Ay chingalo! Ward hoped those two weren't going to bicker everything apart, just when he'd moved the dime off dead center. Accepting that the prosecutor's motive was to enhance his reputation Ward had little faith in the pompous guy backing down.

"It is we that have prior claim," Inspector Dietzen said. "I shall file—"

"Ridiculous," Bajuk Ajakian interrupted, stepping forward. He chuckled as he sauntered around the chamber with an air of unconcern. "My barrister will discredit these witnesses you present for the miscreants they are. No jury will pay credence to gutter-rats and slum-bullies."

"We'll present the evidence in a credible manner," Josephs said, posturing haughtily.

Ajakian continued to scoff as he gestured to Christopher. "Do you believe a jury will consider as credible the testimony of one under indictment for murder? They'll realize it is simply a trade-off. You have only a charade."

"We have a sound case in Rotterdam," Dietzen said.

Ajakian chortled derisively as he passed close to Constable Booker, then sent an elbow into that man's ribs bumping him off balance and momentarily immobilizing him. He spun the constable around and jerked his Webley revolver out of its holster, then shoved Booker into Bivens, knocking that constable down to his knees.

"Now I have control here," Ajakian said, brandishing the weapon to hold everyone at bay. Sneering at them, he sauntered to the table and grabbed a handful of the diamonds. After shoving them into his jacket pocket he started to turn away, then turned back and dipped his hand in for more. While pointing the pistol at the others he took a few steps from the table, then paused and returned to scoop up the remainder.

Grinning self-satisfaction, he slipped behind the prosecutor and pressed the pistol against Josephs' head. "Anyone interferes with my escape will be responsible for the death of the prosecutor."

"No, mon! You go too far." Constable Booker lunged toward Ajakian and threw his burly arm out to defend Byrum Josephs.

Ajakian fired and Booker stumbled backwards, then froze and stared dumbly at the curl of smoke from the muzzle of the gun before crumpling to the floor. Ajakian returned the weapon to Josephs' temple.

Ward made a motion to advance on the Armenian, but froze when Ajakian turned the revolver on him. He held his breath as he stared at that hole in its barrel.

Ajakian sneered and his eyes narrowed, like one about to pull the trigger. Then he jerked around to Inspector Dietzen, who'd moved toward him, and swung the revolver to that man. Ward dared to breathe believing Ajakian didn't intend to shoot, just hold them at bay—had the presence of mind not to use up the bullets needed to affect his escape.

But Ward gasped when the Armenian aimed the gun at Bonbieu. "You gave not a second thought to betraying me."

Everyone flinched at the sound of the discharge. Bonbieu stumbled backwards, a hole between his eyes—to bounce off the wall then collapse.

Ajakian jockeyed the prosecutor around, and pointed the revolver at the Jamaican. "I trusted and admired you."

"No, mon!" Gallyvan's eyes bulged with fear.

Just as Ajakian fired, Josephs twisted his shoulders and flailed an arm, throwing the shooter off balance. Inspector Dietzen lashed out at Ajakian's forearm, knocking the gun away. Ward, Constable Bivens and the chubby DeBeers agent wrestled Ajakian to the floor and pinned him. After flipping him onto his belly, Bivens cuffed his hands behind his back.

Ward struggled to his feet and gaped at Gallyvan writhing on the floor, blood pouring from a hole in his face. The one-eyed Frenchman lay motionless, as did Constable Booker. Henrietta Spiezer examined all three, then shook her head.

They jerked the handcuffed man to his feet, the long hairs he brushed across his bald spot now hanging in his face. "I now have you for willful murder—in my jurisdiction," Byrum Josephs barked at him.

Inspector Dietzen grimly nodded concession. "At least he will no more enjoy freedom, neither here in the Americas, nor in Europe. And I claim credit for clearing the diamond robbery in Rotterdam, as well the murder of the jeweler in Curaçao."

Ward approached Henrietta Spiezer. "I produced the diamonds, which is a bunch more than giving information leading to the recovery of the damned things. How much is that worth?"

"The reward is fifty thousand of American dollars."

"For information. I actually retrieved the things."

"Fifty thousand of American dollars is what is offered and what we pay."

"Write the check."

#   #

## Seventy-Two

Ward sauntered into the Pilgrim's Pride Café and slid into the booth across from Poet. The oldster had in front of him a cup with remnants of coffee, along with a plate of fruitcake crumbs. He'd removed his tie and laid it and his folded suit jacket on the bench beside him. After nodding to each other, both watched Darla strut around in her blue dress with gold buttons, serving patrons at other tables.

She brought beer to Ward and Poet, including one for herself. Ward accepted the Hairoun, as he did the nationalism of Vincentians, and the realization that everybody's got them some pride. "Christopher's off the hook," he announced. "He and his foxy wife can take their motorsailer and resume their nomadic life, assuming they can afford it."

Grinning her enthrallment, Darla dropped into the booth alongside Poet, across from Ward, and grasped Ward's hands. "You have a way of work things out, bold face."

He turned his hands over and linked his fingers in hers. "The truth came out and justice took its course, just like I told you it would."

Darla freed one hand and raised her bottle. "To justice."

After all three clinked bottles, Ward took a swig. Then he announced: "There's more justice. I got a reward of fifty thousand US dollars from DeBeers for recovering the diamonds, and I'm splitting it evenly between the three of us."

Darla gasped. Poet shook his head. "You don't have to. Told you all I want is the exclusive. Called it in right after you called me from the courthouse."

"Hey, super, Pops. When's it running?"

"Tonight and tomorrow. Half the papers around The States will be emblazoned with my by-line. It took a lifetime."

"How much they paying you?" Ward asked.

Poet scoffed. "Those publishers never earned a reputation for generosity when it comes to free-lancers. But my name will be heralded on newspapers throughout The States. You can't put a price on that."

"You get a third," Ward said, "so you don't have to live so poor-assed . . . can buy new sneakers and a whole 'nother bunch of those modish knit shirts. So does Darla. I'd of never solved this case without her helping me put together the pieces of the puzzle."

Tears rilled down her face. "Thank you, mon. True, me earn that money. It not charity. Me provide important pieces of the puzzle."

"Couldn't have wrapped this thing up without the help of both of you," Ward said.

"Now me can send me sweet daughter off to college in Jamaica without financial strain." Darla dabbed at her tears. "Praise God."

"And I can pay my son's tuition to law school," Ward said.

"Praise God," Darla repeated.

"And with your daughter off to school," Ward said, "you won't have all that much to keep you in this burg, slinging hash. How about sailing with me to Venezuela?"

She jerked back, startled. Her eyes brightened and her smile spread across her face. But after a moment, her expression sobered. "What happen to me when you grow tired of this black woman in you South America full of Spanish beauties?"

He threw his hands out and flailed them, grimacing to dismiss that indictment.

"No, mon. To suffer the pain of being jilted one time is enough for any woman."

"How the hell can you rant about being jilted when we haven't even started out?"

"Me never in me life think to live anywhere but here in Kingstown."

"Come on! We're going to sail through the rest of the archipelago—Barbados, Grenada and Trinidad. We'll have the time of our lives."

"No, mon, me doesn't traipse off with some foot-loose sailorman. Sure as God put fronds on palm trees, someday you bold eyes turn to one of those luscious Latins."

He shook his head and sputtered, but before he found words to refute that, she spoke. "Best me remains and find a good mon doesn't have wanderlust and ready to build his life right here."

Ward continued to flail his hands, frustrated by his failure to find words of rebuttal. While their sex had been volcanic, their romance had been rocky at best. It raised doubt of long-term relationship.

"Thank you for asking," Darla said, squeezing his hands. "Me truly flattered. But no, me stays here. You have a cool running."

When Ward's brow arched questioningly, Poet translated her remark. "It's the island expression for bon voyage."

Ward nodded to that and they averted their eyes. Then Darla brightened and asked, "Why you doesn't stay and we build a life together?"

Ward grimaced and shook his head. "This place is too small, without enough to do to keep me interested. I'd always be looking out there at the horizon."

"Then you go, sailorman, and satisfy you wanderlust. Perhaps some day you pass back this way."

Ward turned to Poet. "You ready to sail the Spanish Main?"

"No thanks, new friend. It took eighty years to find this place."

"Another Caribbean island," Ward said. "We'll visit a number of them."

Poet shook his head. "Most of the others are despoiled by tourism. Time has forgotten this wonderful place. I'll stay here, in paradise."

#   #

Epilogue

Ward glanced back at the green hills fading into the hazy distance. The sails snapped in the breeze above his head. How the hell did he know if he'd made the right decision?

Had he walked away for the second time from a woman who'd enrich his life? But how long would he indulge her cantankerous outbursts? And what's the chance of a big-city guy from the Bronx settling for any length of time in a burg the size of Central Park? Naw, he knew damned well wanderlust would eventually induce him to seek distant horizons.

At least he'd left Kingstown with pride, having proved himself a skilled homicide cop . . . again. Those deputy commissioners never awarded him the prize of detective first grade, but he knew damned well he'd qualified. Hell, he'd just proved it . . . again. Now he really felt retired, on a note of achievement.

Shaking his head, he tried to convince himself he hadn't deserted her. He'd asked her to come along. Hell, he begged her. But she had her life and he had his. And the damned twain refused to meet.

Besides, he'd wanted to visit South America since reading about the place and the conquistadors and all as a boy. For all those years he'd yearned to walk in a land of Latin people. Chingalo, imagine being in a world where you don't stick out and get looked down on, and where everybody accepts you without conditions or provisos.

Amazing, when he thought back on his life, the things he'd sought most were respect and acceptance. He wanted his buddies, friends, and co-workers to consider him as simply another American, not a Puerto Rican. It wasn't that he lacked pride in his heritage, but rather that he wanted to be included in that hodgepodge descended of immigrants who called themselves Americans.

He'd attained orgullo by serving in the army, ready and willing to defend his country, then by dedicating his life to protecting society from the predators. Yes, he earned the right to be a proud American.

Yeah, and he wanted those deputy-commissioners to acknowledge that they'd denied him what he deserved because of hard work, professional application and diligent attention to police procedure and detail. He could breathe easy now, having gratified that score. They'd soon get their fill of his puss in the morning newspaper and on the six o'clock news. Screw them anyway.

Look ahead, hombre, not behind. You're on your way to new places and new adventures. Yeah, and he could always return to Kingstown someday.

The End